Dear Mom,

 I hope Dr. K. has been sending you all of my letters. I don't want to bombard with you with too much stuff. I guess I'm just trying to make up for all the time we've missed.

 But you want to know the truth? I'm glad you missed that part of my life. I'm glad you didn't have to see me moping around like a depressed teenage ghost. I can't even imagine what it must have looked like when you found me in the park that night. I can't even remember it. Isn't that sad? I've already seen you, and I can't even remember it.

 But that doesn't matter now, because I'm getting better. I really am.

 Because you found me. Because you're coming back.

 And I can't wait. I can't wait to see you.

 I love you, Mom. I love you.

    Love,
    Gaia

Don't miss any books in this thrilling series:

FEARLESS™

Available from SIMON PULSE

FEARLESS™

GAIA ABDUCTED

FRANCINE PASCAL

SIMON PULSE
New York   London   Toronto   Sydney   Singapore

This book is a work of fiction. Any references to historical events, real people, or real locales are used fictitiously. Other names, characters, places, and incidents are the product of the author's imagination, and any resemblance to actual events or locales or persons, living or dead, is entirely coincidental.

First Simon Pulse edition June 2003

Copyright © 2003 by Francine Pascal

Cover copyright © 2003 by 17th Street Productions, an Alloy company.

SIMON PULSE
An imprint of Simon & Schuster Children's Publishing Division
1230 Avenue of the Americas, New York, NY 10020

Produced by 17th Street Productions,
an Alloy company
151 West 26th Street
New York, NY 10001

All rights reserved, including the right of reproduction
in whole or in part in any form.
For information address 17th Street Productions,
151 West 26th Street, New York, NY 10001.

Fearless™ is a trademark of Francine Pascal.

Printed in the United States of America
10 9 8 7 6 5 4 3 2 1

Library of Congress Control Number: 2003105129
ISBN: 0-689-86019-6

KENNEDY

To my daughters:
Jamie, Laurie, and Susan

Instead of happy little memories, her brain was **alternate** stocked with tons **reality** of masochistic little catchphrases.

GAIA MOORE HAD LOST HER SENSES.

Literally. All the external stimuli had somehow been stripped away—erased and rescinded like some kind of punishment. It was as if she'd fallen into a sensory deprivation tank or a pool of ether. It made the act of waking

Blips and Flashes

a near-impossible endeavor. She couldn't see anything but the bright burning residue of white light inside her eyelids. She couldn't hear anything but a faint high-pitched buzz, agitating her ears with its incessant monotone. There was nothing to taste or smell but the thin, stale air flowing through her dried-up membranes like sterilized dust. Her entire body felt numb and dull—with the exception of her head.

The only thing she could feel was the exquisite throbbing in her head. It felt like it had been detached from her body. It was slumped forward like a chunk of solid rock, her chin digging painfully into her chest, each one of the hundreds of muscles in her face aching individually.

She believed she was conscious. At some point she'd definitely crossed over into consciousness. But she couldn't open her eyes. It was just too bright out there. She tried to squeeze them tighter, but the pain of that flat bar of brilliance just made them water. She could only orient herself by the stale air that enveloped the room and the cold, hard metal of a steel chair beneath her. That was all she had to go on. Because everything else. . . was blank.

That was the only way to describe it. Everything had become inconceivably blank. Blank space. Dead air. White, shapeless light. And nothing. Nothing until that one faint voice. . .

"Miss Moore?"

There was a calm, detached dream voice floating from somewhere in the distance. It was a woman's voice—Gaia could tell that much—but she couldn't place it.

It had no defining features. Nothing deep or raspy enough to suspect, nothing kind or caring to comfort her, just a blank, inflectionless monotone—a subtle hum that blended in with the white noise of what she believed to be central air-conditioning. The droning of the processed air and the electric buzz of fluorescent lighting were causing the most intolerable vibrations in her eardrums.

"Miss Moore, can you hear me? Are you awake?"

Christ, that was a good question. Was she awake? Was she asleep? Dreaming? She couldn't even remember going to sleep the night before. She couldn't remember passing out on her filthy pillow in her empty apartment on East Seventy-second Street. She seemed to have forgotten. . . everything. Everything that had come before this moment.

It was nothing like the usual morning blur. She was accustomed to a certain degree of "blank-slate confusion," as she termed most of her mornings—that first waking moment when she reshuffled all the facts of her life and tried to will herself out of bed. Usually the first moment of every day was reserved for peering into the depressing sunlight or the cold New York grayness and running through her checklist of miserable, life-denying facts: father still missing. . . check; Ed and Sam still hating her. . . check; Natasha and Tatiana still sadistic, murderous bitches. . . check; still living in abandoned Upper East Side hellhole. . . check.

Life still sucking. . . absolute and unequivocal check.

But this was different. This morning—was it even morning? This morning or night, whatever it was, this *moment*—she couldn't even remember what facts she was supposed to check.

"Miss Moore, I need you to open your eyes now. Can you open your eyes, please?"

I'm trying. Will you give me a second? I'm trying to remember where the hell I am. I'm trying to remember where all this pain is coming from.

It wasn't anybody she knew—there was nothing at all familiar the voice. And it was getting louder. Now the woman's tone was more of a demand than a request. She sounded efficient and impersonal—colder than the steel chair or the cool, air-conditioned air. She was speaking as if Gaia were an inmate at a prison or the half-dead victim of a nearly fatal car crash.

An accident. . . ? Could that be it? Had there been an accident?

Open your eyes. You need to open your eyes now. She had to pry them open. Even if only to see what she was dreaming.

Lash by lash, Gaia tore open her painfully sealed eyelids. But she instantly regretted it. The fluorescent light was even brighter than she'd imagined. It seeped into the exposed slits of her eyelids like acid. Each flutter of her eyes stung more than the last. But she had to force it. She had to will her eyelids to press on—to push her focus past the massive glare and the overdose of white. At the very least, she needed to match up a body with that intrusive, unforgiving voice. She needed clues—visual, tactile, anything to place her somewhere in time, anything to kick-start her apparently stalling brain functions.

Her eyes filled with tears as her vision swam painfully into focus.

The first thing she saw was her own knees. They were still attached to her body, thankfully. But they were covered in green cotton pajamas.

Gaia tried to concentrate. What the hell was she doing in green pajamas? She didn't even own a pair of green pajamas. But on closer inspection, she realized that they weren't pajamas. Shapeless pale green cotton pants, a green flimsy drawstring around her waist, a loose wrinkled V neck on her green short-sleeve shirt. . .

Hospital clothes. She was swaddled in thin, ugly hospital clothes.

MAYBE THERE *HAD* BEEN AN ACCIDENT

and she couldn't remember it? A blunt-force trauma to the head— that could have caused some kind of short-term memory loss. . . and that would explain why she was waking up in absolute nowhere land, without a clue as to where she was or who was talking to her. A nurse? Was it the voice of a nurse? She sounded like a nurse—a cold and heartless nurse with a D-minus in bedside manner, but still a nurse. It would even explain the aching pain pulsing through Gaia's temples and rolling down her spine.

But if there had been an accident, wouldn't she be in a hospital gown? In a narrow steel bed, hooked up to an IV and plugged up with plastic tubes? She wouldn't be in these clothes. They looked more like hospital scrubs than a patient's gown. But what exactly were the odds of Gaia having become a nurse or a surgeon in her sleep? Unless she was in a bed and she was only dreaming that she was sitting up? Maybe she never *had* become conscious?

This was ridiculous. She needed to stop contemplating the hundred different implications of her clothes. She had to find the strength to raise her head and wake the hell up. She needed to see more. She needed to know what part of this freakish moment was dream and what, if any, part of it was real.

Finally, with a tremendous effort of her neck muscles, she raised her face and tried to look around. She felt mildly dizzy, like she had been spinning in place, but at least she could see past her own knees. At least enough to gather some information.

Yes, she was in fact in a chrome metal chair. So much for the hospital bed. But still, there was something about the room that was sickeningly antiseptic. It was a small, white, nearly featureless room, and she was seated at its center. There was not one window on the walls, only a single metal door with a small Plexiglas window. There were fluorescent lights across the ceiling that were just like the ones at school, the ugly kind with the sheets of frosted plastic that covered up the bare bulbs. The floor was polished linoleum. The bare walls were as clean as blank sheets of paper. A small metal desk sat across from her, and behind the desk was the owner of that unrecognizable voice: a stranger. A complete stranger.

A new thought raced through Gaia's head. An automatic demand that her father had programmed so deeply into her well-trained mind that it superceded all her frozen synapses and clouded over half notions. It was the first and foremost rule of orientation:

Trust no one. Be suspicious.

She had to stop sifting through her broken thoughts and start doubting—doubting this place and this moment, doubting the alien face behind that metal desk. Even if the situation was totally benign, even if she *was* just recovering from some kind of head trauma, her subconscious insisted that she be wary. It was something in that woman's face. . . a warning. *Be careful.*

The woman was overweight, but not severely. She had a plump, bland face. Her black hair was pulled back into a tight bun. She wore a white short-sleeved *shirt— like a tennis shirt,* Gaia thought. *Or maybe a nurse's uniform?* None of the damn clues would fit together.

"Good," the woman said, with a deeply patronizing lilt. "Now, let's keep the head up and the eyes open, all right?" Her dull brown eyes were fixed on Gaia's. A thick file folder was opened in front of her on the otherwise empty desk, holding a neat stack of papers. She checked her watch and then scribbled down a few notes.

"I'm. . ." Gaia shifted forward in her seat and tried to speak, but her throat felt like torn parchment. It made only the beginning of a sound and then devolved into a dry, phlegm-ridden grunt and then a wave of pain. Gaia swung her head back against the chair and tried to breathe through the sudden nausea.

"Please don't try to move," the woman's flat voice echoed. "It will only increase your dizziness."

Truer, more infuriating words had never been spoken. Gaia's fists clenched tighter as she fought off the aches and pains and the rapid rotation inside her head. Nothing made her sicker or more pissed off than moments like these. Moments of unadulterated weakness—the complete and pathetic lack of control.

Put it back together. Sit your ass up straight, and for Christ's sake, jog your memory. Where the hell are you? You are Gaia. You don't forget things.

She had a photographic memory, goddammit. She could remember names, dates, menus, the smallest defining details of a person's face—a birthmark, a crooked fourth tooth, a barely visible scar, even the brand perfume of someone who she'd only met for five minutes in 1997. But right now, as she tried to flip the last page back in her memory, she was seeing nothing but blank white paper matching the white sterile walls that surrounded her.

She swung her head forward again, fighting off the need to puke and the sharp pains that ran down her numb and rubbery limbs. "Are you—?" Her sentence was interrupted by another dry and crusty cough and the somewhat unexpected slurring of her words. Nonetheless, Gaia was dead set on completing her sentence. No matter how long it took. "Are. . . are you. . . a nurse?"

"No," the woman replied. "I only handle admitting and security. My name is Rosie, and I'll be—"

"Wait," Gaia insisted, raising her hand. It was like trying to lift a cinder block. She quickly let it drop back to her side. "Admitting?" she mumbled, pushing her eyes open again for focus. "Admitting like. . . a hospital?" She was trying to shake the rust from her vocal cords, trying to take back at least a modicum of power in this embarrassingly powerless situation. "So. . . this *is* a hospital?"

"Yes," Rosie said, clearly annoyed by Gaia's willful interruption. "Please don't try to speak. Just listen, all right? You're at Rainhill Hospital. There's no need to be frightened. You should be—"

"What happened?" Gaia interrupted again. Rosie's slow and deliberate tone was only adding to her agitation. If there had been an accident, Gaia didn't need misleading, condescending assurances; she needed facts. And she needed them now. "Was I in an accident?" she pressed. "What happened to me? I can't *remember* what happened—"

"Miss Moore, this is not a conversation for me to have with you." Gaia could read the increasing annoyance in Rosie's pursed lips. "The doctor will help you with your confusion. I can only—"

"*Why?* Why won't you just tell me what happened? Was it a car? Or did someone—?"

"Miss Moore, *please.*" Rosie's eyes narrowed in frustration. She was trying to maintain her subdued tone, but her voice was steadily gaining in volume. "Gaia, it is *very* important that you stay relaxed, all right? Your head will clear much faster if you stay calm, and then I'm sure Dr. Kraven will be able to answer all of your questions. But for now, I need you to—"

"*No,*" Gaia slurred. "Why do I have to wait for the doctor? Just *tell me* what happened. It's a *simple* goddamn question—!"

"All right, I can see you're not quite ready yet." Rosie shot up from her seat and slapped her folder closed. The shriek of her sliding chair echoed off the walls. "I'll give you a little more time. I'll come back in a little while and we'll see if you're feeling better."

"No, wait! Don't go. Just—"

"When you're calmer, Gaia." Rosie turned away and stepped to the metal door, reaching down to a large key ring on her belt and unlocking the plated lock.

Gaia pressed her feet down and tried to push out of her chair, but her legs felt like cheap plastic doll parts. She nearly fell over face first before she managed to grapple onto the base of her chair and rebalance herself. Deep waves of pain shot up through her hollow bones as her wrists shook with weakness. "God*dammit,*" she growled with a rubbery tongue. "*Wait.* I'm plenty calm. I just—"

"We'll talk when you're feeling better." Rosie was already halfway through the door, giving Gaia nothing but the back of her head. The door slammed closed before Gaia could utter another word. She heard the turning of the lock and then nothing. Nothing but white noise.

What the hell is going on here? What is that bitch's problem? Why won't she tell me what happened?

"Fine, let me talk to the doctor," Gaia croaked at the Plexiglas window, hoping it would come out as a yell. "I want to talk to my doctor!"

But there wasn't a sign of Rosie beyond that window. There wasn't even the remotest sign of humanity out there. Just another glimpse of bare walls.

Four bare walls that were closing in on her. She was desperate to tear them down, dying for wide-open spaces—giant parking lots, empty airplane hangars, hundred-mile fields in the Berkshires; even Central Park would do.

Wait. Central Park...

Gaia shut her eyes. Finally something was coming back to her. The park... Central Park... For a moment she could see actual flashes from her memory, flickering on and off in waves of mental static, like a television on the fritz. She saw images of dry leaves blowing up off the ground, dark slabs of rock obscured in shadow. And she remembered footsteps. She could hear footsteps crushing leaves somewhere behind her. Footsteps coming closer and closer. . .

And then nothing. Nothing again. A taste of a memory and then another blackout.

But at least she remembered something from the park.

Was that where it had happened? This phantom accident—this mystery incident that had landed her in the world's most infuriating hospital? Those footsteps. . . *whose* footsteps was she hearing? Who could possibly have hurt her? *She* sent *them* to the hospital—all the muggers and rapists and assholes. It wasn't supposed to be the other way around. It was never the other way around.

Remember, Gaia. Central Park. How long ago was it? Which night was it? Who was behind you?

Just remembering the park was useless. That would have described every night for the last week; she remembered that much. For days she'd been roaming that park like a ghost, looking for any scumbag dumb enough to approach her. She could have been remembering two hours ago or two days ago. There had to be something more specific. There had to be some detail. . . .

A fight. There had been a fight. No, not just a fight, something more. Something worse. Something darker.

Blips and flashes were dripping in again. . . hands squeezing her arms so tightly, she could feel herself bruising. . . her back pressed against the cold, crumbling dirt. Those hands. . . those thick, calloused hands

13

holding down her wrists. . . legs straddled over her, pressing her hips to the ground. . .

Jesus, what are you remembering? Who was he? What did he do to you?

Her eyes darted from wall to wall with increasing rage. She felt sickeningly vulnerable. Her chest began to heave and tighten as she tried to force out another memory. Something to fill in those images. . . She needed it now. She needed to see all of it, much more than she'd needed it before. She insisted on it.

And fractured piece by fractured piece, she finally put something together. Something solid. A real memory was floating in at last. A complete one. A memory of Central Park. . .

IT WAS A SIMPLE EQUATION—COM-

Ass-Kicking Addiction

pletely mathematical, as far as Gaia was concerned. It was what she called the ass-kicking principle:

Life – no family (dead mother + missing father) x a nonexistent fear gene = ass-kicking addiction + no friends to speak of + (no love life whatsoever)^2

Some people turned to heroin. Some to chocolate cake. Gaia turned to ass kicking. Not that she hadn't been known to pound chocolate cheesecake as though the apocalypse were fast approaching. But all that had ever left her with was a ten-second cream-cheese high and a deep sense of regret. No, this was clearly the only coping mechanism that worked. So here she was, scanning the dark shadows of Central Park, trying to feed her addiction. . . .

The sky was a starless shade of black. It was hanging low over Gaia's head like a black hole, swallowing up all the hazy lights from the buildings on Fifth Avenue and Central Park West. The park itself was just as dim and shapeless, each tree falling in line with the damp wind.

Gaia scraped her half-dead Nikes along the gravelly pavement of the path, trying to drum up some attention from some invisible scumbag.

Attention, all skinheads, thieves, and general assholes. I am a young blond teenage girl alone in Central Park at night. Please try to assault me so I can exact some violent justice. You see. . . I need a fix.

Surely there was a preying lowlife couched somewhere in the jagged slabs of rock and the rustling leaves.

By 8 or 9 P.M. it had turned into this: a grim, quasi-haunted forest, replete with dark, winding paths, tall trees that loomed ominously and whispered, and giant rock formations that seemed to live and move ever so slightly in the peripheral shadows. Throw in the newly

15

tarred-over ditch in the middle of the winding road and you had the New York version of a haunted forest: a haunted forest under construction.

Unfortunately, desperate as she was for some mind-numbing action, Gaia was having no luck tonight. No rapists to pound. No skinheads to pummel. It was just the cold, silent wind, blowing through her ears and through the trees and up into that black, lifeless sky. She could already feel the early symptoms of ass-kicking withdrawal setting in: depression, upset stomach, and that unbearable voice in her head. . . .

This is not a life, Gaia. . . . This is not a life. . . .

That was her demon brain's favorite new catchphrase. A constant friendly reminder from her subconscious. As if she didn't know already. As if she needed to be reminded that her life was like a two-day-old helium balloon—floating just above the floor, dropping by little increments every day, withering and flattening and running out of gas. Instead of happy little memories, her brain was stocked with tons of these masochistic little catchphrases:

Your father is dead.

You are romantic poison.

You can't trust anyone.

This is not a life, Gaia. . . (mentioned earlier, but worth repeating).

And those were just the favorites. Those didn't even include the randoms and the daily bonuses: *You look like crap; school is a demoralizing torture device devised by Satan. . . .* Given the opportunity, her nagging inner voice could repeat these little gems as many as five thousand times a day.

She had always wondered what the difference was between hearing those inner voices in her head and actually "hearing voices." Where exactly did one draw the line between troubled teen and full-fledged lunatic? Because wherever that line was, she was quite sure she had crossed it years ago. No one could possibly live through her life and preserve her sanity. Unless that life became nothing more than the struggle to preserve one's sanity. And that was really no life at all.

No life at all. That just about described it.

But then came the miracle. A tiny little miracle. A little gift from God in the form of a cracking twig in the distance.

Gaia froze in place as her ears pricked up slightly and she attempted to trace the origin of the sound. It had come from about twenty feet behind her. . . .

Yes. Thank you, Lord. There is a stalker born every minute.

She began to walk again, veering slightly off the path and into the woods, moving back toward the tarred-over construction ditch. A moment more and she was quite sure she was being followed. *Closer, scumbag. Just a little closer. Welcome to your last attempted rape. . . .*

17

A slight smile sprang up in the corners of Gaia's mouth as she felt her limbs tense and relax at the same time. She was preparing for battle. Though given the particularly dark and desperate mood she was in tonight, there wasn't going to be much of a battle. It was going to be more like a thrashing. She quickly justified in her head that he deserved everything he was about to get. Surely he would limp back to his mugger/rapist compatriots and reiterate the message she'd been sending out for the last week: The solitary female was no longer a species to be hunted.

I can hear you coming. Just a few more steps. A few more steps and—

"Hai!"

Gaia spun her body back and reached for the bastard's wrist instinctively. She knew every target on his body, even in the dark. With her hand firmly planted on his wrist, she unleashed a series of kicks so lightning quick that she didn't even take a breath in between.

His head snapped back as blood splattered on Gaia's already filthy jeans. Then a kick to his shoulder and then to the knee. Then a swift backward kick that forced his entire chest to cave in. There wasn't even time for him to groan or grunt in pain. The combination had already been completed.

Gaia twisted his arm right out of its socket and sent his entire body soaring over her head, watching as the blur of his clothes flew over her and landed in a loud, painful skid across the newly tarred ditch. She could just make out the outline of his body, sprawled out across the new pavement.

She advanced slightly toward him, floating her left hand by her face and holding out her right fist in a firm jujitsu stance. Not that there was any need. She was quite sure this meathead was down for the count.

But a moment more and this supposed meathead did something that no Central Park junkie had ever done. Gaia stiffened with surprise as he suddenly rolled slightly backward and shot back onto his feet. And he didn't stop there. He was already advancing toward her with incredible speed, whipping forward in a complete blur before she could find her defensive stance.

She tried to raise her arms for another punch, but his hands had already dug into her biceps and flipped her over his head and down onto the grass. She felt her entire skeleton shake as she hit the dirt and let out an embarrassingly girlish grunt. She could already feel the bruising at the base of her spine and her shoulder blades.

Suddenly he was sitting on her, pressing her body firmly to the ground as he straddled her hips. Gaia was totally disconcerted. A bolt of hot rage shot up her back. She reached forward to let loose a series of crisp jabs to his head, but his hands had somehow grabbed hold of her wrists, pushing them back into the dirt and restraining her.

So strong. . .

His hands. His thick, calloused hands were taking control, overpowering her. Something about the angle—he knew what he was doing. He knew how to hold her down. Strength had nothing to do with it. No amount of strength would have made a difference. She couldn't break free.

You have to do something, she hollered at herself, hearing the shameful amount of desperation in her own head. *You have to find your way out of this right now. . . .*

His eyes—look at his face.

She'd been struggling so hard that she hadn't even looked at her attacker's face. And only now did she realize. . .

You know him, Gaia. You know him. . . .

AND THEN IT HAD ALL GONE BLACK

again. Her memory had gone blank—like the curtain had just dropped, like her quarter had run out. The past had faded out, and the present had faded hideously back in. Goodbye, Central Park; hello, bright

Textbook Nightmare

white eyesore of a room—hello, cold and uncomfortable metal chair.

It couldn't stop there. The memory could not stop there. It was like her brain was intentionally trying to torture her—tempting her with facts and then ripping them away when she was so close.

Who was he? Who the hell was he? And what had he done to her? Had he done what it. . . seemed so sickeningly like he had done? No. There was no way. Not to Gaia. No way. But the hospital—she was in the hospital. . . . *No way.*

She just needed two more seconds, that was all. Two more seconds of memories. She just had to redraw the face. She had to fill it in again. Was it round or square? Bearded or clean shaven? What color were his eyes? His face had been so disgustingly close. Close enough to touch. But all she could pull up was a shadow. A silhouette. A useless outline.

Think. Go back through it. You're in the park. He rushes you and he throws you to the ground. He holds you down with his own weight and drives your wrists back behind your head. And then you see him. You see his face. You know him. You haven't just seen his face before; you know him. Who?

It was such a pathetic cliché of a bad dream, such a textbook nightmare loaded with cheap Freudian symbolism: writhing helplessly in the dirt, a domineering stranger who wasn't even a stranger pinning her arms back, forcing her to submit—every girl's worst fear.

Except she didn't have any fears. Which left maybe. . . a

dream? Hadn't she closed her eyes? Hadn't she shut her eyes momentarily right after Rosie had shut that door? She thought she had only blinked to collect herself. But hours could have passed between the simple acts of closing and opening her eyes. Her mind could have roamed right into a dream, and she wouldn't have even known it. There was nothing to go on in this cool, existential purgatory of a room—no clock to indicate the passing of time, no windows to reveal a change in the position of the sun. With her body so lethargically glued to that chair, she was eternally stuck in no particular moment at all. She was so tired. Her mind was so out of reach. It was making all its own chaotic choices from moment to moment, without a stitch of permission from her.

Maybe she couldn't remember that man's face because there *had been* no man. Maybe that entire drama in the park had been her own invention. Just an ugly re-creation of her ultimate nightmare. What did she despise more than anything else in the world? What was her worst-case scenario? It was a moment just like that vision—a moment of grossly stereotypical feminine weakness. Losing the struggle, being forced into submission, finally being dominated by one of the hundreds of men she'd faced down in her life. Not just dominated: violated.

It was a dream.

Of course it was a dream. It had to be a dream—a

fiction. It had to be. Her brain had just concocted a conceit to make up for the missing time, to justify falling from blank space into this chair in this eerie hospital. It *had* to be made up, because Gaia was *Gaia*. She wasn't like other girls. The day she was reduced to being like other girls was the day she threw in the towel.

The sudden appearance of Rosie's wide face through the Plexiglas only confirmed Gaia's dream theory. She listened as the lock turned and Rosie cracked open the metal door. Rosie had said that she would come back later. She had specifically said that she would give Gaia more time to calm down. But she had only been gone for a few *seconds*. It was like she'd just closed that door and opened it right back up again. It had certainly seemed to Gaia like only a few seconds. . . but time had passed. Much more time had obviously passed.

"Are we feeling better?" Rosie asked. The royal "we" really needed to be struck completely from the English language. She closed the door behind her and stood at the doorway, gazing expressionlessly at Gaia and waiting for her answer.

"I don't know about you," Gaia replied. "But *I* feel like crap."

Rosie furrowed her brow indignantly. "Right," she uttered. "Well, at least you seem a bit more clearheaded."

Yeah, right. That was a stretch if Gaia had ever heard one. But she had to at least force the appearance of clarity. There was no way in hell she was letting Rosie walk out that door again without taking Gaia with her. Rosie had made the conditions clear before; Gaia just hadn't been ready to accept them. But clearheaded or not, this time she felt a little wiser. She had to appear calm and together or she wasn't leaving this room and she wasn't meeting with her doctor. Rosie was obviously useless to her as far as information was concerned. There was no point in asking her the same questions over and over again. Gaia wished she had just accepted that in the first place, but she wasn't going to screw up her second chance.

"Yeah," Gaia lied, "I feel a little better now." She of course had no idea how much time had passed between "now" and "then." She blinked. "I was just. . . a little confused before, but. . . I'd really like to see my doctor now." *Don't screw me, Rosie. Let me the hell out of this purgatory.*

"That's fine," Rosie said. "You'll be seeing the doctor shortly. Now, if you can maintain this degree of calm, I'll bring you into the common room and we'll try to get you acclimated."

"Acclimated? What do you mean, acclimated? How long am I supposed to stay in this—?" Gaia stopped herself and zipped her lips closed. She could already see Rosie's expression taking a turn for the worse. She had to save her questions for the doctor. "Sorry," Gaia said, forcing a fake smile out of the corner of her mouth. "I mean. . . Yes, I'd really like to get acclimated. Thank you."

Rosie rolled her eyes slightly and gave Gaia one more dubious stare. "Fine," she uttered. She stepped toward Gaia and clasped her hands around her arms, helping her to lift her aching frame to a standing position. She stepped to the large metal door and unlocked it, pulling it open with a loud creak. She grabbed Gaia by the arm and escorted her slowly to the door. "Good," she said. "Now, if you can stay as calm as this while we walk, then we're going to get along fine." Gaia forced one last fake smile and then bowed her head.

Just get me out of here, Rosie. Get me out of this room and to my doctor. I'll figure out the rest from there.

"Better," Rosie said. "Now follow me."

GAIA HAD TO STRUGGLE WITH EACH

Horrific Vision

stride. Her footsteps echoed off the narrow hospital halls, shuffling like strange drumbeats as she stumbled forward in her green cloth slippers. Rosie followed alongside, keeping her hand firmly clamped around Gaia's arm as she guided her across the clean, buffed linoleum floors of the hospital. The more they walked, the more Gaia was sure that she'd dreamed that whole attacker scenario. She was sure there had just been some kind of bad accident. But that still left just about every possibility open—cars, trucks, bicycles. . . .

In spite of her lethargy and her throbbing head, she couldn't help noticing that her body seemed, for all intents and purposes, intact. She could certainly walk. It might be a chore, but she could do it. There didn't seem to be any large cuts, bruises, or surgical scars to reckon with. As far as she could tell, it was her head that had sustained the most damage. And she could only tell that by her headache and her sluggishness and that horrible delusion about Central Park.

In fact, as she drifted past the occasional patient in the hallway, every one of them seemed to be in surprisingly good shape. No dialysis machines, no rolling IVs, no wheelchairs. The patients all seemed to be standing on their own two feet, walking freely and unassisted by doctors or nurses. A few of them did seem to have that glaze in their eyes that mirrored Gaia's overly clouded head space. Some of them even seemed to be sharing in her impeded shuffle of a walk, as if they, too, had been afflicted by an unexplainable excess of gravity—like babies who were just learning to take their first steps. Gaia supposed they might be recovering from injuries of their own—that might explain her own unfortunate infantile shuffle. But somehow that was not her sense of it. She believed something else throwing a wrench in all of her motor functions. The thing she couldn't remember.

They turned a corner, and Gaia nearly bumped into an emaciated middle-aged woman. "Sorry," she uttered.

But the woman gave no response. Not even the slightest turn of her head or grunt of acknowledgment. She stayed perfectly still, her thin salt-and-pepper hair framing her weathered face. But her face wasn't just weathered. It was frozen. Inhumanly frozen. Her jaw was stuck at an ugly, misaligned angle, her eyes half shut and unmoving. It was as if she'd been paralyzed with fear by some horrific vision and had simply never moved again.

Gaia turned back to Rosie's profile. "What's wrong with *her*?"

"Not your concern," Rosie muttered, keeping her eyes straight ahead.

Something about Rosie's response only disturbed Gaia further. An eerie feeling crept up her spine and stiffened her joints. She was beginning to pick up on the very strange energy in this hospital—a dreamlike air of sadness and quiet unlike that of any hospital she'd ever been in. Even burn units and cancer wards seemed like happier places. Every hospital she'd ever visited in New York had more life than this.

That was the first time it even occurred to her.

New York. She had never heard of any Rainhill Hospital in New York.

"Rosie, where am I?"

"I told you. You're at Rainhill Hospital."

Gaia began to hear the din of a large group of people up ahead. It was a very familiar sound, like approaching the cafeteria at school—the dull roar of indulgent loudmouths all talking at once in a room that was too small for them. The sound grew louder as they walked.

"I know," Gaia said. "But *where* is that? In the city? Upstate? I still don't—"

"Dr. Kraven will give you all the wheres and the whys. I'm not a doctor, and I wouldn't know how to handle your condition."

"My condition? What do you mean, my condition? What *condition*?"

Rosie pulled Gaia around one more corner and stopped her at a pair of wide wooden double doors. The cacophony of too many voices was just on the other side. "Gaia," she said with a sigh. "My job was to check your vitals, admit you, and bring you to the common room. This is the common room. So as far as I'm concerned. . . you're home. That's where you are."

Rosie pushed open one of the double doors and pressed her hand against Gaia's back, pushing her slowly through the doorway.

Gaia got her first glimpse of the room and nearly fell forward on her lifeless legs.

Miserable Alternate Reality

THE LONG WALLS WERE BARE. A LARGE black television hung from the ceiling on a metal pole. The TV was turned on—some ultracheesy soap opera with the sound fairly low.

A skinny man in a white uniform was sitting behind a small wooden desk near the door. He was flipping through a magazine. He dropped it immediately when Rosie walked through the door and turned toward Gaia. "You must be Gaia," he said warmly. "I'm Lawrence—welcome to the common room."

Gaia couldn't utter a word. Now that she'd entered this room, she could only stand and stare. It was the most *un*common common room she had ever seen.

It was overcrowded. At least a dozen people of all ages were scattered around. Some were drooped down in worn-out leather armchairs along one wall, looking up at the TV, but most of them were clustered around big round wooden tables—young and old, male and female. A thin, elderly man with precisely trimmed gray hair sat to one side, holding his back very rigidly as he read a newspaper aloud to himself. The paper was yellow and stained. Gaia could tell that it had probably been folded and unfolded hundreds of times. A pair of women in their thirties sat around another table with a deck of cards; they were playing a complicated game. They slapped the cards down very quickly, babbling some incomprehensible fragmented conversation.

A young Asian girl sat leaning on the cement-brick wall in the shadows. She had a yellow crayon held very close to her face. She tore tiny paper scraps from the crayon, held them delicately between her fingers, and then dropped them, watching them float to the floor as she sang some unrecognizable tune to herself in a loud but wispy soprano.

But those were far from the loudest voices in the room.

"I'm his best friend!"

"As *if*!"

Gaia turned to the sharp angry voices of two girls arguing. They were both about her age, standing by the wall toward the back of the room, facing each other down. One girl was tall and far too thin, with long, luxurious black hair and dark green eyes. The other girl was a bit shorter. She had auburn hair that was center parted and pulled back, with a mass of light freckles running down her nose and cheeks.

"He *wants* me to take care of him," the auburn-haired girl squawked. "He's just *scared*, that's all. If you would just stop interfering, then he would—"

"Oh, *bull*," the dark-haired girl spat back. She leaned in and poked the other girl in the chest. "I'm so tired of your insipid *crap*, Tricia. D. can't stand you, can't you see that? He can't stand anyone in this place, and who the hell could? Everyone is freaking *crazy*! And so are all the assholes running this place. All the assholes running this—"

"Language!" Rosie snapped, stepping closer to the girls as she kept firm hold of Gaia's arm. "Paris, watch the language."

Gaia's teeth began to clench painfully as her situation grew clearer.

Paris glared back at Rosie. She was clearly resigned to finishing her sentence regardless of the language. ". . . Running this goddamn prison!" she declared defiantly. "You're *all* crazy," she said, staring steely eyed at Rosie. "Not *me*. . . *you*. I mean, Rosie, when on earth was the last time you undid that freaking bun in your hair? Eighty-two? Eighty-three? You call that *sane*?"

"Second warning, Paris. . ." Rosie stared at her with a stern, threatening glare, and then she turned to Gaia. "Some simple advice if you want to get better, Gaia. Don't act like her—act like *her*." Rosie pointed to Tricia, the girl with the freckles.

Tricia smiled. "Well, thank you, Rosie," she said.

But Gaia had already lost track of the conversation. She didn't need to hear any more. She didn't *want* to hear any more. She didn't want to see any more, either. She understood now. She understood the "where," even if she had no understanding of the "why." They had only been inklings in the hallway, but now all the inklings had solidified. They had melded together into a horrid little heap of understanding. Suddenly it all made sense: Rosie's cryptic, patronizing manner, the sadness in the halls, the glaze in all of their eyes, that poor catatonic woman. . .

Yes, this was a hospital. But not a hospital for the infirm or the injured. These people's bodies weren't sick. It was their heads.

A mental hospital. I am in a freaking psycho ward. I am staring at a pack of lunatics. . . . No. It's worse than that. I'm not just staring at the lunatics. They think that I'm one, too.

Okay, she was obviously still asleep.

Wake up, Gaia. Wake up. You're still dreaming. Pinch yourself, pound your head against the wall, pound someone else's head against the wall if you have to. Whatever it takes. . .

"Paris, please take two steps back from Tricia," Rosie ordered.

"Fine," Paris conceded, taking two long-legged steps.

"*Now* who's playing by the rules?" Tricia taunted.

"Oh, you stupid bitch—!"

"Okay, that's enough!" Gaia interrupted, still struggling to increase the volume in her muted voice. But that always happened in dreams, didn't it? The muted voice. The inability to forge the necessary decibels. It was all just part of the dream. "I've had enough of this dream," she announced. "I'm ready to wake up now."

The cast of invented patients all turned their heads and stared at her in silence. There was nothing more surreal than being stared at by figments of your own imagination. Gaia's frustration increased. Usually the complete awareness of dreaming was the very last moment before waking. But this dream still refused to fade away. It continued to stare back at her defiantly.

She shut her eyes and focused inward, ordering her mind once again to snap out of it, ordering herself to return to that small, featureless room or maybe even her bed back home. But when she reopened her eyes, she was still in the dream.

"Wake up," she ordered herself urgently. "Wake *up*." She didn't even care that she was slurring the ridiculous order out loud.

"Gaia." Rosie stared at her angrily. "I *warned* you about staying calm—"

"Shut up!" Gaia snapped. "Open the door, Rosie. Just open the goddamn door and wake me up!"

"Gaia—"

She knew she couldn't actually run from a bad dream, but she made an irrational turn for the common room door anyway. It was all she could think of to do. As fast as she could, Gaia pivoted in place and broke for the door. But she didn't get farther than about two steps. Running felt like a task she hadn't performed in years. With a loud squeaking noise her shoe slipped on the polished floor and she lost her balance. She threw out her hands to break her fall, but Lawrence had already caught her in his firm grip. And he'd already pricked her with a small needle.

She struggled halfheartedly and stared into his wide brown eyes as he held her up. She was just waiting for Lawrence to fade away. Waiting for all of them to fade away.

Rosie grabbed hold of Gaia's other arm, squeezing much too tightly. The pain seemed so real—the sharp, aching pain from the injection, the viselike grip of Rosie's hand. . . . Gaia couldn't understand it. She couldn't understand why it all seemed so real.

"Let's just take her to her room," Rosie said to Lawrence. "I'll talk to Dr. K." But now Rosie's voice was popping in and out, bathed in a pool of static, along with Gaia's vision.

At least Gaia was finally getting what she wanted. At least this miserable alternate reality was finally disappearing bit by bit. Paris and Tricia were drifting away in pieces, melting into the glaring white light as they stared at Gaia. All the patients looked on with that same blank stare of pity as they melded into the white walls and the wooden tables.

And then all the white finally disappeared from view. Every bit of remaining white faded to black. The dream was finally over. Gaia would finally be able to wake up.

Thank God. It was about time.

What if her unex-
plainable presence
in this hospital
relentless,
didn't
oppressive
have **sadness**
the least bit to
do with any diabol-
ical intentions or
nefarious plots?

GREEN EYES.

They were the first thing Gaia noticed when she awoke. Sad green eyes were hovering over her like a surgeon's, examining her left wrist and then scanning back up to her face.

Psychiatric Incarceration

Gaia tried for a moment to convince herself that they were the eyes of a nurse—that she was finally waking from that nightmare of psychiatric incarceration. She spent the first few flutters of her eyelids basking in her semiconscious state as she ground her teeth together and tried to reinvigorate all the dormant muscles in her face.

She picked up glimpses of the steel-framed hospital bed beneath her and told herself that she'd returned to reality. She'd finally been delivered to a good doctor's hands. She was finally rid of Rosie's condescending threats, rid of her own disturbing delusions. Rosie's bullying eyes had been replaced by the kinder, sadder eyes of this nurse, and Gaia would soon learn which New York hospital she was actually in, how the accident had happened in the first place, and how soon she was going to be released.

But by the third or fourth blink of her eyes, she could see more clearly. And a wave of dismal resignation began to set in.

These were not the eyes of a nurse watching over her. They were the gray-green eyes of a disturbed mental patient—a girl who Gaia had seen before. She remembered her long dark hair and the visible musculature of her agitated face. She even remembered her name. Paris. It was Paris hovering over her hospital bed, sizing her up like a specimen in a science experiment. And somehow or other Gaia had to come to terms with it.

Lying in the same room with this Paris person still made absolutely no sense, but Gaia was hard-pressed to deny it yet again. A dream could only last so long. She could only be fooled so many times by her own perception. Even Gaia's denial had its limits. This hospital. . . this mental hospital and the patients inhabiting it were no dream. And they were far from just a memory. They were real.

Someone had done this to her. Someone had put her in this very real mental hospital. *Who?* Who would have done this? Who would want to lock her up in the freaking twilight zone like this? And more importantly, *why*? Could Loki have anything to do with this? That didn't make any sense—Loki was totally out of the picture. Natasha? She'd already been taken into custody. The lack of answers was so exhausting. Why couldn't she just remember? Why couldn't she remember what had happened? How long had she even been asleep? The questions were starting to pile up much too quickly for her throbbing head. And shutting her eyes wasn't going to make them go away.

Paris wouldn't seem to go away, either. And her relentless stare was beginning to make Gaia extremely uncomfortable.

"What?" Gaia grunted, her eyes meeting Paris's.

Paris jumped to attention. Apparently she hadn't quite noticed Gaia waking. The moment Gaia uttered a sound, Paris backed away in a lightning-quick turn and jumped into the adjacent hospital bed, fixing her glance in the opposite direction.

Gaia stared a few more moments at the back of Paris's head, but then her eyes were compelled to take in the rest of the unfamiliar room. She shook her head slowly as she began to scan the perimeter.

The hospital room's "decor" consisted entirely of two adjacent hospital beds, one minuscule bathroom with a flickering fluorescent light, one wooden closet door, one metal-framed chair in the corner covered with black vinyl, and one small Plexiglas window sunk into the center of the opposite wall.

Window. Finally, an actual window. Maybe she could find some kind of clue outside to orient herself further. Without even thinking, Gaia slipped her aching, lethargic bones out of bed. She shuffled herself gingerly past Paris's bed over to the window and pressed her forehead to the thick, warm Plexiglas, squinting as the sun penetrated her maladjusted eyes. She felt like she hadn't seen sunlight in days. But as her vision began to focus, she only found herself more baffled.

Sand. Sugar-white sand stretched out from the concrete walls of the hospital, leading out about fifty feet until it hit a massive fence topped with twirled barbed wire. Beyond the fence there was only water. A huge expanse of dark blue water spanned out as far as the eye could see into the horizon, forming a pristine line between water and light blue sky.

One thing was for sure: This was not New York. *What happened? What the hell happened to me?*

"Haldol," Paris muttered.

Gaia whipped her head around from the window and stared at Paris, who had picked up a book and buried her head in it so far that her face was completely hidden from view.

"What?" Gaia asked curtly.

"Haldol," Paris repeated coldly, keeping her face hidden. "That's what happened to you. You've been asleep since yesterday."

Haldol. That was what Lawrence had pricked her with in that common room—a big whopping dose of Haldol, the tranquilizer to beat all tranquilizers. Gaia had read all about the different sedatives in her psych class: Thorazine, Mellaril, Nembutal. And the more she investigated the lethargy in her limbs and the thick clouds in her head, the surer she was that she'd been doped out on the stuff since the moment she woke up in this place. That was why her head weighed a ton. That was why every step felt like it was taking place underwater. She wasn't recovering from an accident—someone had drugged her. And they'd done it before she'd even gotten here. They'd done it back in that elusive chunk of time that she still, quite infuriatingly, could not remember.

She tried yet again to force out a memory from the past twenty-four hours, but she was coming up with nothing but a bigger headache. The last thing she wanted was another fake memory to fill in the blank space. *Come on, Gaia. Remember. Remember something real this time.* But all she was drawing were painful blanks. That part of her brain simply would not function. The drugs. It had to be the drugs that were making her forget everything.

"I can't *think*," she complained, knocking her fists against her head to try and shake something free.

Paris peered out from the side of her book and gave Gaia another clinical, suspicious stare.

"*What?*" Gaia spat, with a surprising amount of hostility. There was something deeply offensive about this girl's judgmental stares. "What are you looking at?"

Paris blew out a condescending puff of air and rolled her eyes. "Paranoid schizo," she muttered to herself, returning to her book. "Just what I need. Another paranoid schizo."

"*Excuse* me?" Gaia forced her body to straighten and stepped closer to Paris's bed. She was still teetering slightly from side to side, but she wanted to be standing up for this. Up and in Paris's face if possible. "What did you just say? Who's a paranoid schizo?"

Paris placed her book down on her lap and locked her eyes with Gaia's. "Why don't you take another Haldol?" she suggested. "You're doing what's known here at Rainhill as 'acting up.'"

Gaia's jaw clenched with indignation. Paris was clearly under the mistaken impression that Gaia was just the newest psycho in this loony bin. And if there was one thing Gaia could not tolerate, it was being treated like a crazy person. Paris seemed to be just a little confused as to which person in this room was sane and which one was the mental patient. Gaia had already seen a glimpse of her attitude in the common room, but if she thought she could dole out the same crap she was giving Rosie, she was sorely mistaken.

Gaia was all too ready to say something to that effect, but she forced herself to hold back and reconsider.

There was no point in explaining herself to a total stranger with sanity issues. She knew that the wisest choice was to steer clear of the patients altogether and focus on her fact-finding mission. She shook off Paris's patronizing glance and dragged herself over to the door. Surely some doctor or nurse would be able to provide Gaia with some kind of useful information—some semblance of facts that would explain how she had gotten here and what she needed to do to correct the egregious error and get her ass back home, where she belonged.

41

She turned the doorknob and tugged on the door to head out into the halls. But it wouldn't open. She must have been even weaker than she'd thought. She placed both hands on the door and tugged as hard as she could, but the door wouldn't budge.

"It's locked," Paris explained, as if Gaia were too dumb to comprehend the notion of a locked door. "We're both on lockdown until lunch. Rosie is big into discipline. Me for my little outburst and you for. . . you know, whatever's wrong with you."

"There's *nothing* wrong with me," Gaia moaned. She tugged at the door three more times irrationally.

"Of course not," Paris replied in an unbearably deadpan tone. "Why would you be in a mental hospital if something were wrong with you?"

Ignore her, Gaia ordered herself. *Just ignore her.* "You don't know what you're talking about, okay?"

"Whatever," Paris replied. "You just keep working on that door, then. Crazy is as crazy does. . . ."

"All right, enough!" Gaia croaked. She pounded her hand against the door and whipped back around to face down Paris. Three minutes in this room and she'd already had far too much of Paris's clinical stares and her ill-informed, obnoxious, presumptuous mouth. Gaia would have to set just a few things straight. If she could keep the room from spinning.

"Look," she groaned, leaning back against the door for support, "you don't know me, and I don't know you. You have *no idea* who I am. I am not supposed to *be* here. I don't even know how I got here. This is all just somebody's screwed-up scheme or somebody's tragic error. Either way, I am not a paranoid schizo or any other kind of schizo, all right? *You* are the mental patient, and *I* am a sane person from New York who is in an unfortunate predicament. Okay?"

Once Gaia had completed her little diatribe, she began to feel guilty. She didn't know any more about Paris than Paris knew about her, and she certainly hadn't intended to insult the mentally ill. Insane or not, Gaia sure as hell knew enough about despair, and the last thing she wanted to do was rub someone else's sadness in their face. Especially a complete stranger whom she was quite sure she would never see again. "I'm sorry," she uttered. "I didn't mean to say—"

Paris interrupted her with a caustic little laugh. "It's no problem, Gaia."

Gaia's eyes narrowed with suspicion. "How did you know my name?"

Paris rolled her eyes. "Rosie called you Gaia in the common room. What, did you think I was part of the big CIA conspiracy or something?"

Gaia couldn't possibly have explained how reasonable a possibility that was. But her silence only seemed to increase the glint in Paris's eye.

"Uh-huh." Paris sighed. "Yeah. Well, just for your information, I'm actually the only sane person in this place. And regarding your little monologue there, I might as well tell you that it's pretty much word for word what every single paranoid schizophrenic has said to me on their first day. 'This is all a mistake. . . . This is all somebody's *scheme*. . . . They're all out to get me,' et cetera. If you'll pardon the cliché, I've really heard it all before."

"Yeah. . . I may *sound* paranoid," Gaia uttered between clenched teeth, "but if you knew a thing about me or my life, you would know that in my case it's all true, okay? It just so happens that people really *are* out to get me, and this really *is* a mistake."

"Are you sure about that?"

"What?"

"Are. . . you. . . sure. . . about. . . that?" Paris repeated herself, as if she were speaking for the hard of hearing.

"Of course I'm sure about—"

"How do you know?"

"What?"

"*How do you know?*" Paris swung her legs over the edge of the bed to face Gaia head-on. "Why are you so sure you're here by mistake?" Her piercing green eyes were nearly pinning Gaia to the door. "Why don't you take a look in that bathroom mirror there? I may have a few aggression issues, but you. . . Check out the freaked-out look in your eyes right now. I'd say you're no different from the rest of the freaks out there. I'd say you're probably cuckoo for Cocoa Puffs. You don't even know how you got here. You have no idea what's going on. Maybe you're *supposed* to be here. Have you even considered that little nagging possibility? Think about it, roomie. Think about it. . . ."

Gaia couldn't bear to be referred to as Paris's "roomie." She was ready to spray out a barrel full of venom at Paris, the world's most provocative stranger. But halfway through her windup, she found herself struck by an unexpected silence. She had suddenly found herself unable to say a word. Because in spite of everything, Paris had a disturbingly decent point.

It was the one possibility Gaia had yet to consider. What if her unexplainable presence in this hospital didn't have the least bit to do with any diabolical intentions or nefarious plots? What if it wasn't a mistake at all? Maybe a decision had been made, and that was the part she couldn't remember. Maybe someone had finally decided to do something about the relentless, oppressive sadness that had been slowly squeezing the life out of her for the past five years?

Maybe someone had finally decided to put Gaia Moore out of her misery.

I suppose there comes a time in everyone's life when they must stop for a moment and consider just exactly how much their life sucks. I, for instance, have reached that point in my life approximately ten times a day for the last five years.

Of course, there is always the guilt and the self-flagellation that follow. I know, at least rationally, that the average Ethiopian child or Korean refugee has it far worse than I do. I am not starving. I have access to all the amenities of modern society—or at least I did until today. I do, of course, as anyone's grandmother would remind me, have my health. At least, my *physical* health. But still. . . compared to the average American teen (whatever that means), I'd still have to say that I'm way up in the ninety-ninth percentile on life's suck-o-meter.

I know self-pity is the devil, and I ought to be constantly

searching for the silver lining, blah, blah, blah, but I'm pretty sure that my silver lining has long since tarnished to a vicious shade of black. There's just been way too much death in my life for a silver lining. Way too much death, way too much loss, and *way* too much alone time. I've spent close to a third of my life alone.

I suppose I've said it a million times or at least thought it a million times: *Someone should just lock me up and throw away the key. I've had enough of this miserable existence. My life is a project that has failed. It just hurts too much. I'd be better off in a padded cell with three squares a day. . . .*

I've certainly thought it enough times. . . . I just never thought it would actually happen.

Could it be that simple? Has someone finally wised up and called the white coats on me? Did they decide it was time to put me away? Did they decide to get me off ass kicking and get me on

Prozac? Or Haldol or Thorazine?

Because if that's the case. . . then I need to have a *major* talk with them. Whoever "they" are.

I need to explain to them that this is *not* the answer for me. No freaking way, nohow. I would rather live out my life as a fearless freak of nature than live it out in green cotton hospital scrubs. I will take depressive vigilante justice over white walls and locked doors any day. I will take eternal grieving and endless sadistic plots to assassinate me. I will take a lifetime of loneliness over a lifetime of doing the Thorazine shuffle.

All right, I admit it. Maybe I haven't been careful enough about what I've wished for. Maybe I've overdone it with my dreams of throwing in the towel. But I've more than learned my lesson here.

This is not where I belong, no matter how screwed up I may be. If someone thinks I'm supposed to be here, then they are sorely mistaken. I just need to explain that to the people here at the hospital—starting, I think, with the world's most presumptuous psycho roommate. I need to straighten my limp ass up, shake off these drugs, and explain to all parties involved just exactly to what extent I do *not* belong here. I need to make them shut up, wise up, and show me the exit. And if words don't do the trick, then I'll need to explain it with a solid roundhouse kick and show myself out.

Because that is me. That is who I am. And who I am is one thing I have not forgotten.

SOMETHING IN GAIA'S EYES HAD

changed. Her bleary-eyed, drug-addled confusion seemed to go up in smoke. Her limp, dysfunctional posture straightened right up as if she'd gotten a sudden infusion of adrenaline. Her schizoid bug eyes settled into a sharp, pinpointed glare. And the glare was aimed directly at Paris.

Psycho Roommate War

Paris considered herself the least fearful person in the hospital by far, but something about Gaia's new expression was honestly a bit frightening. It was nothing like the defensive stares she'd given Paris before. It was downright threatening. And when she took her first steady step in Paris's direction, it took everything Paris had not to retreat back to the headboard of her bed.

"You know what?" Gaia said, moving with a slightly tigerlike quality toward Paris. Her dirty blond hair was falling in thick, matted tendrils over her preying eyes. "I think we may have gotten off on the wrong foot here. I don't think we've been introduced in the appropriate *context*."

Her words were polite enough, but based solely on her eyes, Paris was beginning to wonder if it might not be time to holler for security before Gaia tried to take a bite out of her ear like Lizzie Huffington had done on *her* first day.

"That's cool. . . ," Paris uttered, peering through the window of the door to see if there were any orderlies nearby.

Gaia stepped to the vinyl chair in the corner and dragged it across the floor with a deafening screech that echoed off the bare walls. She pulled it up to within two inches of Paris's bed and sat herself down so that they were damn near nose to nose. Paris pulled herself back ever so slightly in the bed but tried to maintain eye contact. All paranoid schizos were different—Paris had seen all kinds. Some of them would freak out on you if you made eye contact. But she got the distinct impression that with this particular girl, it was actually best to maintain eye contact.

"So let's start from scratch, shall we?" Gaia suggested. Paris made sure not to flinch when Gaia presented her hand. "I'm Gaia."

"Paris," she replied cautiously, offering her hand in return. Gaia's handshake was beyond firm. Her grip felt like a piece of industrial machinery. She'd somehow managed to shake off the Haldol. It was like she had willed the drugs out of her system. Or maybe they'd just finally worn off.

"Yeah, I know," Gaia said. "Paris. Well, Paris, I'll tell you what I want to do. . . ." Gaia was yet to even blink. Paris stiffened her own posture just to try and stand up to Gaia's penetrating stare. "First of all, we're going to clear things up once and for all regarding our respective degrees of sanity. And then I'm going to ask you a few questions, all right?"

"Right. . . ," Paris mumbled tentatively. She still couldn't believe that she was feeling threatened by another patient. She never felt threatened by other patients. They were always threatened by her. That was how she kept all the crazies at bay. But something about Gaia was different. It was like she had suddenly turned up her "power" knob to match Paris's level, and Paris was still mentally stumbling to regain a sense of equal footing. She could think of only one other patient whom she'd ever viewed as an equal—it was, of course, the same patient she'd been thinking about ever since they'd dumped Gaia into that bed. But she didn't want to think about Ana. She never wanted to think about Ana again.

Gaia cracked her knuckles and leaned forward. Her words were crisp and deliberate. "First of all, I'm just getting my bearings here, but the apparent general consensus seems to be that I am crazy. You, for example, have even given me your own little uninformed diagnosis: a paranoid schizophrenic. A diagnosis that strikes me as odd coming from you, the only mental patient in the room."

"Look, I was just trying to give you the facts before they—"

"No, there's really no need to speak yet." Gaia thrust her hand forward to silence Paris. The menace in her eyes was barely veiled.

Paris swallowed hard and let out a deep, frustrated breath. She wished that Rosie weren't such a fan of these lockdowns. She wished she had never even begun any kind of dialogue with her roommate. After everything she had been through with Ana, she should have learned her lesson by now. Never talk to your roommate. Nothing good ever came of it.

"As I was saying," Gaia went on, "you provided me with your own little diagnosis, and I tried to set you straight, but I don't think I did a very good job of it. And it is *very* important to me that we clear up your error in judgment right now. I figure if I can clear it up with you rationally, then hopefully I'll be able to clear it up with *them* rationally so I can be on my way. See, that way, violence won't be necessary."

Paris's eyes drifted toward her bedside cabinet. There was an engraved metal paperweight in the top drawer that her school had sent her as the world's worst get-well gift. It was the only thing she could think of to use as a defense if Gaia truly flipped out on her. But she'd have no time to get to it with Gaia sitting only inches from her face.

Just stay cool, she told herself. *You've dealt with worse than this. Remember when Bible Jerry tried to exorcise your demons with Rosie's stun gun? You can handle this.*

But in Gaia's case, she wasn't so sure. She still didn't know a damn thing about this girl's history. For all she knew, Gaia had killed someone out there, gotten off on an insanity plea, and ended up here. . . in Paris's goddamn room. It made a sick kind of sense, actually. Put the craziest person at the hospital in the same room as the sanest person at the hospital. That was just the kind of crap Rosie and Dr. Weissman would pull on Paris. Just to watch her suffer. Just to scare her into submission.

But the last thing Paris had any intention of doing was submitting.

"Just forget I said anything," Paris huffed. "Just relax, all right? I wasn't trying to start some kind of psycho roommate war here, okay?"

"Well, that's just my *point*," Gaia shot back. "There's not going to be any kind of psycho roommate war because I am not a psycho. And according to you, neither are you. You're not a psycho. . . right, Paris?" Gaia searched much deeper into Paris's eyes, clearly challenging Paris's sanity right to her face.

"*Right*," Paris assured her with a pissed-off frown.

"Gee," Gaia offered with deep sarcasm, "have I offended you?"

"Whatever," Paris muttered, keeping her eyes fixed on Gaia's.

"Because if I have, then I think maybe you're beginning to get my point. You asked me if I was sure I didn't belong here. Well, my answer is hell, yes, I am sure. You asked me how I knew, and the answer is *because I know*. I know I am not crazy. Depressed, yes.

Miserable, you bet your ass. But crazy enough to be put away? Nuh-uh. No way. I just know it, that's all. I know me. So that only leaves one question: How do *you* know, Paris? You said you were the sanest person in here. But how do *you* know you're not crazy?"

Gaia's penetrating stare was beyond annoying. Paris felt the sudden impulse to reach back and smack her right across the face just for asking that idiotic question. Her sanity had been challenged enough by Dr. Weissman and Rosie and all the rest of them—she didn't need to hear that kind of crap from a new patient. She knew full well what she was doing in this hospital, and it had nothing to do with insanity.

But the longer she spent trying to concoct the best answer to Gaia's question, the less she felt like smacking her in the face. Because when all was said and done. . . Paris's answer was really no different than Gaia's. She knew she wasn't crazy because she knew it. That was all. Because she knew herself better than any shrink or security bitch knew her.

And after searching a few extra seconds for an answer that would somehow make her seem superior, she found that only the simplest of words actually fell from her mouth.

"I know because. . . I just know," she uttered.

The anger in Gaia's face began to subside. There might have even been the slightest hint of a smile at the corners of her mouth.

"Right," she said. "I just have to take your word for it, don't I? So then here's the deal: If I have to take your word for it. . . then I guess you'll just have to take mine." Gaia locked her eyes with Paris's. "Make sense?"

Silence filled the room. Somehow Gaia's logic suddenly seemed to make a rather unavoidable amount of sense. And even more important, she'd actually used logic to make her point. Paris had never met a mental patient in this hospital who had used logic to make a point. Except, of course, for Ana. Back in the early days.

In that brief silence Paris began to realize that Gaia hadn't exactly been trying to scare her or rip her to pieces. It was starting to seem like she had only been trying to make a point—a point about both of them. About how they each defined their sanity. And in that moment Paris could feel herself beginning to identify ever so slightly with Gaia—to feel some faint sense of kinship. That is to say, she was maybe beginning to like her just a little bit. And that was the last thing she wanted. That was exactly the mistake she'd made with Ana, and she'd sworn to herself that she'd never make another friend in this place. But still. . . having even a remotely normal exchange was providing an undeniable hint of relief.

"Fine," Paris agreed reluctantly. "I'll take your word for it. For now."

"Fine," Gaia confirmed. "And I'll take yours." She completed their pact with an almost imperceptible nod. She relaxed back in her chair as a more peaceful silence filled the room. The silence seemed to seal the deal. They had officially agreed to consider each other sane until proven insane.

Eventually Gaia leaned back toward Paris, though this time it was much less threatening. "Well, then, as one theoretically sane person to another. . . where the hell are we?"

"It's called Rainhill Hospital; it's—"

"No, I *know* that, but *where*?" Gaia pressed. "That's not New York City out there, that's for sure."

"Oh," Paris said. "Florida. Fort Myers Beach. Are you from New York?"

Gaia didn't answer. She looked too busy trying to accept the notion that she was in Fort Myers Beach, Florida. When her eyes finally met Paris's again, she seemed able to muster only one question.

"Who the hell do I talk to about getting out of here?" she asked.

Paris blew out a pitiful little laugh. "Well, you can talk to your shrink. But it's a totally useless endeavor. Believe me, I've tried. And tried and tried. Useless."

Gaia looked none too pleased with Paris's response. "Well, what if I want to just bypass the shrink? What if I want to skip the talking altogether and show myself out?"

"What, you mean escape?"

"Yeah. That's what I mean."

Even entertaining the thought made Paris a little sick. It pushed her back in time to her first few months in this place. All those conversations with Ana. All those escape plans and all that naive optimism, when she'd actually believed that she might someday find her way out of Rainhill. She didn't want to indulge in that thinking for even a moment. It was too depressing. And depression at Rainhill was the kiss of death.

"Don't even think about it," Paris said, keeping her voice quiet as she checked the door again. "Just do yourself a favor and put it out of your mind."

"Oh, come on," Gaia said, lowering her voice. "There must be some way to—"

"No," Paris insisted. "There isn't. Not without. . . Oh, forget it."

"Forget what? What were you going to say?"

"I said *forget* it!" Paris snapped. Now Paris was the one who sounded crazy, and she knew it. But she refused to converse any further on that depressing topic. It only made her think of Ana, and of Jared, and of how very long she had been cooped up in this hellhole without any choice in the matter.

"All right, all right, *relax*," Gaia said. "Jesus. I was just asking."

Paris lay back in her bed and tried to toughen herself back up. Two minutes of company behavior and she already felt weaker than she had in months. This was exactly why she avoided all real conversation in this place. It just got way too sad, way too quickly. She had to maintain her distance.

Gaia took a couple of deep breaths. "Can I just ask you one more question?"

"What?" Paris muttered, looking at the same patch of blue sky that she'd been staring at for months.

"Before. . . when I was waking up and looking around. . ." There was a touch of caution in her voice. "You kept staring at me. You kept giving me these weird looks. Why were you staring at me like that?"

Paris debated how to answer the question. For some reason, she decided to be truthful, in spite of her better judgment. "I was just thinking about someone, that's all."

"Who?"

"My old roommate, I guess. You're just the first roommate I've had since her. She was one of Dr. K.'s, too."

"Dr. K.? Is that Dr. Kraven? Rosie said I could talk to Dr. Kraven. Is he supposed to be my shrink?"

"Yeah," Paris said.

"Wait. . . how did you know he was my doctor?"

"Your ID bracelet." Paris pointed down at Gaia's blue bracelet with the little plastic dot at the center. Then she held up her own bright red bracelet. "I have Dr. Pain-in-the-ass Weissman. You have Dr. K."

"Oh." Gaia seemed to consider this for a moment as she examined her ID bracelet. But then she lifted her quizzical eyes back up to Paris's profile. "Well. . . what happened to your old roommate?"

Paris turned her head farther toward the window and away from Gaia. She knew she shouldn't have been honest. Not with a girl who was going to ask so many goddamn questions. "I don't want to talk about it," she breathed.

Gaia didn't seem to know what to do with that answer. "Well. . . is she still at the hospital or. . . ?"

"No. She's gone."

Gaia paused again, uncomfortably. "You mean. . . *gone* gone or—"

"I just *told* you I don't want to *talk* about her, all right?" Paris whipped her head back to Gaia and shot her a razor-sharp "back off" glance. "Jesus, what are you, *deaf*?"

"All *right*," Gaia squawked. "Will you relax, please?"

"Well, I *would* relax if you would stop asking me all these goddamn questions!"

"Look, you brought her up, I was just—"

"Yeah, well, that was a *mistake*, and now I'm correcting it. I don't want to talk about her. I don't even want to *think* about her."

The lock on the door suddenly turned with a loud snap as Vince, one of the orderlies, hurled it open and stepped through the doorway. "Lunch!" he barked rudely. And then, just as quickly as he had entered, he turned around and barreled down the hallway.

Gaia turned to the doorway and then back to Paris. She looked unsure as to what to do or say next. Paris swung her legs back over the edge of the bed and tried to tone down her bitchiness. She really hadn't meant to take out all her Ana issues on Gaia. Gaia had enough to deal with right now, what with having just recently woken up in hell.

"Look," Paris said. "I'm sorry. I didn't mean. . . Let's just eat, all right? When was the last time you ate?"

"I have no idea."

"You're probably starving, right?"

"I guess, but. . . can you just tell me—"

"Gaia, *please*. I don't want to talk about her. Let's just eat some repulsive institutional food. I'm trying to be nice. If you want me to go back to being a bitch, it's really easy. You can go right into that common room by yourself and sit with any psycho of your choice. . . ."

This potential scenario seemed to hit home. Gaia let out a long, frustrated sigh and then she nodded. "Fine," she uttered. "Let's eat. I'm hungry."

"Good. I'll introduce you to our gourmet cuisine. And when we're done eating, I'll show you where to puke."

One night at Denny's. One stupid night at Denny's.

That's the only reason I'm in this place. That's it. It would be laughable if it weren't so pathetic.

It basically goes like this: One random night in February, my dad decides to take us all out for a Scram Slam dinner. Me, my boyfriend, Jared, and my mom. That was Dad's idea of splurging. Scram Slams at Denny's.

It was like the one night out of a hundred that he wasn't pissed at me for something. I hadn't skipped any tests in a while. I hadn't snuck over to Jared's to spend the night. I hadn't missed any curfews or scraped up his precious car. We hadn't had any screaming matches in a few days, and I hadn't cursed out my mother for just sitting by while he hollered at me for making his life such a chore. We were actually all getting along for more than five minutes.

I couldn't even believe he'd
invited Jared along. He was
always blaming Jared for my
"attitude problem." He always
said that if I weren't so
obsessed with my boyfriend, then
maybe I might actually study for
something—maybe I might give up
on my whole "problem-child routine,"
as he called it, and stop pissing
my life away. My theory was that
he had just forgotten what it
actually felt like to be in love.
He had probably loved my mom at
some point. Like maybe when they
got married. Or maybe before they
had me. But on Denny's night he
was actually being civil. I don't
know why, but Jared and I were
trying to make the most of it,
anyway. We were playing it as
Seventh Heaven for Dad as we possibly could. Jared was calling
him "sir"; I had put on something
that wasn't black. Mom even told
a few very bad jokes.

And the good mood actually
lasted for a while. About forty-
five minutes, I'd say.

I don't really remember exactly when it all went wrong, but of course it did. Dad, being the idiot that he was, went ahead and ruined a perfectly good evening by mentioning something to me about college applications. I said something bitchy and then excused myself to go to the bathroom so I could cool down and try to salvage our Denny's extravaganza.

But when I got back from the bathroom, things just got worse. It's kind of a fog at this point, but it all started with the look on Dad's face when I got back to the table. I made one little follow-up comment about not going to college, and he just started barking at me to sit down and shut up. And then I started barking back at him—you can't talk to me like that, you can't tell me what to do, all the usual stuff. And then it all just turned into a big ugly Denny's spectacle. He was barking, and I was barking, bark, bark, bark, and then the whole damn restaurant started barking for both of us to shut up, and then, yes. . . I broke a window.

That's it. That is the sum total of my lunacy. I got pissed at my dad and I smashed a Denny's window. *That* was the big "last straw" that got me tossed into Rainhill. What a joke. Dr. Weissman just loves to quiz me about it. She loves to sit there and listen, nodding with that dumb-ass smile as she gets me to go through that stupid night over and over again. As if a broken window was such a big deal that of course I'd require long-term in-patient treatment to "change my ways." It's a bunch of bull, and she knows it. She and I both know what's really going on. We know what I've really been doing here all this time.

My parents just don't want to deal with me. That's it. That's what it's all about. They don't want to deal with me anymore. My dad was just so *overwhelmed* by his rebellious teen daughter, so ashamed to be the father of a screwup that he just wanted someone else to step in and fix all his lousy parenting. He wanted someone else to deal with his "problem child" so he could have his dinner in peace and play his golf on Sundays without wondering what little embarrassing teen stunt he was going to have to deal with next. And of course, my mom wasn't going to say a word. She wasn't going to fight for me to come back home because she never fought for anything.

Everyone's just waiting for Dr. Weissman and all the rest of them to "fix" me. The way they try to fix everybody here. The way they "fixed" Ana.

Well, it's not going to happen. Never. No one is ever going to convince me that a broken window means that I'm insane. My dad doesn't have to love me. But he could have at least found a way to deal with me. The same way I've had to find a way to deal with this place.

Whatever. It's his loss.

a mental
patient
with a
black
belt in
karate

**flight
risk**

FLORIDA. FORT MYERS BEACH, FLORIDA.

How was that possible? How the hell was any of it possible?

Disturbing Little Mystery

Gaia wasn't sure she could wait until after lunch to puke. The stale reek of C-grade institutional food had penetrated her nostrils from the moment they'd entered the common room. It made the cafeteria at the Village School seem like afternoon tea at the Plaza. What was that added stench that seemed to float off all hospital food? That sickening combination of rancid sweet and rancid sour—as if it had all been stirred up in some industrial-sized vat and sealed up in large white cans marked Food. Whatever it was, Gaia wasn't sure she could stomach it.

She wasn't even sure what was more upsetting, watching the patients all line up for their lunches in their sagging robes and hospital scrubs like prisoners of war or watching them sit crunched together at those large wooden tables with their soiled trays and their miniature containers of milk like a bunch of disturbed oversized kindergartners at snack time. Who in their right mind could possibly think that you could cure someone of depression in such a dismal environment?

Ultimately Gaia had no choice but to turn her head down to the linoleum floor and try to shut them all out. She stood silently in the food line behind Paris and tried to contemplate her next move. But that was next to impossible, given her and Paris's totally fruitless conversation. Every time Gaia had tried to extract some information from Paris, she only seemed to strike at yet another painfully exposed nerve. She had gotten completely stonewalled on the subjects of any kind of official release from the hospital or any potential routes of escape. Not to mention Paris's rather eerie reluctance to talk about her last roommate—the roommate with whom Gaia apparently shared a doctor. That disturbing little mystery was more than a bit discouraging. What the hell had happened to her? What could be so awful that Paris wouldn't even offer a few simple words on the topic?

One thing was for sure. There was no point in making a blind run for it if Gaia didn't even know where she was going. She could just imagine the outcome of that. She knew that she'd finally shaken off the majority of her Haldol lethargy, and yes, at full strength she could probably take down half the orderlies in this place in one shot. But what if all the orderlies were as massive as that dude who'd unlocked the door and announced lunch? Then she'd definitely need to be firing on all pistons. And what if she wasn't quite at full strength? Or what if she came up against a dead end in her run for it? Eventually they might just gather enough help to restrain her, and then what?

Then they'd know they had a flight risk on their hands. Not just a flight risk, but a violent flight risk.

A mental patient with a black belt in karate... This was, without question, a hospital's worst nightmare. One violent episode and they'd shoot her so full of Haldol, she probably wouldn't even remember her name. No, the blind run was definitely out. At least until she had tried talking some sense into them as she had done with Paris, at least until she could gather some more information about the lay of the land.

It was all so discouraging. Every ounce of it. *Fort Myers Beach, Florida...* It was all just melting together into a big gelatinous mass of hopelessness and nausea in Gaia's stomach.

Still, there was at least something about Paris that Gaia felt she could trust. At least Paris wasn't mumbling to herself as she stared at ten-year-old newspapers or singing to herself as she peeled the paper off crayons.

No, that wasn't quite fair. It was more than that. In spite of Paris's hypersensitivity to certain questions, Gaia did honestly believe in the girl's relative sanity. Gaia was, of course, going on sheer instinct, but right now there was very little else to go on. There was just something about Paris—something that somehow reminded Gaia of herself. It could be as simple as Paris's general disdain for most of her peers or her deep wells of alienating attitude, but Gaia had a feeling that it ran deeper than that. Even though she didn't know a damn thing about the girl.

Gaia finally reached the five-foot-tall box of stacked trays and pulled her shrink-wrapped lunch from one of the bottom slots. The stench at close range nearly knocked her off her feet.

She took two reluctant steps toward one of the round tables, but Paris's hand grabbed firmly to her arm and held her back.

"No, no," Paris muttered from the side of her mouth, pulling Gaia closer to her. "You don't want to eat next to Soylent James."

"Who?"

Paris flicked her head in the direction of an older man with a mop of dusty black hair and thick Coke-bottle glasses. "Soylent James. You know that movie *Soylent Green*, where it turns out that the stuff everyone's been eating is actually people? Well, Soylent James is convinced that Rainhill cuisine also happens to be made entirely from people, and he talks you through it bite by bite."

"Okay," Gaia uttered, swallowing hard to fight off reverse digestion. She turned toward another table.

"*Uh-uh*," Paris whispered urgently. "Not Christina Karetsky. Obsessive food thrower. She fixates on new patients, and then you're dodging oatmeal for days."

"All right, will you just lead the way, please?" Gaia begged.

"Over here," Paris said, guiding Gaia to a smaller

but empty table all the way at the back of the room by the concrete wall.

They settled down in their chairs, and Paris immediately began to eat. She had obviously built up a resistance to the hospital's food over time. Gaia was in fact starving. She probably hadn't eaten for at least twenty-four hours. It was really the one and only reason she'd agreed to have lunch before researching her immediate release. But the moment Gaia peeled the plastic off her dark brown tray and got a glimpse of the enigmatic brown mass at the center of her plate, her reflexes kicked in. She shoved the tray against the wall, dropped her head in her hands, and focused on her breathing.

"I can't do this," she complained. "I am not doing this. I need to talk to them *now*. Dr. Kraven, or the administration, or *whoever*. Now."

"Chill *out*," Paris insisted. "I already told you, talking to those assholes isn't going to do anything. They don't listen, Gaia. They don't care."

"Well, they'll listen to me. I'll make them listen."

"Fine, go ahead and scream your head off. All you end up with is a lockdown, or the quiet room, or Rosie's personal favorite, bathroom cleaning." She sighed, then sat up straight.

"Oh, crap," she muttered.

Gaia's head darted back up. "What?"

"No, don't walk this way," Paris pleaded to herself. "Do not walk this way. . . ."

"What? What are you talking about?"

"*Tricia, the teen zombie,*" Paris whispered. "She's coming this way."

Gaia followed Paris's finger and saw a girl headed toward the table with a smile that had been borrowed from a 1950s toothpaste commercial. Gaia remembered Tricia from her first trip to the common room. She remembered her short, center-parted auburn hair and the mass of light freckles spreading down from her nose. She remembered that Tricia and Paris had been arguing about something or someone. Most of all, she remembered that Rosie had offered Tricia up to Gaia as the model of a well-behaved patient at Rainhill.

Gaia hated her already.

"*HIIII,*" TRICIA BELLOWED, NEARLY knocking Gaia backward with her blinding ebullience. Gaia had been a little too distracted to notice it the first time, but now with only that one syllable spoken, she could hear Tricia's Midwestern accent. "Can I sit here?"

"No," Paris muttered.

"Oh, shush, Paris, don't be such a frown hound."

A frown hound? Tricia placed her tray on the table

and plopped down in the empty chair next to Gaia. *Right* next to Gaia. "I'm Tricia," she said, grinning. "Gaia, right?"

"Right," Gaia mumbled.

"Well, Gaia, you're going to have to ignore her," she said with a smile, referring to Paris. "Paris has been having a bad day. For about the last three months." Tricia let out a bright girlish giggle, as if to share it with Gaia. But Gaia's face only grew stiffer.

Tricia interrupted her giggle and crossed her arms dramatically, staring at Gaia. "Uh-oh." She sighed. "Now, you see. . . a few minutes with Paris and you've already got it, too."

"Got what?" Gaia asked.

"A case of the *frowns*," Tricia explained. "It's okay. It happens to the best of us. I wasn't too excited my first day here, either."

Not too excited. That somehow that did not sufficiently describe Gaia's state of mind.

"Well, at least you're getting some of your color back." Tricia reached her hand over and pinched Gaia's cheek. Gaia's fist clenched for a reflexive punch, but she managed to keep it under the table. She was reserving it for the next time Tricia tried to touch her.

"God, I was really worried about you yesterday," Tricia went on. "My heart *so* went out to you, looking so lost. The first day is definitely a doozy. But I swear to you, it gets better. It gets so much better. Like, my first day or so, I was totally a mess. But in a few days the whole mess just started to rise up and drift away, like I'd put it in a big giant hot air balloon and let it float off into the bright blue sky, you know? Like I'd—"

"*Tricia.*" Paris pounded her hand on the table.

Tricia's eyes widened with surprise. "What?" she asked innocently.

Paris shook her head with disdain. "She's having enough trouble dealing with the mystery meat. Your incessant motormouth is only going to make her more nauseous."

Tricia placed her hands on her hips and puffed out her chest. "Why don't you lay off, Ms. Mean Jeans? I'm just trying to let Gaia here know that things are going to get a lot better." She turned back to Gaia. "You know how I know things are going to get better?" Her sly little smile suggested that she was about to share some kind of delicious secret with Gaia.

She leaned forward and placed her left hand next to Gaia's. "Because we both have Dr. K." She grinned. "Oh my God, Gaia, he is the best." Tricia was practically swooning. "Truly. The absolute best, hands down. No offense to Dr. Weissman," Tricia added, with a quick nod to Paris. "She seems like a supersweetie, too."

"None taken." Paris sighed, with a roll of her eyes.

"But Gaia," Tricia said. "Seriously. You don't even know how lucky you are. Dr. K. is just. . . There's just something about him. Something gentle and kind.

Something different. He went through it all with me, piece by piece, you know? All my old crazy issues. Believe me, girl, I was *deluded*. Oh God, I was such a crazy-daisy. But Dr. K. . . . I don't know. . . personally, he changed my life. A total one-eighty. It was kind of a miracle. Not to mention the fact that he looks just like George Clooney." Tricia grinned sheepishly, and Gaia winced in pain.

Paris cringed, too, as she turned to Gaia. "In case you haven't figured it out yet, Tricia is in love with her shrink."

"*Ew*," Tricia groaned, swiping at Paris's shoulder with a flaccid girlie slap. "Shush your *mouth, Paris*. I am *not*."

"You're blushing, Tricia," Paris muttered. "It's called *transference*. Look into it."

"Okay, whatever to *you*. I'm eighteen years old, and he's, like, thirty-eight. I am not in love with my therapist; I just admire him, that's all."

"He's forty," Paris said.

"No, he's not; he's only thirty-eight. He won't even be thirty-nine till next August."

"Not that you care."

"Okay, will you cut it out?" Tricia insisted. "I just wanted Gaia to know that she's in good hands, that's all. And that she's lucky." She turned to Gaia. "He hardly ever takes on a new patient. It's been a couple of months since—"

"*Enough* about the great Dr. K., all right?" Paris

76

tossed her fork down in the middle of the slop on her plate. "I'm sick of hearing his goddamn name."

Gaia was sick of it, too. She was sick and tired of hearing about her supposedly genius therapist. She just wanted to meet him already. She just wanted to meet the great Dr. K. right now and get her hall pass, or her get-out-of-jail-free card, or whatever it was she needed to return to the civilization of humans.

"I need to talk to him," Gaia announced, standing up out of her chair. "I need to talk to Dr. K. right now."

"Gaia, I'm telling you," Paris complained. "It's not going to do you any—"

"Now," Gaia interrupted.

"You go, girl," Tricia said with a grin. "Wanting to get better is totally the first step. But you have to wait for your appointment. He only—"

"I'm not waiting for anything."

Gaia was not going to waste any more time. She was going to find Dr. Kraven, even if it meant opening every door of every hallway in the entire hospital. But she had only taken one step from their table when the deafening clatter of falling food trays stopped her in her tracks.

Everyone's attention zoomed in on the corner of the room where the sudden ruckus had broken out. The sound of one man's maniacal shouting had become the common room's main attraction.

"I swear to God, I'm gonna rip those eyes right out of your head!" he howled, shaking his fists wildly in the air.

He was a rather obese man, and he had knocked down a full cart of lunch trays, spilling the food all over the floor. When Gaia moved her head slightly to the left, she could see that he was towering over a much younger boy who had fallen to the floor. He was screaming down at the boy with a vicious array of curses.

The boy tried desperately to shield himself from the man's onslaught by raising his arm over his face, but he was slipping in all directions, tangled up in puddles of mashed potatoes and mystery meat, looking utterly terrified. He couldn't have been much older than thirteen or fourteen.

Tricia leapt out of her chair. "Oh my God, D.," she uttered, making her way through the overexcited crowd and kneeling down next to the boy to tend to him. He looked a little too tall for his age and awkwardly skinny. His blondish brown hair was falling in stringy, shaggy bangs over his bright blue terror-stricken eyes. Tricia turned around on one knee and glowered at the screaming man. "Leave him alone, Marvin! You're scaring him to death!"

"He was giving me that look again!" Marvin, the obese offender, growled. "He knows I can't stand that *look*." Marvin stared back down at the cowering boy and then knelt closer to him, pointing his thick finger right in his face. "Don't you look at me again, junior, or I swear to God, I'll rip your skin right off your freakin' face. I'll—"

"All right, Marvin, enough!" one of the orderlies shouted. It took two orderlies to latch onto each of Marvin's arms. They tugged him slowly away from the boy, dragging his flailing six-foot frame toward the door as he continued to look back with a maniacal glare.

"Don't you look at me!" he repeated. "Don't do it, boy!"

"He can't look at you if you're in the quiet room," one of the orderlies said as they finally tugged Marvin out of the room and out of sight.

The common room went momentarily silent. But it took only seconds for the crowd to turn right back to their meals and their incessant chatter. Encounters like these were obviously par for the course here at Rainhill.

When Gaia turned back to the boy, however, she saw that he wasn't nearly as unfazed as the rest of the crowd. He was still literally shivering with fear. Tricia tried to wipe the foodlike slop from his clothes and help him off the floor, but he was resisting her. He kept batting Tricia's hands away, trying to stand up by himself. But the floor was just too slippery.

The boy finally managed to get back onto his feet, and then he stepped over to one of the empty tables and sat down. He was clearly trying to collect himself after his traumatic little showdown with Marvin. But if Gaia had gone by the devastated look in his eyes, she would have thought he had just been nearly murdered. Tricia immediately sat down next to him with a stack of napkins and continued her maternal routine, trying to wipe him clean and give calming affectionate strokes to his back. But once again the boy seemed to want her nowhere near him. He kept batting her arms away like she was a menacing insect.

It took a few more moments of observation before Gaia truly noticed what had happened to her. Only a minute or so before, she had been totally focused on one goal and one goal only: to head out into those halls and find her apparent shrink of all shrinks, Dr. Kraven; to get out of this place by any means necessary; and to do it now. But right in the middle of that most crystalline mission, she had suddenly found herself totally fixated on this poor slop-covered thirteen-year-old boy. She absolutely could not take her eyes off him. There was just something so sad about him. Something about his awkward skinny frame and his terror-stricken eyes just made her heart split down the middle.

It seemed that Gaia's savior complex was still very much intact. Even in the confines of this hospital, the sight of any weak and helpless individual being bullied by someone twice their size made her skin crawl and her fists clench. If those orderlies hadn't stepped in so quickly, Gaia would have had Marvin pinned to the ground by now, his face forcibly shoved into piles of crap-colored mystery meat. Because in spite of the urgency of her own predicament, this was something she simply could not abide. She could not tolerate the assault of such a frightened and helpless young boy. Whether she knew him or not.

Freaky Random Words

"WHO IS THAT?" GAIA ASKED, CASTING a glimpse back at Paris.

"That's D.," Paris replied dismissively. "He's our resident spook. Not that they aren't all spooks."

"'D.?'" Gaia asked. "Just the letter *D*? That's his name?"

"As far as I know. No one really knows that much about him. I mean, besides all the stories."

"What stories?"

"Oh, please," Paris muttered, sipping from her milk carton. "He's just been here too long, that's all. He's been here longer than anyone else. Except maybe Catatonic Elsie. Everyone just loves to tell stories. There's a million of them. You know, he was raised in captivity at the hospital like some kind of monkey, that kind of stuff. Or he has psychic powers, he has no parents, blah, blah, blah. . . . It's all made up. Big deal, his folks have never visited? *My* folks have never visited. So frikkin' what? People just like to make crap up about the resident spook."

"What do you mean, 'resident spook'?" Gaia turned back and watched as Tricia continued to struggle with D., shoving napkins in his face and trying to make eye contact.

"I mean, I'm with Marvin on this one," Paris said. "Marvin may be a deranged psycho, but he's right. D. is always just standing there staring at you—staring at your face or staring up at the top of your head. It's just disturbing. And he hardly ever says a damn word. He spits out some chunks of gibberish about colors or something, and then he just goes back into his own little world. I don't even think he can make a full sentence. I mean, I guess it's kind of sad watching him wander around aimlessly all the time, saying, like, two freaky random words a day, but honestly, it *really* starts to get on your nerves when he just stands there staring at your head. You just kind of want to shove him into a closet or something so you don't have to deal with those spook eyes."

"People are assholes," Gaia muttered. "He's just a kid. I don't see what's so spooky about him."

"Yeah, well, you're nuts."

Gaia whipped back around and gave Paris the evil eye.

"*Kidding*," she said, holding out her hands. "Only kidding. You don't want to lose your sense of humor in this place, believe me."

"Right," Gaia mumbled, turning back to the boy. "Well, I'm going to see if he's okay."

"Be my guest," Paris said. Paris's voice drifted back into the crowd as Gaia approached D. and Tricia.

You're wasting time, a voice in her head reminded her. *You just need to find Dr. K. and get out of here.*

She would find him in just a second. She just wanted to be sure this very sad kid was all right—one good deed before she got the hell out of Rainhill. She was, after all, one of the few mentally intact people in the room. The least she could do was give one of the sadder cases an encouraging pat on the back. She knew what it felt like to be the freak in the room. Even in a room full of freaks. She had felt like a lab monkey plenty of times in her life. And she certainly knew what it felt like to have no parents.

"Are you all right?" Gaia stood at the table and tried to get D.'s attention. His stringy bangs were hanging over his eyes, blocking his peripheral vision. His mouth stayed locked in the post–traumatic-terror position.

"He's *fine*," Tricia cooed, trying to soothe him with repulsive baby talk as she repeatedly pushed the napkin at his mouth. "Big bad Marvin just scared him, right, D.? He's just a big bad Mr. Mean Jeans, sweetie. That's all. Don't you even worry about him, Dee Dee. Don't you worry. That's just Marvin's disease talking."

Gaia rolled her eyes. The kid wasn't four years old; she didn't see why Tricia had to treat him like it. "I don't know about his disease," she said. "I just know he was an asshole."

"*Hey,*" Tricia squeaked, turning to look up at Gaia. "*Gutter mouth.* D.'s upset enough as it is without having to hear that kind of language." She turned back to D. "You just had a little spill-spill, didn't you Dee Dee? . . . Yeah. . ." D. shoved her hand away.

"I don't think he wants a napkin, Tricia. Hey. . . are you all right?" Gaia spoke with more authority this time. She'd walked over here to be nice to the kid, not to be ignored. All she was looking for was a friendly nod, and then she'd be on her way.

D. seemed to finally register the voice coming from above him. He followed the voice and inched his head up toward Gaia. She'd gotten a good enough sense of the patients here to know she should be ready for anything. But the moment D.'s hair fell back from his eyes, something in his deeply traumatized expression changed. The moment he got a glimpse of Gaia, the pain seemed to slowly melt from his face.

Suddenly he looked nothing like the damaged, terrified boy she'd seen cowering from across the room. His eyes widened, reflecting all the stark fluorescent light in the room like little pieces of cobalt blue glass. The corners of his mouth began to turn upward, and most unexpectedly, he drifted up from his chair. Suddenly he and Gaia were standing face-to-face. And just as Paris had warned, he began to stare, unblinking, into Gaia's eyes. This was obviously his ritual with every one of the patients. "D.?" Tricia beckoned from her seat.

"D., sit down, sweetie, you're bothering Gaia. *D. . . .*"

Tricia sounded almost annoyed. The world's most annoying girl was suddenly annoyed. But in this one very odd case, Gaia was not. This strange boy's probing eyes didn't seem to bother her in the least. Maybe it was just her lack of fear. Maybe it was her inability to be spooked, even by the resident spook.

The longer D. examined her countenance, the more his entire expression seemed to shift. More and more, his entire face seemed to register something Gaia could only describe as. . . wonderment. That was the only word she could think of. As if he'd seen something wonderful about her face. Something she obviously had never seen.

"D., that's enough," Tricia said. "Leave her alone, honey. Come sit back down with me, all right? Don't worry, Gaia. He's always staring. People just make him uncomfortable and he gets too scared to talk. D., come sit here."

"Yellow," D. uttered in a gentle raspy voice. A wide, unfettered grin spread across his cheeks as he circled his finger just outside the edges of Gaia's face. In spite of his freakish behavior, Gaia found herself glued to the boy's eyes. There was something almost trance-inducing about him. She didn't even budge when his finger suddenly moved so unexpectedly close to her skin.

"That's right, sweetie," Tricia said. "She has blond hair." Tricia reached for his hand, but he slapped it away.

"Nuh-uh," D. snapped, shaking his head. He circled Gaia's face again with his finger without actually touching her. *"Yellow,"* he repeated more emphatically, glimpsing just above her head. "Glorious, glorious yellow. . ." His joyful eyes stayed fixed just above her head.

Glorious yellow? What on earth could that possibly mean? Was he talking about her hair? Gaia had no idea. She only knew that he'd meant it, in his own bizarrely cryptic way, as some kind of compliment.

For the first time Gaia found herself bothering to wonder about a fellow patient. What had happened to this poor kid? What had left him spitting out cryptic words and staring at people like he had just come down from outer space? What made him cower in terror like that? How had he become the resident spook?

She searched deeper into his enthralled eyes, but before she could find any answers, his eyes changed again. Slowly but surely the fear began to seep back into his face. For a moment Gaia wondered what it was about her that had changed his expression back to one of terror. But as she followed his gaze, she realized that he was no longer staring at her. He had shifted his stare to the people coming up from behind her. Whoever they were, they'd turned the kid right back into a terrorized victim in seconds. Gaia turned to look behind her.

Rosie. Rosie and one of her pumped-up, white-shirted minions. Of course D. was terrified of Rosie.

He was terrified of bullies, and Rosie was the god-damn queen bully.

"Hi, Rosie." Tricia smiled, reeking of kiss-ass.

"Tricia." Rosie gave Tricia her closest approximation of a smile. But her bureaucratic frown returned the moment she turned back to Gaia.

"All right, Gaia, it's time," Rosie said.

"Time for what?" Gaia asked coldly.

Rosie gave her another one of her icy glances. "I thought you'd be more excited. It's time to meet Dr. K."

"Finally," Gaia said. She had turned to follow Rosie when a hand grabbed hold of her. She turned back to find D.'s long, delicate fingers wrapped around her wrist.

"Nuh-uh," he uttered as the fear built up in his eyes. "Yellow. Yellow glorious."

"D., honey, let go of Gaia," Tricia said, grabbing hold of D.'s other hand and trying to guide him back down to his seat.

"*Yellow*," he repeated, squeezing tighter on Gaia's wrist and staring urgently into her eyes.

She was beginning to see just how screwed up D. was. He was so irrationally terrified of Rosie, he couldn't even let Gaia stand next to her. And what was he talking about? What exactly was his obsession with the color yellow? Gaia had thought it was some kind of compliment. Now she wasn't so sure that it wasn't just one of the only words he spoke.

D. tried again to grab at Gaia, but Rosie stepped in

front of her, giving D. a threatening glare. "Sit down and stay quiet," she ordered. D. nearly fell back against the table, backpedaling. He shut his mouth and plopped down in his seat. "What happens when we don't stay quiet, D.?" Rosie added, hovering over him. D. was already shaking in his cloth slippers, but of course she had to hover over him, what with her pathetic little power trip. Gaia wanted to pound a hole in Rosie's face, but that was thankfully the last of Rosie's unnecessary threats to D. She turned back to Gaia and grabbed one of her arms. "Vince. . ." She signaled to her beefy orderly—the same oversized frat boy with the blond buzz cut who'd unlocked Gaia's door earlier. Vince grabbed Gaia's other arm and they began to escort her out into the hall.

"Nuh-uh," D. groaned from back at the table. Gaia twisted her head around to get another glimpse of him. "Yellow," he whimpered. "Glorious. . ." Tricia tried to console him, but he wriggled his shoulders free of her touch.

Gaia felt so sorry for him, whatever on earth was wrong with him. If it had been anything other than Dr. K., she would have tried to stick around another minute to calm him down a little more. But this meeting with the doctor was far too important. It was, in fact, all that mattered now.

Besides, in spite of her strange little bonding moment with D., Gaia knew there was no point in getting attached. Not to D. or to Paris, either. For one thing, she had the distinct feeling that no one was ever going to be able to truly help that poor boy. And much more important, she wasn't going to be here long enough to make any new friends or tend to any more victims.

Because she was getting out.

Glorious yellow. Yellow glorious. Brighter than the big yellow circle in the sky.

They're all gray. All their heads. Gray and green like vomit. Brown like mud. Red like blood. Crimson blood from their heads, vicious black from their eyes, dripping down on their white coats.

There was no more yellow. No more yellow until her.

She's yellower than the circle in my pictures. Yellower than the paint. Even yellower than Ana.

Glorious, glorious Ana.

Her head turned black and blue.

And red. Red like blood.

Don't go, Glorious Yellow.

Don't Ana. Don't Tricia. Don't look at their heads. Don't turn black.

Please.

She knew
that she was
probably the
only **incurable**

person on **power**

this planet

trip

who would

not be

afraid at

this moment.

KENNEDY

I'm almost jealous. Gaia gets to have her very first session with Dr. K.

I don't think it's ever as good as the first time. I mean, my first few sessions with Dr. K. were the real lifesavers. They were the ones that really cleared all the icky spiderwebs out of my head. They were the ones that woke my crazy-daisy head up. I'll never forget them. I'll never forget what Dr. K. did for me and for my whole poor family, who had to put up with me.

I'm not ashamed to admit it. I used to be Looney Tunes.

I used to think I was a farmer named Daisy. No, that's not a joke. Farmer Daisy. A living cartoon. I used to babble and dream and babble and dream about "the farm." A big green farm in my head. In Oklahoma. With sheep and horses and pigs and cows. I thought my father was named Merle, and he wore overalls and drove a tractor. I thought my mom was named Nellie, and she knitted sweaters out of sheep's wool. I thought I had a brother named Jack and a sister named Jill. Jack and Jill. Wonder how I came up with those names. . . .

Of course it was all just a giant bucket of delusions. I didn't live on a farm in Oklahoma. I lived in a six-bedroom house in Winnetka, Illinois. My backyard was my "farm." My parents are named Victor and Alexandria, not Merle and Nellie. I don't have any brothers and sisters, and my name is not Daisy. It's Tricia. Tricia Keller.

I made it all up. Well, *I* didn't exactly make it up. My mind made it up for me. To protect me. See, I made up this whole Farmer Daisy girl with this perfect life so I could protect myself from some terrible trauma that happened to me as a child. I still haven't been able to remember what the actual trauma was yet. Dr. K. thinks I saw something really horrible happen and I don't want to remember what it was. I don't know yet. I guess it happens to more than a few young girls, this whole imaginary-life thing. There's even a name for it: "DID," dissociative identity disorder. Dr. K. explained it all to me. This is basically how it works:

If you have some sort of major trauma as a kid—like if you saw something too horrible to imagine or if there was some kind of awful, supertragic death in your family—then sometimes you just can't deal with it. So you kind of "go away" in your head. The trauma is just too much to take, especially for a little girl, so you start to make stuff up so you can cope—the same way a really lonely kid can make up an imaginary friend so they don't feel so alone.

You might just change the facts in your head, convince yourself that the really bad thing just didn't happen: "I didn't see anyone get hurt," you'd insist, or, "Nobody hurt me." Or you might take it *way* further than that. You might be so scared to deal with that trauma, you might go *so* far away in your head that you actually kind of turn yourself into this other person. This person who doesn't have any of those problems. This person who has this whole other life. That's what I did. That's why I made up Daisy.

I guess at first my parents just didn't know how to deal with it. They probably didn't know that much about psychotherapy, and they'd probably never heard of DID. I think they must have thought I was just putting on my own little play all the time—like I was some kind of budding actress getting ready for my Oscar-winning role as a farm girl. I don't really remember it all that well. Maybe they were just too ashamed to try and get me help. That's understandable. No one wants a crazy-daisy for their only daughter.

But my delusions started to get worse. Much, much worse. It

had all been just roosters and cornfields. . . and then I started to see the most horrible things. Well, only one thing, really, but it's too horrible to think about. I don't even like to talk about it anymore the way I used to. Dr. K. says that's all right. He says I never need to talk about it again if I don't want to. He says that horrible delusion was just some kind of sick mental metaphor. But he's going to help me bring out that trauma the right way—through the right therapy and through all my treatments. He's going to keep me safe through the whole process.

He really has saved my life. I only hope he can do the same for Gaia. I bet she has DID, too. I know that's Dr. K.'s specialty. And I know her disease must run pretty deep if she's getting the privilege of his treatment. I can see it in her eyes—she's got some nasty-blasty demons to shake. I don't even want to think about

how long she's probably been suffering.

But she'll make it through.
I'll help her any way I can.
.She'll make it back to reality. With Dr. K.'s help, I know
she will.

GAIA HAD NO IDEA WHY THEY WERE gripping her arms so tightly. As if she had any intention of running. This was all she'd wanted in the first place—to meet her doctor, to straighten this whole mess out. She'd practically screamed as much to Rosie in that quiet room. Nonetheless, Rosie and Vince were digging their beefy hands

Absolutely Sane and Average

into her biceps, stepping slowly and deliberately, like a goddamn funeral procession.

"Can we pick up the pace here?" she asked.

There was no response other than Rosie squeezing tighter on her arm. Of course she had to squeeze tighter, what with her incurable power trip. She obviously had no idea what Gaia could do to her if she really wanted to, if Gaia hadn't been sure that aggression would only dig her a much deeper hole of misunderstanding.

Rosie led her down a few more colorless hallways and around a few more corners until they finally slowed to a halt at a white door that was identical to the rest of them, with the exception of the slim metal lettering at its center:

Rehabilitation.

Could they maybe be a little more specific? That could mean anything.

Rosie opened the door and pulled Gaia into a small hallway. But Gaia held up momentarily at the threshold. She had to stop for a moment. Because it was the first glimpse of real color she'd seen in this entire place.

Behind Gaia were the white ascetic halls of the hospital, devoid of the slightest flare or detail. But ahead of her were actual signs of life. The linoleum floor was a warm beige color. The walls were a pale shade of blue. But what truly made this hallway so different were the paintings. Two colorful paintings on either side of her, suspended by thin translucent wires that hung from the ceiling.

"We're *walking*," Rosie said, giving Gaia a slight tug to get her moving again.

Gaia stared at the two paintings as she passed them. Each one was another burst of chaotic colors, fused together in seemingly abstract shapes. Bright yellow ringlets and deep crimson branches. Chunks of lavender piled onto a blast of lime green. But when she looked a little closer, she realized that they weren't just random blotches of color. There were actually subtle hints of human figures just under the surface. Male and female forms, wrapping their hands around the colors or somehow living inside them. A stroke of blue made up a woman's dress, or the green became an expanse of grass where a man's abstract form lay asleep. Gaia decided quickly that she hated the paintings. They had too much color. They were trying so hard to be beautiful that they quickly became very ugly. Even a little disturbing, if you looked closely enough.

At the end of the hall was a pale blue metallic door. Rosie reached down to the large key ring on her belt and unlocked it, taking a firmer hold on Gaia's arm.

"Dr. K.?" Rosie called out flatly.

As the door cracked open, a bright shaft of sunlight shone into the otherwise dimly lit surroundings. The door fell open the rest of the way, and Gaia was quite sure that the tall man standing before her was the celebrity himself. The man of the hour. As it read in slim metallic letters on his door, *Dr. Michael Charles Kraven, M.D., Ph.D.*

Gaia was immediately caught off guard. Tricia was actually right: He did look a little like George Clooney—not that that meant much to Gaia. His white doctor's coat was hanging open over his heather-gray T-shirt and khaki pants. He was surprisingly young looking and physically fit—with thick, sandy brown hair that was just barely graying at the temples and a warm, unpretentious smile.

Once he'd fully opened the door, however, the smile dropped off his face and annoyance took its place. Before he had even said hello, he flashed a critical glance at Rosie and Vince and pulled their viselike grips from Gaia's sore arms.

"Rosie, don't make me tell you again," he complained. His voice was deep, laid-back, and confident. "We are not running a prison here; this is a hospital."

Rosie looked perturbed, to say the least. "Safety

first, Dr. Kraven," she said in a clipped tone. "For all I know, she's a flight risk."

Goddamn right, I'm a flight risk.

"Right," Dr. Kraven muttered, rolling his eyes almost imperceptibly. "Well, I'll take it from here, Rosie, okay?"

Rosie pasted a dead, resentful smile across her face. "Of course, Doctor. Would you like us to bring her into the—"

"I think we've got it under control." He smiled. He almost managed not to sound as condescending as he was actually being.

There was a brief and tense silence between them.

He's telling you to leave, Rosie, Gaia wanted to say. But she held her tongue.

"Of course," Rosie said, clenching her teeth into a pathetic imitation of a smile.

"Thanks, Rosie." His wide smile was a clear-cut kiss-off. Rosie was clearly dismissed.

Gaia couldn't help but take a little pleasure in this reversal of power. She cracked a slight smile as Rosie and Vince turned around and shuffled back down the hall-way with no one to bully for at least the next few minutes. As they closed the door behind them, it echoed loudly off the pale blue walls and the ugly paintings.

Gaia turned back to Dr. Kraven, but she'd forgotten to wipe the last bit of smile from her face. He caught the tail end of it and shared the slightest knowing smile of his own.

"I'm sorry about that," he said. "That woman is such a royal pain in the ass."

Gaia had no idea how to respond to this. She was slightly floored.

"Just so you know," he added, "I'm not the one hiring the security around here."

This was not at all how she'd expected Dr. Kraven to speak. This was not at all how she'd expected him to *be*, in spite of Tricia's glowing recommendation. She had expected to launch into a massive diatribe the moment she laid eyes on this Dr. Kraven person. Perhaps even beat him to a bloody pulp until he gave her the key to the front door of this place. But now that she'd actually met him. . . she found herself somewhat at a loss for words. Unable to speak, yes, but suddenly breathing a little easier than she had in the last twenty-four hours. This was a good beginning. This was an excellent beginning. Here was a remarkably normal psychiatrist who would surely listen to reason.

"God, I'm sorry," he said with a slight laugh. "Where are my manners? I'm Dr. Michael Kraven—you can call me whatever you want. I hear a lot of 'Dr. K.' Or 'Michael' is fine. I only request that we steer clear of 'Dr. Mike' because that's got that 'Dr. Phil' sound to it, and you really don't want to get me started on Dr. Phil. I don't think you want to get any psychiatrist started on Dr. Phil." He put out his hand. "And you, of course, are Gaia. Hello, Gaia."

"Hi," Gaia said, trying to sound absolutely sane and average. She placed her hand in his and gave it a firm shake.

"So, the way they brought you in here, I'm sure you've got a lot of questions," he said. "What do you say? You want to sit down and talk?"

Good. Yes. Perfect. Talk. That was exactly what she wanted to do. She wanted to sit down and talk.

"Absolutely," Gaia replied. "I thought you'd never ask. I thought no one would ever ask."

Dr. K. laughed. "Well, don't worry about that," he said. "One thing we definitely do here is talk. Come on in and sit down." She gave herself a brief moment to actually enjoy the warm sunlight coming in from his window—a much larger window than the one in Paris's room, a much better glimpse of the sun and the white sand and the crystal blue ocean. A much better glimpse of the outside world.

Maybe she'd be back there sooner than she'd thought.

Basic Teenage Ups and Downs

"WHY DON'T YOU HAVE A SEAT OVER here," Dr. Kraven suggested. "I just need to check your vitals, if it's all right with you."

"No problem." Gaia smiled, trying to make her "affable grin" as genuine as possible. She promised herself that she would not make one remotely aggressive move until she had attempted the calm and collected approach. Right now, she was feeling particularly confident that would do the trick.

She let her eyes roam around his office. It was reasonably spacious, with a combination of a few high-tech medical machines and the calm colors from the hallway. The walls were the same shade of blue, and the floors were the same shade of beige. There was a small desk in a corner of the room with a few piled folders and a flat-screen monitor. But the most notable feature by far was that window— a wide window along the back wall. It framed what under any other circumstances would have been the most beautiful view of the ocean Gaia had ever seen.

She took a seat in the metal examination chair at the center of the room as Dr. K had suggested. Once Gaia settled in, she realized that there was still one more of those ugly paintings hanging on the wall directly in front of her. It was a little bigger than the others, hanging from the ceiling like a massive eyesore. It was packed with an even larger array of excessive colors. Splotches of deep ugly brown and bright silver and ruby red. Something about it annoyed Gaia even more than the ones in the hall. No, it didn't just annoy her; it made her uncomfortable. It gave her the creeps. She turned her eyes away and stayed focused on the doctor.

Dr. Kraven sat down on a sleek blue rolling chair and rolled himself smoothly over to Gaia's side. He placed his hand around her wrist and held it gently as he checked his watch for a pulse reading.

"Did you paint these?" she asked, giving her best approximation of preliminary chitchat. Best to soften him up a little, she figured. She knew she couldn't say what she felt like saying: *Get me out of this hellhole before I start cracking people's skulls open.* That would not really meet her nonaggressive standard for this very delicate and desperately important conversation.

"Oh, no." He smiled, peering into her eyes with a small penlight. "One of my patients loved them so much, I thought they'd make him more comfortable. I guess they just grew on me after a while."

"Uh-huh." She nodded.

"Can you breathe in for me?" he asked. He placed his stethoscope against her chest and listened closely.

Okay, that was enough preliminary chitchat. The time was now. It was time to make her point as calmly and succinctly as possible.

"Look, I'm sorry," she said, "but see. . . none of this is necessary. There's nothing wrong with me. There's been some kind of mistake here, and I think you can help me clear it up." She was proud of her calm delivery.

Dr. K. pulled his stethoscope away and pushed back a bit in his chair, focusing his thoughtful brown eyes on Gaia's. "What kind of mistake?"

Good. Thank you. Thank you for listening. She stared deeper into his kind eyes and searched as hard as she could for a truthful answer from him. "Okay. . ." She clasped her hands together, trying to look as peaceful as a Buddhist monk. "Okay. . . the truth is. . . I'm not really sure how I got here. I'm not sure who brought me here because I think I was drugged—" *No, don't say that. That sounds paranoid as hell. You're smarter than that, Gaia. Come on.* "I mean, I'm not sure I was drugged. It's not even really important how I got here. The main point is, someone brought me here by mistake. And most important, they did it without my permission. You can correct me if I'm wrong, but I don't think that's even legal."

"Well, it depends on the circumstances of your admittance," Dr. K. replied.

Gaia wasn't sure how to respond to that. She of course could not remember the circumstances of her admittance.

"Sure, of course, I understand," she lied. *Stay cool. Cool and collected.* "Well, regardless of the circumstances, the essential point I'm trying to make. . . is that I don't belong here. I mean, I've had plenty of struggles in my life, and I've had plenty of the basic teenage ups and downs"—*oh, Lord, that's a good one*—"but I don't belong in a mental hospital." She laughed. "And I certainly don't belong in Fort Myers, Florida. I live in New York. This is a mistake. It's a misunderstanding."

"Well, I understand," Dr. K. replied.

"You do." She sighed. "Good. That's good." Gaia's entire body relaxed back into the chair. She'd known he could be reasonable. She'd known it.

"Believe me, I certainly understand how you're feeling," he said.

Her muscles tensed up again. She brought herself forward in the chair once more. "Um. . . no," she explained. "It's not how I'm 'feeling'; it's how it *is*. See, that's precisely my point. I know the difference between what I *feel* and what actually *is* because I am not mentally ill. I know that I'm not supposed to be here. Someone may have *mistakenly* thought I was, but that's my point. They were mistaken."

Dr. K. dropped down into a more casual position, resting his elbows on his knees, leaning closer to Gaia. "First of all, no one said you were mentally ill, Gaia. Personally, I don't even know what that means. And if there have been some misunderstandings, then we should definitely talk about them. But mistake or not, you know, you do have a shrink sitting right here. Do you want to talk about some of those struggles you mentioned? Those basic teenage ups and downs?"

Gaia's eyes narrowed with anger. "*Don't* patronize me." She pointed an accusing finger at him in spite of herself. "I'm trying to be cool about this. I'm trying to talk straight to you about a *ridiculous* mix-up. They didn't just make a mistake, they made a *massive* mistake, and I'm telling you, you need to *fix* it. So don't talk to me that way, and don't look at me that way."

"What way?" Dr. K. searched deeper in her eyes.

"*That* way. Like I'm a mental patient!" she barked. "I am *not* a freaking mental patient!"

"Gaia. . ." Dr. Kraven spoke with deep calm and patience. "I need you to stay relaxed, all right? We can talk this all through. I want to hear everything. But I need you to try to lie back in your chair while we talk. Can you do that for me? Is that cool with you?"

Gaia could feel the blood rising in her face. She wasn't controlling the conversation. She wasn't controlling herself. She was veering off course. *You're losing him. Control your temper. Say something reasonable.*

"Look, if I could just make a phone call," she said, trying not to visibly simmer. "I haven't seen one phone in this place. If I could make a call back home, I'm sure we could clear this up in a few minutes. Can I just make a call?"

"Usually we like to wait a week or so before patients start calling home," he said, shrugging slightly. "It gives them a chance to settle in without any additional stress."

"But I'm *not* a *patient*—"

"But I was going to say," he interrupted, with an outstretched hand. "I was going to say—if you would try to stay calm—that I might be able to make an exception. So, if you could make that call. . . who would you want to call?"

"Well, I'd. . ." Gaia's voice tapered off after her first few syllables. "I'd. . ."

She had been so thrilled at the notion of getting that phone call that she hadn't really stopped to consider it: Just who exactly would she call? Her sudden inability to complete the sentence was one of her more sickening moments at this hospital. Because it was a sentence she wasn't sure she'd be able to complete.

WHO THE HELL COULD SHE CALL IN

Electroshock

the city? Who was left in her vacuous black hole of a life? Who would vouch for her sanity? She had no idea where her father was, and Ed hated her guts. Not only that, but he'd seen her completely lose her mind more than a few times. He'd seen her behave like an absolute schizo over and over again to the point where he couldn't even deal anymore. He would probably be thrilled to know she was finally receiving some intensive psychiatric assistance.

Sam? She'd accused Sam of trying to murder her, for God's sake. Yet another stellar advertisement for her sanity. For all she knew, Ed and Sam were the ones who had gotten together over coffee and signed her up for this nightmare.

Who else? Natasha and Tatiana wanted her dead.

They would have told Dr. K. to let her rot. They could have put her in here, too, just to be rid of her for good. So who did that leave? Who was Gaia supposed to call when she had no friends and no family? Dmitri? She hardly even knew Dmitri and he hardly knew her. They weren't even related. What was she supposed to say? *I found this old man locked up in my uncle's terrorist compound. He used to work for a mercenary terrorist organization. He'll vouch for me.* That would pretty much drive the last nail into Gaia's increasingly lousy sanity defense.

There was no one. No one in her life. No one to call. "You look sad," Dr. Kraven said gently. "Did I say something to make you sad?"

"What? No," Gaia insisted. *Jesus, will you keep it together? Now is not the time to lose it, you idiot. Block it out. Block it.* She clenched her jaw and tightened her fists, forcing herself to throw off the ten-ton weight of loneliness and depression that was trying to crush her flat against the black leather chair. "I'm fine."

She caught a glimpse of Dr. K.'s deeply sympathetic expression. And it made her extremely pissed off.

Anger slowly began to replace all the uninvited sadness. The last thing she needed was this random doctor's pity. "I'm *fine*," she repeated, giving him a much more pinpointed glare. "I just have to think of the right person to phone, that's all. I just want to be sure someone is home."

110

The lie made her want to vomit. It was poking more holes in her already tattered pride. This was one thing she never did. She never lied to sound more well-adjusted than she was. She might despise her miserable life, but she wasn't ashamed of it.

"Well, what about your parents?" Dr. K. asked, searching Gaia's eyes. "Wouldn't you like to call your parents?"

Jesus, was he *trying* to rip her heart out? What was this, "make 'em cry" therapy? Was that Dr. Michael Kraven's specialty—finding your weak spots and driving a sharp blade right through them? There was no way she was going to answer that question in any amount of detail. She was not about to tell this man, whom she was trying to convince of her total normalcy, that her father had barely been in her life for years, that he had been kidnapped by any number of her enemies. She was not going to tell him that her mother had been shot by her sick, twisted uncle and thet Gaia had watched her die in her father's arms on the kitchen floor in California.

"I can't call them," she muttered.

"Why not?" he asked.

"Because I can't, that's all."

"But wouldn't you like—?"

"Because they're *gone*, all right? They're gone." She felt two feet tall telling that fact to a total stranger. Poor little orphan Gaia, sitting there in paper-thin hospital scrubs, in a freaking dentist's chair, telling her life story to Mr. Sensitive Doctor Guy. She felt sick and naked. And of course, more pissed off.

"Well, what happened to them?" Dr. K. took a pen and a small pad out of the front pocket of his white coat. "Let's talk about your parents."

"*No,*" Gaia moaned, nearly digging holes into the thick leather arms of the chair. "I didn't come here for a goddamn therapy session! I don't need my head examined; I need you to let me the hell out of here. I came here to fix this screwup!"

"Gaia. . . ," he uttered cautiously. "If you can't lean back in your chair, then I'll have to cut this session short. And I don't want to cut this session short. Just lean back, okay? Lean back. I know you're a little scared right now, but you have nothing to be afraid of."

"I'm not *afraid,*" she snapped. "I am *never* afraid. That's not what is going on here. I just don't think you're listening to what I'm telling you."

"Now that's not fair. I *have* been listening, Gaia. I *am* listening to you. And I want to hear more. I'd like to talk some more about your parents—"

"No! No, that's not what we need to talk about. We need to talk about the *mistake* that's been made here." She couldn't help herself. She couldn't stand to have him jotting down notes for some case file that wasn't even supposed to exist. He might be much kinder than Rosie, but he was ultimately treating her the same way—like a mental case. "I don't want to talk about my parents; I want to talk about—"

"Well, that's okay. We don't have to talk about your parents now. What about never being afraid—can we talk about never being afraid? How exactly does that—?"

"No, I don't want to talk about that, either." She groaned. She could just imagine trying to tell him that she had no fear gene. Then he'd really think she was a lunatic.

"Well, has that always been the case?" he asked. "Have you always been unafraid? Even as a child? You know, sometimes certain events in our lives can—"

"I said I didn't want to talk about that! That's not what I came here to talk about. You wouldn't even understand—"

"Now that's not true, Gaia. Believe it or not, that's not so unusual." He jotted down another note on his pad. "I've had many patients in the past who have mentioned feelings of fearlessness and—"

"No, it's not a *feeling*; it's a *fact*. And I am not a patient!"

"Well, okay. Then let's talk about the fact. How often would you say you experience these feelings of—"

"Jesus! I'm *not* crazy!" she shouted. She slammed her hands on the chair again, much, much harder than she had before. The thud echoed up to the ceiling. She could practically feel her patience snap, deep inside her chest. "Stop talking to me like I'm crazy!"

Dr. K.'s eyes grew steady and careful. "Gaia, I asked you before to stay calm."

"Do you think I don't know what that sounds like? 'I'm never afraid'—I *know* what that sounds like to you. But you don't *know* me. You don't know a damn thing about me, do you?"

"Gaia, please. . ."

"Well, I'm not getting messages from outer space on the TV, I don't talk to Elvis, and my neighbor's dog is not Satan! If you would just stop giving me all this shrink crap and listen to me, then I wouldn't be yelling right now. But you are not *getting* it. You're not getting the big picture here, and you know what? You are *really* starting to piss the living *crap* out of—ow!"

Gaia's eyes darted down to her left arm just in time to see Dr. Kraven pulling out a small syringe. She'd been so busy freaking out, she hadn't even noticed him inject it.

"It's a gentle muscle relaxant—it's nothing," he assured her. "It's a precaution, Gaia, not a punishment, okay? We just needed to calm you down a bit. You might start to feel a little strange in a few minutes. You might start to feel a little paralysis, but there's nothing to worry about."

"No, no more drugs," she spat. "No more drugs."

"It was just a precaution, Gaia. It's as much to protect you as to protect me, all right?" He capped the syringe and put it back in his front pocket. "Now listen. . . ." He moved closer and gave her an encouraging pat on the leg. "I promise you, you'll be able to make some calls very soon. You're still very agitated right now. And it's not such a good idea to call home in the state you're in. After a couple of treatments, when you're in a better state of mind, we'll have you call home, all right? We'll even bring in your parents."

"I told you, my parents are gone."

"Well, Gaia, we're going to talk about that, too. We're going to talk about your feelings about your parents and about your condition in general. But we'll go nice and slow, all right?"

"Condition? What *condition*? I don't *have* any condition."

"We don't have to worry about that now, okay? We need to be really patient. Let's just wait for that muscle relaxant to kick in, and then I'm going to give you a little treatment, and then we'll talk some more. We'll talk about your condition—we'll talk about some of your misconceptions."

"What misconceptions? I don't have any misconceptions. My *conception* is that I've been trapped in a freaking loony bin in Florida and I want to get out. So thanks for your time, but I'll just be showing myself to the door."

So much for the calm and rational approach. This conversation was ridiculous. It was utterly useless to Gaia. She reached for the handles of the chair to push forward, but her hands didn't respond to her brain's demands.

What the hell?

She tried to push out with her legs. But her legs wouldn't move, either. Her neck, her chest, her head... completely numb. Nothing would move.

"What is going on?" she growled. But her mouth could hardly form the words. It was as if her entire face were stuck behind a metal mask—as if her entire body had been dosed with a gallon of novocaine. "What the *hell*?" she squeezed out through immovable lips, shooting poison darts at Dr. Kraven with her eyes.

"Gaia, it's totally normal," he assured her. "It's just the muscle relaxant. I told you there would be some paralysis."

Some paralysis? She couldn't move a muscle in her entire body. Her head fell back against the headrest like a chunk of solid rock, leaving her with no choice but to stare directly at that painting—that ugly, horrific, modernist painting. She wanted to kick and scream and break the great Dr. K.'s face off his neck, but she couldn't even talk anymore.

"It's just to keep your body safe during the treatment, Gaia. That's all. Now, you've already told me you don't get scared. So this should be a cinch. I promise I'll be right here with you the entire time, okay? I won't leave your side."

What the hell was he talking about? What treatment did he mean?

Dr. Kraven leaned over her and reached down

under the arms of her chair. "Okay," he said. "Don't let the wrist and ankle guards freak you out. They're just one more safety precaution." He reached under each of her armrests and brought out two leather straps, fastening each one around her wrists so that they were tied down to the chair. Gaia couldn't make a move to stop him.

What are you doing, you son of a bitch? What the hell are you doing?

He quickly rolled down to the extended base of the chair by her feet and pulled out a long strap, which he fastened around her ankles.

Move, Gaia. Jesus, make your body move.

He rolled his chair back up to her head and reached behind the headrest of her chair, pulling some mechanism that she was infuriatingly unable to see over the top. But she could feel it as it settled over her head—two foam sponges pressing tightly above her temples.

I know what this is. Jesus, I know what this is. . . .

Wrists and ankles restrained. . . body unable to move. . . conductors above each temple of her head. . . ECT. *Electroshock.* Gaia wasn't in this room to defend her sanity. She'd been brought into this room for shock treatments.

Get away from me, she wanted to howl. *Don't come near me.* Her heart was pumping triple time, but it was of absolutely no use to her immobile body. All she

117

could do was growl at him over and over, straining her vocal cords with each useless muted roar.

"Gaia, please," he said gently. "Don't worry. You won't even remember any pain, I promise."

I'm not worried, you asshole. I just want rip your face off. You liar. You lying piece of crap. You haven't been listening to me at all. I'm not crazy.

He reached over to a metal cabinet by the chair and brought out a small syringe with a greenish fluid floating inside the vial. He pricked the side of her neck with it just below the back of her skull. Then he reached back once more and brought out a thick foam sponge shaped like a small candlestick. As if he'd done it a hundred times before, he cracked open her paralyzed mouth and placed the sponge between her teeth like a horse's bit.

She growled again and again, ripping her vocal cords to shreds, wishing to God she could bite his fingers off.

"This is just to protect your tongue," he said with the same kind, laid-back voice that had lured her into the chair in the first place.

You're going to pay for this. Somehow. I swear to God.

"Okay," he announced as if they were about to go on a field trip. "We're all set. Now, try to just relax your mind, Gaia. I'm going to be right here."

With that, he turned behind him to one of the high-tech machine Gaia had hardly even paid attention to when she'd first walked in. There was a series of black dials along the right side of it and a hefty chrome lever on the left. Three digital readouts were spread across the top panel—each vertical bar pulsing up and down in green light. Dr. K. slowly turned up each of the black knobs, and a deep electrical hum spread through the room. Gaia could only lie there like a corpse and watch it happen. She watched the green bars on the equalizer each climb a little higher. He was raising the voltage.

Then he simply placed his hand on the chrome lever and Gaia knew. . . .

She knew that she was probably the only person on this planet who would not be afraid at this moment.

BLACK BINDER—Case #27DG

Attending
physician: Dr. Michael Kraven
Patient ID: Gaia Moore 2747
Diagnosis: Acute DID with bipolar II disorder;
recurring paranoia
Treatment: High-impact K-cycle ECT with lysergic
acid diethylamide + phentedrine;
intensive psychotherapy

Notes: Patient was highly aggressive and agitated
in initial state. Severely paranoid. But
she was converted to a nonaggressive and
receptive alpha state after administration
of treatment. Brain waves were reduced to
between five and eight cycles per second.

Once hypnotic theta state was secured,
patient spoke to me at length about her
post-traumatic delusions and the acute
emotional aftermath that has worsened over
the course of the last five years.

Initial session was administered solely
on the subconscious level—should register
to patient only as lost time. Second
session should successfully transfer to
alpha-only administration. Patient will
then consciously recall corrected facts as
needed. This cycle will be administered for
a period of five to ten days, depending on
the discovery of appropriate levels of
lysergic acid and phentedrine and patient
response.

History: Patient's primary traumas occurred at ages six and twelve, both resulting in dissociative identity and imagined episodes of domestic violence. Resulting fictional identity includes grandiose delusions of large-scale conspiracy and protracted childhood fantasies of fearlessness.

Prognosis: One of the patient's family members has provided me with necessary factual information to counter patient's delusional re-creations of prior events. This should make the elimination of false identity move at a far more rapid pace, without incident. We've already begun work on correcting her delusional interpretations of the dominating traumas from her past. Expect a full recovery.

Future Actions:

1. Monitor patient closely.
2. Confer with Dr. W. on potential DID treatment setbacks.
3. Inform R., V., and B. of potential security issues.

Additional Notes:

1. Prep T. accordingly.
2. R. binder: Inform Y. that the process is under way. Deprog. stage 1.

This little fiasco had thrown her off so completely.

odd boy

GAIA HATED HERSELF FOR HIDING.

Hotshot Secret Agent

She despised herself. This wasn't her. This wasn't *fearless*—hiding in the bedroom like some average little kid. She was *twelve years old*, for God's sake. Nothing was supposed to scare her. Nothing.

God, she wanted to smack him. She wanted to smack him so hard, that jerk. That *asshole*. Why did he have to drink? Why did he have to ruin a perfectly good vacation by drinking again? And why did he have to get so violent? Why did he have to be so mean to her mom? God, she wanted to smack him. But she couldn't budge. She couldn't budge from that ugly bedroom. She could only stand there like a coward with her hands over her ears and watch him screaming at her mom through the crack in the door. Screaming and throwing things all over the room.

Why did he have to ruin everything? Everything had been going *fine*. They'd all been getting along for a change, having a little bit of *fun*, even. He and Gaia had been playing a game of chess; her mother was in the kitchen cooking beef stroganoff—they looked just like a real family for a few minutes. That was what this stupid trip to the mountains was supposed to be for. That was the whole reason they'd taken this vacation in stupid San Rafael, California—so that Dad would be nice for a change. So he could take a vacation from his stupid security guard job. So he'd stop drinking all the time and coming home from work screaming about how he should have been some kind of hotshot secret agent for the CIA. So he'd treat Gaia and her mom like his family for once instead of his verbal punching bags. Or, in her mom's case, not just a *verbal* punching bag.

That asshole. That mean, drunken *jerk*.

One comment. Her mom had made one stupid comment about him looking for a better job, and now he'd gone off again.

If you hit her again tonight, I swear to God. . . I'll turn fearless, and I'll come out there and I will beat the crap out of you, Dad. You won't scare me the way you scare Mom, you understand? You may scare me right now, but once I turn fearless. . . you better start running.

Wait. . . .

What is that? What's in his hand?

No, Dad. Put it down. Put that down, Dad.

"I'll do it!" her father screamed. "Believe me, Katia, I'll do it!"

A gun. He had his gun from work. He had his gun from work pressed against his forehead.

"Is this what you want?" he hollered at her mother. "You want me to do it,? Because I will! I don't give a crap anymore, Katia. I don't care. Why don't I just put this whole family out of its misery? Why don't you just take the insurance money and find yourself a real man? Believe me, I'll do it! I'll pull the goddamn trigger right now and make us all a hell of a lot happier!"

"No!" Gaia cried from the bedroom, hurling open the door. "Stop it, Dad! Stop it!" Tears had suddenly begun to pour from her eyes.

"Tom, *stop*," her mother cried. "*Please.* Look what you're doing! Look what you're doing to her."

"Stop it, Dad," Gaia pleaded, trying to breathe between her suffocating sobs. "You're *scaring* me. You're scaring Mom!" She threw her arms around her father and tried to hug him. "Please. Please."

"*Gaia.*" Her father tried to tug her off him. "Gaia, stop it. Let go of me!"

She kept struggling to keep her arms around him, to stop him from using the gun.

"Gaia, god*dammit!*" He clamped his hand onto her arm and pushed her down until she was clinging to his knees.

"Tom, stop!" her mother howled. "You're hurting your daughter!"

Her father got so frustrated that he actually pushed Gaia down onto the floor just to subdue her. "Stop it, Gaia, do you hear me?" His shouts grew louder and louder as he pushed her to the ground and held her against the floor. "Stop this right now! This has nothing to do with you."

"Let me *up*," Gaia pleaded. "Dad, let me *up*."

"Leave her alone!" Gaia's mother howled. She threw

her hands around his wrist and tried to pull the gun from his hand. "Give me the gun, Tom. Let go of the *gun!*"

That was when Gaia heard the sound.

The sound was like a bomb going off. The sound of the gun.

It made Gaia deaf. It was so loud, it made the whole room shake.

Gaia's mother's eyes got wide. She stared at Gaia's father like she was in a trance—like she was frozen in time. And then she began to stumble. She stumbled backward in two shaky steps.

Gaia didn't understand. She didn't understand what was happening. Why was it so quiet all of a sudden?

"Oh my God," her father uttered. The gun fell out of his frozen hand. "Oh my God, Katia. . . I didn't. . . That wasn't. . ."

Her mother stumbled backward to the kitchen doorway. And then she fell down. She collapsed in a contorted heap on the kitchen floor.

"Katia!" her father shouted. He left Gaia on the floor and crawled across the carpet, pulling Gaia's mother into his arms on the floor. "Katia, I had the safety on. I thought I had the *safety* on. Oh God, oh God, please. . . Gaia! Pick up the phone, all right? Pick up the phone and dial nine-one-one."

Gaia was frozen on the floor. She couldn't move. She watched as a stream of blood began to pour from a splotch on her mother's head, gathering in a thick black puddle on the white kitchen tiles. Her eyes were closed. . . .

"*Gaia!*" her father screamed. Gaia looked up at his face and realized that now the tears were falling from *his* face. "Nine-one-one! *Call nine-one-one. Now!*"

"Mom. . . ?" Gaia uttered, crawling back toward her mother. "Mommy. . . ? Mom? Dad, what did you do?"

"It was an *accident*, Gaia, just call the ambulance!"

"Mom?" Gaia breathed. "*Mom? Mom?*"

"JESUS. WHAT THE HELL WAS THAT?"

Vicious Black

Gaia muttered out loud, shoving the stiff white sheets off her sweat-soaked body.

It was one of the worst nightmares she'd ever had, that's what it was. Some hideous concoction that her own sick brain had brewed up just for her own displeasure.

God. It had seemed so real for a second. Like she really was twelve years old again. Every detail of that house seemed so real—the creaky door to the bedroom, the ugly maroon carpet, the tiles on the kitchen floor. . . . She didn't want to think about those tiles. She never wanted to think about those blood-soaked tiles again.

But she couldn't get them out of her mind. She couldn't get any of that miserable dream out of her mind. Her head just felt so strange. . . .

Where had she even come up with such a nightmare? How could she even allow her mind to concoct such a ridiculous version of that night? Her father screaming and yelling with a gun to his head? *Gaia's* dad? A drunk? A security guard? It was all so ludicrous. Ludicrous and, well, ugly. There was no other word for it. Even if Gaia had sat down and tried to *invent* some kind of "sadder version" of her life (as if that were possible) and of *that night*—the night that Loki had snuck into the kitchen and shot and killed her mother—she would never have been able to conceive of these ugly versions of her parents. Even in a dream it had shocked her profoundly because it seemed so real. It was like she had spent ten ungodly minutes in some alternate universe.

Stop thinking about it. It was just a nightmare. You've had a ton of nightmares.

But never one like this. This one almost seemed more like a memory than a dream. It felt like she had been reliving something, not imagining it.

Whatever. Get it out of your head.

She needed to sit up, that was all. Dreams always lingered in her head until she got up off the pillow. She pressed her hands down against the bed and hoisted herself up against the headboard. Her sun-soaked surroundings finally came into focus. And as they did, Gaia realized that she wasn't alone.

D. was there; Gaia recognized him instantly.

Neither of them moved. Gaia squinted, her eyes watering from the glare of the sunlight. D. stood at the foot of the bed, right beyond the steel bedposts, his green hospital shift drooping off his narrow shoulders.

What the hell. . . ?

There was no way to tell how long he had been standing there. Gaia could tell, from her blurred, peripheral view of the rest of the room, that Paris's bed was empty. . . and that the door was standing open. The hospital was quiet this morning. Gaia could hear nothing but the thin, distant hum of the air-circulating machinery. Far off in the distance somebody laughed; the sound could have been coming from miles away.

They were alone.

Gaia wasn't alarmed. It had surprised her to see D. standing there—it was disconcerting to wake up and realize that somebody has been watching you sleep— but wasn't that what this odd boy *did*? Just show up, whether you wanted him to or not? Show up and refuse to leave? It was strange, but it was hardly threatening.

In fact, D. was about as far from a threatening figure as Gaia could imagine. He seemed so gentle. Even lying in bed, she didn't feel helpless or vulnerable with him there. Not like. . .

. . . *not like when?*

Gaia wasn't sure. Something had come into her head, a blurry, vague memory. Lying down, being pressed downward into the cold ground. . . helpless, unable to move. . .

. . . Nothing. She couldn't remember.

D. looked at her intently, as if suddenly worried. . . and then he smiled.

It was a small, fragile smile, barely noticeable, but Gaia appreciated it. When was the last time she'd seen a smile like that? A simple, unaffected grin—not the crass leer of somebody trying to sell you something or get you to like them. Just a twitch of the mouth to indicate happiness or pleasure. Such a simple thing.

Gaia smiled back.

It was strange—sitting in this narrow, stiff bed, miles and miles from home, she was smiling, and it was a completely honest, natural thing to do. Gaia wondered vaguely when the last time was that she had smiled and meant it.

"Glorious," D. said.

"Hi."

Gaia heard her own, raspy voice—the morning voice nobody was ever around to hear. She cleared her throat, reaching to brush her hair away from her face. "Good morning, D."

"Trouble," D. said, pointing at Gaia. "Dark trouble."

"What?" D. was pointing at Gaia's head, she realized. *Glorious. . . glorious yellow. . .* He had said that before, hadn't he?

130

"Come see." D. was walking closer—he stepped around the bed, his shoes squeaking on the linoleum floor. In the distance Gaia could hear voices and the sound of a television—just another beautiful morning at Rainhill. "Come to the red."

The red?

D. was right in front of her, reaching for her pajama sleeve and pulling on it. Up close, his eyes were a penetrating ice blue, like those of a soldier in a navy recruiting poster. Normally Gaia didn't like when people got close to her like this—intruded on her personal space—but right now she didn't mind. There was something about the way that D. looked at her that made it all right.

"Come now. Come see." D. continued tugging on Gaia's sleeve.

"Wait—" Gaia was wondering how to politely break this off. She liked D., strangely enough, but she hadn't even gotten out of bed yet—she wasn't ready to go off on some excursion with him. "D., wait—I'm still in bed."

"*Yes.*" D.'s eyes lit up. He nodded urgently. "*Her* bed. Same bed—same girl."

"What?"

"Yellow, yellow. Ana's bed. Ana's head cooker." D. was pulling on Gaia's sleeve more frantically. It wasn't fun anymore. *This is a mental patient,* Gaia reminded herself. *He may be cute or friendly, but under the skin he could be Jeffrey Dahmer.*

But she didn't believe it. Every single element in

D.'s face conveyed peacefulness, gentleness. He was just excited, that was all. Maybe that was his problem, a hyperactivity disorder or something.

"Come see, come see!" D. wasn't giving up easily—he bounced on his toes, trying to get Gaia to follow him. She reached down, ready to gently pry D.'s fingers from her arm, and she saw her own blue plastic bracelet.

Dr. K.

In a sudden, forceful rush all her memories of Dr. Michael Kraven came back. The digital readouts on the machine, the green fluid in the cold glass hypodermic. . . and that slick, smug smile of his. That *humble* smile that seemed to say, "Let's politely agree how terrific I am." And then. . .

And then what?

She couldn't remember. It bothered her. She usually remembered everything, in greater detail than she even wanted to. But now, trying to piece together what had happened after Dr. Kraven had put her into that chair, she was drawing a blank.

What had he done?

That son of a bitch. . . Gaia could feel anger welling up explosively inside her.

"No! No!" D. had let go of Gaia's sleeve. He was staring at her face, looking frightened. "Dark now. Dark now."

"What? D., no—everything's fine." Gaia realized what had happened. D. must have seen something in her face when the fury at Dr. K had come over her. It must have frightened him. "D., don't worry. I'm fine. I'm not mad."

"Okay." D. sounded dubious. He gave her a penetrating look, as if trying to judge whether she was telling the truth.

"It's not you—it's the *doctor*," Gaia explained. "They made me see this doctor yesterday and—"

Gaia stopped talking because D. had suddenly covered his face with his hands. It made him look ten years younger—it was like watching a small boy.

"You don't want to hear about that?"

"Vicious black."

Gaia wasn't sure what that meant. But she was glad she'd been reminded of Dr. Michael Kraven, Ph.D., and his machines and green fluids and "treatments." D.'s entrance into the room was almost like a hotel's wake-up call: *Good morning, Gaia. It's time to get out of bed. . . and get the hell out of this nightmare.*

I just have one question: Who
the hell came up with this therapy crap in the first place? No,
I know the answer to that. It was
that Freud guy. Sigmund freakin'
Freud.

Sigmund, I've got a question
for you. What the hell were you
on, man? What were you thinking?
When exactly did you decide that
we were all going to feel *so much*
better if we had some chick in a
white coat sit across from us in
her little black swivel chair,
smile and nod a lot, and make us
repeat ourselves every freakin'
day until we want to puke? I
mean, come on, Sigmund. Is that
medicine? Could you really sit
there with a straight face and
call that science? What science?
The science of bitching?

That's what we do every day.
Me and good old Dr. Barbara Pain-
in-the-ass Weissman. *Every goddamn day.* I sit there in my
stiff-as-a-board, piece-of-crap
chrome hospital chair. Dr. Weissman

sits there in her ergonomic, superplush Mercedes of a swivel chair. . . and I bitch. I bitch and moan. And then I bitch some more. And then I do a little more bitching.

"Let's talk about that night again, Paris," she says. "Um, not today," I say. "I really think it would do you some good," she says. "Okay," I say. "You're the boss, right?"

And then begins day eight hundred million of my bitching, featuring yet another whirlwind of mind-boggling, never before heard revelations. Including such mind-blowers as:

I'm a pissed-off teenager. My God, what a *shocker*.

My dad's an asshole. Your *dad*? Your very own flesh and blood? An *asshole*? *Impossible*. We'd better keep you locked up right here in Satan's *ass* of a mental hospital.

And so it goes.

God, I just can't stand her. Dr. Weissman and her funky little shag haircut and her little "I'm

smart *and* sexy!" tortoiseshell
glasses. And that *smile*. That
*screw you, you're never getting
out of here* smile. Sometimes, when
she quizzes me again about that
stupid night, I want to jump over
to her and just spin the living
crap out of that chair. Spin it
like it's the goddamn wheel of
fortune and just watch her twirl
and twirl like a bad cartoon.

It was a broken window, Doctor! A
broken window at *Denny's*, no less.
Not exactly an upscale joint. It's
not the end of the world, you know?
I didn't go into some deep
fetal-position suck-my-thumb depression. I didn't go postal on anyone's
ass. So why won't you treat me like
a freaking human being? If you're
not going to let me out of here,
then how about a couple of phone
privileges? How about some
clothing privileges so I can take
off these butt-ugly green jammies?

Or how about this, Doctor? How
about you give me some of Jared's letters? Is that really so much to ask?

She won't, though. I hate to

sound like one of the freaks, but
this whole place is full of con-
spirators. They won't let me call
Jared; they sure as hell won't let
me see him. I know they're not
sending him any of my letters, and
they won't give me *any* of his. I
know it's my dad's idea. I know
it. He always hated Jared. Always.

But I thought maybe these
"trained professional psychia-
trists" might be just a little
more enlightened than my bow
tie-wearing father. I mean, is
Dr. Weissman really that dense?
What's supposed to make me happier and more well-adjusted?
Another day at psycho Rainhill,
or talking to the only person in
this world I've ever loved who's
actually loved me back?

Dr. Weissman is just like my
dad. She's obviously never been in
love either. She has no idea that
love cures everything. It cures
all of this stuff—depression,
aggression, boredom, loneliness,
rage. It sure as hell cures a bad
attitude. I could be sitting in

the back of Jared's broken-down, dented-up truck, eating a box of Ritz with Cheez Whiz and I'd still be in freaking heaven. It's not exactly rocket science.

I don't know, Sigmund, you tell me. What were you thinking when you invented this therapy crap? I'll tell you my personal theory, Dr. Freud. I think you were trying to drive us all insane.

Just Troubled

"SO, YOU'RE FINALLY AWAKE," PARIS said as she entered her hospital room. She'd been waiting for Gaia to wake up so she'd have someone to talk to. But what she hadn't counted on was that Gaia would be having company over.

"Who invited you?" Paris barked at D., who was clinging to Gaia's side.

He flinched, then burrowed himself deep into Gaia's arm.

"Did you stay up all night, or—"

"Don't do that," Gaia said sharply.

"What?"

"Don't talk to him like that." Gaia was sitting on the edge of her bed now, leaning in to look at D.'s face. She seemed very concerned. "You're scaring him."

"If he doesn't want to be scared," Paris said, kicking off her shoes and letting them thump loudly to the floor, "he should stay away from me."

"He's a kid," Gaia told her. She seemed very serious. "He's just a kid, Paris. D., everything's fine. Don't—"

"Hate," D. complained. "Hates me."

"You got that right," Paris said with a yawn. "Gaia, don't encourage him. I'm warning you—it's not a good idea. He's harder to get rid of than a headache. Get *OUT*!" Paris clapped loudly. The blast echoed harshly through the room. "Get out of here, D., I am not kidding!"

Covering his face, D. ran from the room.

"In real life," Paris said lazily, "the life I would be living if I weren't at Rainhill. . . in that life, there would be no retarded thirteen-year-old boys. It's just—"

"He's not *retarded*." Gaia had stood and was pulling on a clean hospital shirt. "Can't you tell? He's smart. He's just troubled. Anyway, why frighten—?"

"I don't care, I don't care," Paris said, wincing in disgust. "I swear—one day here and you're already beginning to talk like those psychos. A week from now *you're* going to be all 'associative disorder' and 'vicious black.' Before—"

"No." Gaia had pulled her hair through the cheap shirt's neck hole and was flipping it back, standing up. It was nearly painful how familiar it was—how much Gaia reminded Paris of Ana. "There isn't going to be any 'week from now.' I'm leaving. A week from now I'll be gone."

"You *think* you're leaving," Paris said quietly. She was leaning back against the wall, her bare feet curled in the blankets. She wouldn't look at Gaia. It was just all so familiar, and she didn't want to deal with it. "But you're not."

"I won't accept that." Gaia was putting on her shoes. "I just need to find—"

"Find what? There's nothing to find. There's nobody to talk to. There's no way *out*, girl. *Believe* me. Weren't you going to talk to your amazing doctor and get him to let you out? What happened to that brilliant plan?"

Gaia was tying her shoes, and she stopped. Paris watched as Gaia froze, clearly thinking. Clearly confused.

"I'm not sure," Gaia said quietly.

"*I'm* sure. You tried to tell Dr. George Clooney that you're sane, and he smiled and nodded and didn't listen to a word you said. You can't—"

"Paris—"

"—*talk* to these people. I've been trying for months to get my boyfriend's *letters*. My boyfriend, Jared, has been writing to me and they won't even give me the goddamn letters, Gaia." Paris was shouting now. "The one thing that would make this bearable. Don't you understand what you're dealing with? They don't care. They don't *care* about how much I love my boyfriend, they don't care about anything except their, you know, rules and regulations and doses and lockdowns and—"

Paris stopped. She stopped because she was ranting, and she knew that people didn't like that, no matter how right she was. But she also stopped because of the look on Gaia's face.

Gaia was staring at her, as if something had just come clear in her head. Her eyes were wide. "Your boyfriend," Gaia said.

"Yeah?" Paris didn't get it.

WHAT WAS IT? WHAT WAS IT IN

Fried-Up Memory Banks

her head? Some kind of lingering thought that Gaia couldn't place. Some kind of lingering black muddy invisible cloud of a thought in her fried-up brain. All she wanted to do was climb out of that bed and go find Dr. Sadist Kraven and slap him right across his kindhearted face. But now there was this thought. . . this other thought. This half of a confused thought.

About boyfriends. Boys. . .

Boys and love. And that name. . . Jared.

Who the hell cares about Jared?

Jared. How could she be thinking about Jared? Jared was Paris's boyfriend. Was this some kind of aftereffect of the tranquilizers? Confusing the particulars of other people's lives with your own?

No. Not Jared. That wasn't the name. That wasn't the name she was trying to pull up from her fried-up memory banks. But it sounded like Jared. Or. . . no, it was more like. . . *Jake.*

Jake. She was thinking about Jake.

"Gaia. . . ?" Paris was standing right there, but she sounded miles away. She was waving her hand in Gaia's face, but Gaia had to ignore her. She had to. "Hello? Earth to Gaia. . ."

"Shhh." Gaia couldn't listen. She kept her eyes fixed on a blank point on the linoleum floor to keep her brain concentrated—to keep it moving in a linear fashion.

Because she was remembering something. Something real this time. Something very real. A face hovering just inches from her own. . . his hands pressing against her wrists. . . pressing her into the dirt. No, not just the dirt. . . the *grass*. In the park. Central Park. . .

"JAKE?"

Extreme Pissed- offedness

"Jesus," Jake panted, trying to catch his breath. "Who did you think it was, the freaking *Boston Strangler*? What the hell is the matter with you?"

Gaia wasn't sure what hit first, her deep, crimson-faced embarrassment or her overwhelming guilt. She had just unleashed one of her deadliest combinations on Jake Montone and hurled him into a mound of fresh tar. And she hardly even knew him.

Somehow that made it even worse. If she'd accidentally pummeled a good friend, at least they might have been able to laugh about it in twenty years. But

Jake was hardly a good friend. Jake was nothing more than the super-annoying new kid, the egomaniacal karate jock who always seemed to be messing with her. Now, unfortunately, he would forever be known as "that kid that Gaia tried to kill for no apparent reason."

Nice going, Gaia. Brilliant. Beating up innocent schoolmates. You haven't done that since you were six years old. She and Jake might have been through a little sparring match at school, but this. . . even a conceited asshole like Jake didn't deserve this. She didn't blame him for fighting back. But what on earth was he doing here in the first place?

Jake was sitting over her, bruised and battered by her irresponsible hands and feet. Blood was dripping from the side of his mouth, and skid marks ran all along the side of his neck. Black tar was spread all over his leather coat and his face.

Gaia rolled her eyes back and let out a loud, frustrated groan, hoping that might cover over at least a percentage of the guilt coursing through her veins. "I'm so sorry," she uttered. "That was a total accident, Jake. . . . I was just. . ." There wasn't much else to say. She wasn't about to launch into an explanation of her deranged ass-kicking addiction. "I should have looked first."

"Um, *yeah*," Jake spat between short breaths. "I always say, 'Look before you try to beat the crap out of someone.' You know you've got some serious issues?"

He might be an innocent schoolmate, but he still had the ability to piss her off instantly.

"I said I was *sorry*. What the hell are you doing out here, anyway? I thought you were a rapist."

"I was just looking for *you*," he squawked in his defense. "I was going to talk to you about the karate team at school. Now I'm not so sure you wouldn't try to kill one of your opponents."

She stared at him doubtfully. "You were looking for me in the middle of Central Park at nine o'clock?"

Jake glared back indignantly. "Are you paranoid or something? Your doorman said I'd just missed you. He said you were headed toward the park, so I figured I'd catch up to you. Which obviously I did." He referred back to his scraped-up, tar-covered body. "Now I'm a *rapist*? Nice. Real nice."

"I didn't mean *you* were a rapist, Jake. I was looking for *actual rapists*." That was not at all what she had intended to say, but this little fiasco had thrown her off so completely.

Jake stared deeper into her eyes with a look of utter bafflement. "You were *looking* for rapists. . . ?"

Don't look at me like I'm crazy, Jake. I already know I'm crazy.

She could see the whites of his green eyes reflecting in the dark. He leaned a bit closer, examining her more carefully. But the sudden closeness of Jake's face sent a rush of blood up her chest that she could only describe as. . . *extreme pissed-offedness.*

In that blip of uncomfortable silence Gaia finally woke up to the infuriating position of their bodies. She had been so busy arguing and swimming through her guilt, she'd barely even registered this annoyingly domineering configuration. Now she was all too aware of Jake's strong hands holding her wrists in the dirt, and his athletic thighs squeezing against her hips, and his face only inches away.

"Can you get off me now, please?" she snarled through clenched teeth.

"I don't know. . . . Are you going to try to crack my ribs again?"

"If I'd wanted to crack your ribs, I would have just cracked your ribs. Now get the hell off me."

"God. What happened to 'I'm sorry, Jake'?"

"I *am* sorry. But you should get off before I smack you on purpose."

Jake's eyes widened with disbelief. "Oh, really? How?" he challenged her.

"How what?" she hissed.

"How exactly would you hit me right now, Gaia? I've got you pinned."

"Jake, if you want to play *Fight Club,* go find one of your latent homosexual jock buddies to wrestle with, okay? Consider this your last warning. . . ."

Jake shook his head at her with the most condescending

concern. "What are you even doing out here at this time of night, Gaia? I mean, what if I *was* some sicko? Think of this as a self-defense lesson. Say I'm a mugger. You tell me how you could possibly hit me now that I've got you totally—"

Gaia slipped her hand through Jake's grip and cracked her fist right across his jaw. It made a hell of an ugly sound and sent him toppling off her and into the dirt. But it thankfully shut him up. She'd been trying to avoid hurting him any further, but he really hadn't given her much of a choice with that little patronizing monologue. Besides, she knew he could take a punch or two. He probably deserved three.

"God*damn*," he groaned, massaging his jaw as Gaia sprang back to her feet. "I was just trying to help. Was that really necessary?"

"Consider it a self-defense lesson," Gaia replied, brushing herself off.

"Oh, that's it," he announced, jumping back to his feet and taking a karate stance. He pushed the dark brown hair from his face and began to circle Gaia playfully. "Come on, let's go," he taunted. "Try that punch again. See if you can get it by me this time."

He circled her slowly, inviting her into an impromptu sparring session as he flashed a slightly bloody smile. Gaia didn't think it possible, but as she examined Jake's strangely innocent Oregon grin, it occurred to her that she might have discovered the one human being on this planet who actually loved a good fight even more than she did.

"Jake, I'm sorry for kicking your face in. But I really think you should go home now."

"Come on, one punch." He smiled.

Gaia cocked her head. "Are you sure you're eighteen? Because I'm getting more of a twelve-year-old vibe. . . ."

"Hey, I'm not the one out here looking for rapists." He leapt a step closer, giving Gaia no choice but to take a defensive stance.

"Yeah, well, *you* were looking for *me*," she replied, sidestepping him with graceful ease. "And that's just as sick, believe me."

Now they were circling each other with disciplined caution—knees slightly bent, arms limber and prepared. Gaia couldn't help herself. If a stupid nighttime sparring session with Jake was the best she was going to get tonight, it would have to do. Besides, his Italian "J. Crew dude" good looks could stand a few bruises.

"Go home, Jake—I'm hazardous." She flashed a fake kick to make her point and then pulled back quickly. "And you can forget about the karate team. You're right—I'd just end up killing some poor quote-unquote *black belt* like yourself."

"Oh, damn!" He chuckled, shifting smoothly to his left-handed stance. "Are you questioning my black belt now?"

148

"No, I think it's incredible that you can break fifty boards with your ass. Very useful."

"Now you're complimenting my ass? Gee, I'm honored."

"Oh, I'm sorry. Did I say your ass? I meant your head. I just keep getting the two confused."

Jake thrust out his left hand, and Gaia blocked it with a resounding thwack. But Jake didn't flinch even slightly. They were still just feeling each other out.

"Three words, Gaia. *Anger management training*. Look into it."

"That's funny. I was just thinking you should look into asshole management training. . . ."

"Okay." He smiled. "You obviously think I'm going to make the first move here, but believe me, you won't even know when it's com—"

Jake's face suddenly contorted with pain. His entire body lurched forward toward Gaia, nearly knocking her to the ground. And then he collapsed. He fell back into the dirt like a rag doll. As if something had hit him from behind. Something invisible and dead quiet. Something hard and fast and merciless.

Gaia's eyes darted all around the dark perimeter of the park. She couldn't see a thing. Nothing but trees and shadows. She dropped down next to Jake and grabbed his shoulders.

"Jake? Jake?"

Jake wasn't answering. She wasn't even sure he was

breathing. Her eyes darted up again and scanned every inch of the park, looking for a target, looking for *anything*.

"Jake?" She shook his torso as hard as she could. "Jake, Jesus, *talk*. *Say* something, for chrissake. Jake!"

There was
no reason

overwhelming

to **emotional**

wonder

effect

if she was

dreaming or

insane.

JAKE.

Gaia was reeling from the memory—and from the way it ended, abruptly, like a lamp being unplugged. She had no idea what had happened next.

Obedient Pussbags

What had happened to Jake? Was he all right? What the *hell* had happened next?

But something even more urgent was occurring to her.

If Jake had been there. . . maybe he had seen what happened to her.

For the first time there was a connection. Some strand of reality, of her actual life, that connected to this horrible experience. There was no reason to wonder if she was dreaming or insane. The disconnection, the feeling that she'd just been removed from her life and placed into a different one, like a kid sneaking from one movie to the next in a multiplex—that feeling was gone.

"I have to make a call," Gaia told Paris.

"Fat chance." Paris snorted derisively. "Phone privileges are—"

"No, I need to make a call." Gaia came closer to Paris's bed. "I need to find a phone and make a call. Right now. Where's the phone?"

"They won't *let* you." Paris sounded like she was

talking to a small child who didn't understand the rules people had to follow. "Only obedient pussbags like Tricia get to use the 'patient communication facilities.'" She recited the phrase like she hated knowing it. "You can't just go do it. You can't even try; you'll get into trouble and—"

"Will you show me where the phone is?"

Paris crossed her arms, looking away. "I'm not going to encourage this," she said.

"Fine."

Gaia left the room. She could hear Paris calling her name behind her. She didn't listen. The bedroom was one of a series that faced into a plain, undecorated corridor. The walls were bare white, recently painted. Gaia randomly turned to the right and started walking. Her shoes squeaked on the worn-out linoleum.

If she could contact Jake, maybe she could figure this out—and find a way to get away from this place. Paris's comments about what it would be like here after a week were very much on Gaia's mind. The idea of being here for days. . . for weeks. . . of getting used to it, not *minding* it. . . was unbearable.

"Gaia, wait!"

Behind her, Paris was stumbling out of their bedroom, still pulling on her shoe. "Gaia, hang on! Don't do anything stupid."

"I'm not." Gaia kept walking. *I'm doing something smart—for the first time since I got here.*

Gaia turned a corner into another white, feature-less corridor. There was nobody around. There were no signs or labels on the doors, but Gaia was beginning to get her bearings; she knew that the common room was somewhere straight ahead.

"Gaia, stop!" Paris's shoes squeaked as she swung around the corner behind Gaia, struggling to catch up with her. "You're wasting your time."

"Fine."

"Gaia, they're going to bust you if you try anything," Paris said. She was out of breath—she'd had to sprint to catch up.

"Uh-huh." Gaia stopped at an intersection. More drab hospital corridors, going left and right. There were people around—two orderlies in white outfits, standing by a bulletin board, holding clipboards. The orderlies were laughing, as if one of them had just told a particularly good joke. Beyond them, on the wall, Gaia saw a blue metal sign, with a picture of a telephone receiver, and an arrow pointing off to the left. She turned in that direction.

A tremendous crash rattled Gaia's eardrums. She stumbled, nearly falling.

Call nine-one-one! Now!

Her father's voice, in her head. Suddenly it was like the lights were too bright. Gaia tried to keep her footing.

"Sorry," one of the orderlies said. Gaia looked over and saw that he'd dropped his clipboard. It had slapped the floor loudly, making her jump. It had sounded like a gunshot, but it was a dropped clipboard. That was all.

So why was she picturing tiles? White tiles. . . and a red stain?

Her dream. Gaia remembered her dream. . . her father the drunken security guard. Where had *that* come from?

Who cares, she told herself firmly. *Figure it out later. Get moving now.*

She sprinted forward again.

"Gaia, *wait*!" Paris was hurrying to catch up. The orderlies watched them go by, without seeming to care too much one way or another. "Gaia, believe me, you're making a mistake—"

Gaia came around the next corner and stopped.

The sign hadn't lied. The corridor ended in a widened area, where a wooden door stood partially open. The door had a glass window—Gaia could see a tall, skinny young man with bright red hair talking intently into a black telephone receiver. A big, muscular guard leaned on the wall next to the phone alcove. A nightstick hung from a worn-out leather strap on his belt. He had a thin black mustache, drawn like a pencil line across his face. The guard looked as bored as a human being could look without being dead.

When she saw the phone, Gaia breathed a sigh of relief. She had been worried that it would be a *pay* phone. . . and of course she didn't have any money.

There's four dollars and fifty-nine cents in my jeans pocket, she thought firmly. *From the park. From that night. In my jeans.* That was reality. That was the real world, *her* world, love it or hate it, and she was going to get back to it.

Gaia walked toward the wooden door with the glass window, and that was when the big, beefy guard pushed away from the wall and stood facing them. He still looked bored, but now he looked confused, too. Gaia was moving directly toward the phone alcove door. The boy inside saw her—his eyes moved as he continued to talk.

"Just a second," the guard told Gaia. "Do you have a phone pass?"

Gaia looked at the guard. And while she smiled at him, she shifted her weight onto her left leg.

NEVER IN HER ENTIRE LIFE HAD

Paris seen someone move so fast.

The guard—Stephen—had stepped toward Gaia, asking for her pass.

It was exactly what Paris had expected him to do. She had the next minute mapped out in her head: Gaia would

Blame and Morality

say she didn't have a pass, and Stephen would tell her that she couldn't be around the patient communication facilities unless she had one. And Gaia would plead that she really needed the phone, as so many patients did.

But that wasn't what happened at all.

Instead Stephen came over and asked if Gaia had a pass. . . and suddenly Gaia became airborne.

In one fluid move, like a ballet dancer, Gaia had shifted her weight onto her left leg and leapt into the air, spinning as she rose, her right leg swinging around like a deadly pendulum to smack against Stephen's head.

Stephen's eyes rolled, and he collapsed to the floor like a sack of laundry. He hadn't even moved, Paris realized. He hadn't had *time* to move. He was out cold.

Paris was so shocked, she stopped breathing. Her jaw hung open—she knew, because she could see her face reflected in the phone alcove's door. Her mouth was like an O, superimposed over Bible Jerry, who was staring out through the glass, looking as shocked as she.

Gaia had landed on her other foot. She stood balanced, her leg still out, her arms raised like some kind of Zen master ninja fighter. She had landed so well that her shoes hadn't even squeaked. The whole thing had happened so quickly that the echoes were still ringing through the corridor.

It was incredible. It was like something out of the Olympics or a Bruce Lee movie—the kind of thing that made a crowd gasp. *Did Gaia really do that?* Paris wondered as she stared down at Stephen, who was lying on the linoleum unconscious. His nightstick was trapped under him—he hadn't even managed to get it unstrapped.

How had she done that?

"I need to use the phone," Gaia was saying. Gaia's perfect pose was suddenly ruined; she lost her balance, just for a second, stumbling as she stepped forward, and she had to steady herself against the wall. Paris figured that anyone who had spun in the air and landed on one foot—even *without* kicking a weight lifter in the head along the way—was bound to lose her balance. It made Gaia seem human again and not like a killer machine or a wild animal.

"I need the phone now," Gaia told Bible Jerry.

"Put the evil away from the midst of thee!" Bible Jerry yelled. His Adam's apple bobbed furiously. The phone receiver was clutched in his hand. Paris saw that he was cowering back against the far wall of the phone alcove. "Keep me from evil, that it may not grieve me! Thou knowest the people, that they are set on *mischief!*"

"Give it a rest, Jerry," Paris said—but quietly. It was supposed to come out sounding tough, but Paris heard herself practically whispering. She was still stunned by what Gaia had done. And Stephen, on the floor, was *literally* still stunned.

"I'm sorry," Gaia said, pulling open the phone alcove

door. It didn't have a lock, or Jerry would have locked it—he looked that frightened. Gaia's blond hair swung as she shot forward and plucked the phone receiver out of Jerry's hand. He didn't resist—he darted past her, out of the alcove, and ran away. He was going to get more orderlies. Paris could tell from the look on his face. Whoever Gaia was going to call, she had to do it fast.

I'm going to get in trouble, Paris realized. *Just by standing here, I'm in trouble. I shouldn't have let Gaia do this.*

And that was funny, because how could Paris have *stopped* her?

But Rosie and the others weren't exactly thrilled with debating the finer points of blame and morality. Paris knew it well. She was here, so she was in trouble.

Gaia was dialing the phone, Paris saw. Ten digits— long distance.

New York.

Paris realized that she could leave. She could walk away right now and nobody would ever know she had anything to do with this. Bible Jerry wouldn't remember that she had been there—all he could remember was who begat whom and what was going to happen on the Day of Revelation. Already Paris was hearing approaching footsteps; it was close, but she could still make it if she darted off in the other direction.

She stayed where she was.

Inside the alcove Gaia was squinting, covering her

other ear, listening to the phone. From in there Gaia probably couldn't hear the approaching footsteps. Paris took a few steps back so that she could peer around the corner past Stephen's unconscious form and see down the other corridor, the direction that Rosie and the others would probably come.

Standing guard.

Catching Gaia's eye, Paris pointed frantically at her own wrist. *Hurry up.* Gaia got the message and nodded tersely, like she was concentrating on listening to the phone. But then she looked back at Paris and mouthed the word *thanks.*

I'm in so much trouble, Paris thought. It had been a while since the last time, she realized. She'd actually been on pretty good behavior, if you didn't count that stupid argument with Tricia a couple of days ago. A near spotless record. She'd even been on her way toward getting clothing privileges. That was all over now.

And it didn't bother her at all.

GAIA WAS WEDGED INTO THE PHONE alcove. It was a small room, the size of a closet, lit with a harsh overhead lightbulb in a cage. The room smelled

A Simple Jujitsu Kick

bad; Gaia wondered if the odor she smelled came from the red-haired patient who had yelled Bible quotes at her. Whoever or whatever she smelled, it made her want to hold her breath.

The phone wasn't in particularly good shape, either. It was an old push button, and the numbers were worn off. The small table it sat on had been scuffed and stained several times over.

Outside the alcove Paris had moved to one side to check the corridor for oncomers. Gaia was impressed that Paris had done this without being asked. It wasn't the kind of thing you'd expect someone to just *do*—especially someone you'd known less than twenty-four hours.

Looking down, Gaia saw that the door couldn't be locked. She could probably hold it shut, but not for long. With enough people trying hard enough to get in, it would only be a matter of time before the door got pried open. All she could do was prolong her phone conversation a few seconds.

If she even got through to anyone.

She lost a little bit of time getting Jake's number from directory assistance. The robot voice recited the digits, and Gaia had to clamp the phone to her head just to hear. On the second repeat she was confident that she'd heard all the digits. Glancing back out through the glass, seeing Paris standing guard, Gaia dialed.

I'll do it! Believe me, Katia. I'll do it!

Gaia closed her eyes. That was from her dream—

the weird nightmare she'd had right before waking up. Her father, unshaven and drunk, waving a gun. Gaia couldn't understand why the dream was still haunting her; it seemed to linger in her memory, as if it were important. As if it were more than just a dream.

Gaia didn't have time to think about it now. The phone was ringing. She could hear the soft hum a thousand miles away. . . in Manhattan. The homesickness was so strong and so unexpected that it nearly brought Gaia to tears. She never would have predicted it—that the mere sound of a New York dial tone could have such an overwhelming emotional effect. But suddenly she nearly wanted to cry. A phone was ringing in New York. She could picture it so vividly: the soot on the sidewalks, the garbage cans behind the Chinese restaurants, the Calvin Klein posters in the bus shelters, the way the street looked after the rain. The taxicabs, the delivery vans that roared past in the traffic as if they were trying to knock over pedestrians like bowling pins. The New York sun, hazy, shining on the East River like sparkling glass.

I want to go home, Gaia thought. It was the simplest, most basic, most primal thought anyone could have. In her mind the empty East Seventy-second Street apartment called out to her like a friend patiently waiting for her to return.

Miles away, in New York, the phone rang again. Gaia had lost track; she didn't know how many times it had rung. She felt dizzy again and weak—just as she had after kicking the orderly. It concerned her: a simple jujitsu kick had made her lose her balance and nearly faint. She had no idea what was wrong with her.

Oh God, I want to go home, I want to go home so bad.

Outside the glass Paris moved. Suddenly she snapped her head around, staring into the distance. And her eyes widened. From where she was, Gaia couldn't see anything—but she could hear approaching footsteps. She was running out of time.

The phone picked up.

"Hello."

It was an older voice—Jake's father.

Outside the phone booth Paris was gesturing, trying to get Gaia's attention. Now Gaia could hear a loud commotion outside, as if a lot of people were coming.

"Mr. Montone!" Gaia yelled. "Mr. Montone, can you hear me? It's Gaia Moore! G—"

"We're not here to take your call," Jake's father said. Gaia realized that she was hearing an answering machine recording. "But if you wait for the beep and leave a message, we'll get back to you as soon as we can." Immediately Gaia heard the tone that meant she was being recorded.

"This is Gaia Moore calling for Jake," Gaia blurted. She was straining to talk as clearly, loudly, and quickly as she could. "Gaia Moore, Jake's friend from school. Jake, I'm in trouble."

"You stay *right there,* young lady!"

That was unmistakably Rosie's voice, from outside the phone alcove. Gaia could see Paris backing away as Rosie and four orderlies suddenly came into view. No wonder their approach had made so much noise. It was like she'd brought a platoon.

"I don't remember what happened," Gaia yelled into the phone. She was trying as hard as she could to speak clearly. "I'm sure you're not exactly thrilled to hear from me. But listen, Jake, I'm at a place called Rainhill. Fort Myers B—"

Beeeep. The answering machine cut her off.

Rosie was right there, in her uniform, with her hair pulled back in that same overly tight bun. She was pulling the door open. The orderly beside her had his nightstick out—and there were three others behind him. Rosie reached in and pressed the button on the phone's base, ending the call. The other orderlies were right there, obviously getting ready to pry her out of the alcove.

There was no way to fight. There just wasn't enough room. She was trapped in a small closet, with four orderlies and an obese woman right there, trying to get her out. She was going to lose—there was no way she could get past them. Especially in her weakened state.

"Get away from me, you storm trooper," Paris snarled—Gaia couldn't see Paris, but she could hear her—her shoes were squeaking on the linoleum as the orderly struggled with her.

"Gaia," Rosie said. Her face was a foot from Gaia's. "Look at me. Look behind me. There are four orderlies here. Whatever lucky punch you landed on Stephen, I strongly doubt that you can get past all five of us."

She's right, Gaia thought. It bothered her immensely. Because ordinarily it wouldn't have been true. Four rent-a-cops were nothing; she could have knocked them all out in less time than it took to say their names. Rosie had no way of knowing that.

But Gaia couldn't do it. She was too weak, too tired, too confused. Even without the disadvantages of trying to fight from inside a closet.

"So, are you going to come out peacefully," Rosie went on in her dry, clipped tone, "or are you going to get into even more trouble with me?"

Gaia leaned back against the wall of the phone alcove. The smell was getting to her—she was yearning for the cooler, cleaner air out in the corridor.

"I'll come out peacefully."

Rosie nodded and backed up. The four orderlies stepped back, too. The way they moved, they looked like Nazis, the ones from those old Harrison Ford movies.

The moment she was out of the phone alcove, the orderlies grabbed her upper arms, holding her firmly. They weren't messing around—they must have known what she had done to the other orderly.

Paris was standing to one side, her hair snarled around her face. She couldn't adjust it, since her arms were pinned, too, by the other orderly. Her green eyes were narrowed defiantly. She held her head up straight.

A few patients had come around, evidently to see what all the noise was. They stood some distance away down the corridor. A nurse had shown up, Gaia saw—he was bending over the fallen orderly, holding a big plastic ice pack, trying to wake him up.

"Gaia," Rosie said, "you've picked the wrong friends."

"Screw you," Paris said. Down the corridor, at least one of the watching patients gasped.

Amen, Gaia thought.

Had she left an understandable message? That was the big question. Gaia tried to remember as the orderlies lockstepped her forward. They seemed to be taking special care to squeeze and hurt her arms. Had she managed to say the name of the hospital?

Gaia's memory, unfortunately, was perfectly clear. She hadn't managed to say "Florida." And she hadn't said "hospital," either.

Had she said *anything* meaningful?

And even if she had, so what? What would Jake care—if he even got the message anytime soon? If he could make any sense of it? Jake was probably nowhere near that phone—he was probably in karate class or at the movies or something, wishing he'd never met Gaia Moore. Assuming he was all right.

And what if he *wasn't* all right? What if he was missing? Gaia imagined that as the orderlies took her and Paris away from the phone. She imagined Mr. Montone calling the police, the FBI, frantically looking for his son. . . and then, a couple of days later, getting an incomprehensible phone message from some girl Jake had met. . . .

There was just no way to know. And Gaia realized that it was going to be very hard to try that trick again. She knew from experience: Once they knew you could fight, the whole game changed. You'd lost the advantage of surprise.

Waste of time, Gaia thought dejectedly. *All just a waste of time.*

"You're starting out on the wrong foot," Rosie told her. "Believe me, you're going to regret it."

Story of my life, Gaia thought.

THE BATHROOM DOOR SLAMMED AND

James Bond and Superman

locked. Gaia watched as Paris went over and began scrubbing the urinals. She knelt on the dirty tile floor, her thin green hospital pants darkening as they touched the damp tiles.

"Come *on*," Paris said, glaring over her shoulder at Gaia. "Start."

"But—"

"You heard her," Paris said doggedly. The porcelain squeaked as Paris scrubbed it. "You have to. If you don't, you're screwing *me* over. Classic disciplinary technique: Divide and conquer."

"But—"

"Maybe in New York the toilets clean themselves," Paris snapped. "Here it's a little different."

Gaia went over to the other end of the row of urinals. The smell was even stronger—it made Gaia's head swim. She held her breath and knelt on the floor, facing the rightmost urinal. Her face was vaguely reflected in the curved porcelain.

Go ahead.

Gaia smeared some cleanser on the sponge and began scrubbing. It was hard work. The sponge dragged, squeaking over the tiles.

BANG. Gaia flinched. A gunshot: The sound was deafening, overwhelming.

Except that there hadn't been a sound. Gaia was confused; she had actually flinched, but the gunshot had been in her head.

The tiles.

Staring at the tiles, Gaia was back in her dream again. *Is this what you want?* Tom Moore yelled, waving the gun. *I don't give a crap anymore, Katia! I don't care.*

Scrubbing the urinal, Gaia firmly told herself to forget the dream. The dream bothered her. It was *wrong,* factually—like nearly all dreams were. But this dream was wrong in a detailed, exact, precise way that was unusual. Gaia tried to avoid looking at the tiles; for some reason, the way they looked kept pushing her mind back into that crazy dream.

Paris is mad at me, Gaia thought, glancing over at the other girl. She didn't exactly blame her, either. Why hadn't she *listened* to Paris? Why had she been so determined to get moving rather than strategizing?

"I'm sorry," Gaia said awkwardly.

Paris didn't say anything. She kept cleaning.

"Listen," Gaia started again. "I know I just got here, but—"

"Locker room."

Gaia was sure she'd misheard. "What?"

"The orderlies' locker room," Paris said. She was squinting, scraping some bit of nameless goo from the edge of the urinal. "Behind the kitchen, past the bedding closets. There's a locker room." Paris turned her head, finally looking at Gaia. "That's the way out."

"What?"

"We figured it out," Paris went on quietly. "Ana and me. There's a way to do it, at a certain time of day. . . but we couldn't put the plan in motion."

"Why not?"

Paris didn't answer. She kept cleaning.

"Paris?" Gaia switched the sponge to her other hand—and realized that she'd already done that. Her left arm was tired, too. "Paris, why couldn't you put the plan into motion?"

"Personnel problems," Paris said. "I need Jared to make it work."

"Uh-huh," Gaia said. She remembered the amazing Jared from earlier—the way that Paris talked about him, the guy was a combination of James Bond and Superman. Gaia wondered how Jared was supposed to help—it sounded far-fetched.

"And I don't have a partner anymore," Paris went on. "Ana's gone."

"Where'd she go?"

"They got her."

They?

Paris was beginning to sound pretty paranoid herself. *She is a mental patient, after all,* Gaia reminded herself. *Someone checked her into this place. Why am I assuming she's sane?*

Because I'm sane, Gaia thought furiously. *And she doesn't seem so different from me. That proves it, right?*

Gaia wasn't sure. Her logic had sounded so reasonable the day before. But now it seemed faulty, here kneeling on the floor with the ammonia and urine smells penetrating her nostrils. Not exactly the choice activity for sane people.

"So where'd you learn to fight like that?"

Paris asked the question haltingly, in a bored tone—like she didn't want to sound *too* impressed.

"It's a long story."

"I'll bet." Paris had already finished a second urinal—she was clearly an old hand at this.

"Your big plan," Gaia began. She was thinking about the view out the windows—the endless white sands she'd seen. "How did it work? Did it involve the beach, or—"

Paris was shaking her head. "You can walk out on the beach, no problem. You just won't get very far. There's an electrified fence."

"Okay." Gaia was starting to feel claustrophobia closing in. She had held it at bay for a while, believing that she'd find a way out. But now it was starting to look like there *wasn't* a way out—just a mysterious plan that had never worked, anyway. One thing was clear, though: Paris could be the key. It was pure luck that had put them in the same bedroom, probably the only stroke of good luck in this whole nightmare. Maybe Paris wasn't much good as an escape artist. . . by herself.

"Paris, I'm sorry I got you in trouble." Gaia meant it. "I'm sorry you're getting punished."

Paris shrugged. "I get punished a lot."

"Paris."

Paris turned her head and looked at Gaia. A strand of black hair fell over Paris's eyes and she brushed it back with her wrist.

"We're going to escape," Gaia said quietly. "You and me, together—we're going to get out of this place."

One of the faucets behind them was dripping; Gaia hadn't noticed until right then. Paris was still looking at her, arching her back to soothe a cramp in her arm.

"Yeah," Paris said. "Okay."

Suddenly a clattering noise came from the door. Both girls jumped and then made a big show of resuming their cleaning. They were both scrubbing diligently as the door swung open.

"Howdy, girls."

A young male voice. Gaia looked over and saw Vince, the buzz-cut orderly from before. Another, taller orderly was behind him. Vince was walking in, carrying his brass key ring.

"Paris, you been a bad girl again," Vince said pleasantly.

"Screw you," Paris said without looking.

"I'm here to get Gaia Moore," Vince said, looking at Gaia. "You Gaia Moore?"

Gaia looked back at Vince. He had come into the room, and the other orderly was standing behind him. The door was still open. "I'm Gaia," she said.

"Time for your shrink session, Gaia," Vince said breezily. "Come on—I got to take you over there."

Shrink session. Gaia felt a wave of revulsion rising through her. Dr. Kraven and his smooth, snake-oil voice. Dr. Kraven's office, with its digital processors and padded chairs and electrified sponges and hypos full of green fluid.

No, thanks.

"Hey, Butch," Paris said suddenly, rising to her feet. She smiled at the other orderly. "You didn't say hello. Don't you like me anymore?"

"Paris," Butch said. He had a low, gravelly voice.

"I swear, Butch—all you do is follow this loser around." Paris was walking toward the sinks, her wet arms held out. On her way past she flicked a glance down at Gaia.

"Who you calling a loser?" Vince said, smiling. He seemed to be enjoying himself. Vince was watching Paris cross the room—he wasn't looking at Gaia at all. And the door was still wide open.

"I'm calling *you* a loser, loser," Paris told Vince. Gaia had put her sponge down slowly and was checking her shoes—the laces were tightly tied and tucked away. Gaia had learned that lesson the hard way: Make sure your shoes are tied first. "I mean *look* at you— does your mama cut your hair or—*oops!*"

Paris kicked Gaia's bucket over. With a loud splashing noise the dirty, soapy water poured out all over the floor. The gray, sudsy puddle spread quickly, moving toward Vince and Butch's white shoes.

"Sorry, I'm sorry," Paris said, bouncing on her toes, her hands against her mouth.

"Damn it, Paris—" Butch and Vince were moving quickly, backpedaling away from the water. They moved against the wall as the puddle spread, its suds hissing.

173

As if on cue, Gaia propelled herself toward the open door. Her feet slapped against the wet tiles, sending wide splashes across the room. Gaia bolted right past Vince and Butch and through the door, out of the room, before they had a chance to react.

"Oh, *damn*—," Vince yelled at Butch, thwacking him on the shoulder and pointing toward the door. "*Come on!*"

The two orderlies ran frantically toward the door. They both immediately slipped in the soapy water— their legs pinwheeled straight up into the air, and they fell, side by side, splashing loudly to the floor.

"Losers," Paris said quietly.

GAIA COULDN'T EVEN BELIEVE WHAT she'd been reduced to. Running like a child— like a *girl*—just to escape two pathetic goons. She should have had them lying flat on those grimy tiles in three seconds. **Freaked-Out Nightmare** They should have been eating soapsuds, wishing they'd never met her, wishing they'd never gotten their tragic, low-paying lackey jobs at this hospital. But she just couldn't trust herself. Not with that freaked-out nightmare slicing through her head in painful blinding flashes. Not with those awful blips of total confusion slowing her down—interrupting her motor functions like someone was just slapping away at her mental pause button.

It wasn't fear. It wasn't like she was afraid of those goons; she just didn't trust herself. How pathetic was that? She didn't trust herself to fight. Her supposed addiction. Her one means of quasi survival. It was cutting in and out on her, tucked away somewhere in that black cloud in her brain.

But she couldn't let them catch her. They weren't putting her back in that chair. There was *no way* they were putting her back in that chair. No more psycho alternate universe dreams. No more gunshots in her head, no more images of her mother, no more screwed-up confusion. No more Dr. K.

So, what now? What came next? She'd reached the basement. Maybe even the sub-basement. There were thick black steaming pipes on all sides and large steel electric meters hanging dangerously close to her head. The dark gray paint seemed to meld together on all sides, messing with her perspective and her depth perception until she felt like she was trapped inside a cardboard box. *Where now? Which turn to make?*

But there really were no turns to make. A move in any direction would just leave her bouncing off the walls like a lab rat in a cage. Which was way too appropriate a metaphor.

A bony hand clasped her shoulder from behind. Her unreliable reflexes forced her to grab the wrist and pull back for a swift punch. But once she turned behind her, she tugged back her hand.

It wasn't Vince's thuggish hand on her shoulder. Those weren't Butch's doltish, colorless eyes gazing at her. They were guileless silver-blue eyes, overflowing with intelligence. Those unselfconscious, alienlike eyes that glowed with a kind of ethereal kindness that she just hadn't seen enough of in her life. Her mother had always been capable of expressing that sort of kindness with her eyes. Sometimes her father. But that was to be expected from parents. She'd just never expected to see it in the eyes of a complete stranger. Then again, looking at D. didn't feel exactly the same as looking at a stranger.

D. turned his face up toward the ceiling, listening as the loud stomping feet traversed the stairwells. Then he turned back to Gaia and searched the edges of her face. "Not scared," he said, clearly referring to Gaia.

"No," she replied, riveted by his young eyes. "I'm never scared. But they're going to find me anyway."

"They won't," he said. With that, he grabbed her hand, pulling her quickly toward the basement wall, then farther past the boilers until they came to a rusted steel door hanging off the wall by only one hinge. He tugged her inside, and Gaia was nearly blinded by the metal-encased lightbulb hanging down from the rusted ceiling. Or maybe she'd just been blinded by all the colors.

Torture Chamber

AT FIRST IT LOOKED LIKE A MINIA-ture kindergarten classroom. Every wall was covered with bright-colored drawings on crooked sheets of construction paper, taped up haphazardly with slabs of Scotch tape. The small deserted utility closet couldn't have been much more than six by six, leaving Gaia and D. cramped awkwardly at its center, almost as if the walls were closing in on them. But Gaia didn't feel the least bit claustrophobic with D. In fact, it was the opposite. Though she could not possibly explain why, entering D.'s tiny makeshift gallery seemed to untie some of the knots in her chest and reduce the pounding in her head. Maybe it was just the childlike drawings all around her. But walking through D.'s rusty door gave her that same childhood feeling of coming back home after a long and miserable day at school.

Ugh. Home. She didn't want to think about home right now. It only reminded her of the dream.

177

D. slid by her and grabbed the handle of the hanging door, tugging it as near to closed as it could get with a piercing metallic creak. Then he ducked under her and grabbed a rusted plastic maintenance bucket from the corner, flipping it upside down and placing it under her as a seat. Gaia dropped down on the bucket and took in a series of deep breaths.

"Thanks," she said, checking to make sure the door was closed. She took a few more breaths, slow and easy, as they sat together in the quiet and stillness of his little studio.

Something about D.'s presence was so calming. It helped Gaia think. The thick black cloud in her head began to lift a little. She breathed a little easier. She felt a little bit stronger—a little bit more like herself.

D. finally pulled up a bucket of his own and grinned at her knowingly.

"What?" she asked.

He reached out and ran his hand just along the surface of her head. "Yellower." He grinned with that same disarmingly comforting smile. "Just now."

He pulled away and clasped his hands.

"What is yellow, D.? My hair?"

"Head," he replied, waving his young hands wildly over his own head. "Glorious yellow."

Gaia still couldn't make heads or tails of that statement or any other statement of D.'s. But the glee in his face was somehow infectious, and before she knew it,

Gaia was smiling. Her eyes drifted back to all of D.'s colorful drawings. And as she looked closer, she began to realize that they weren't at all like the work of a kindergartner. The colors were bright, and the images were rough, but there was a deep sophistication to it all. The total opposite of that primitive junk in Dr. Kraven's torture chamber.

She remembered what Dr. Kraven had said to her before frying her brain. He'd said that the paintings were there to try and comfort one of his patients. . . .

D. . . . Of course it was him. It had to be. A cheap attempt to win over this oddly color-obsessed boy. Her eyes darted down to his left wrist, and she realized the simplest and most obvious detail that had somehow floated right by her in their first encounters. Maybe she hadn't noticed it because it was so worn out, tattered, and faded. It was far paler than Gaia's, but it was still blue. A pale blue ID bracelet with the transparent little dot at the middle.

She was struck by an unbearably painful image. An image of this frail and gentle boy strapped into Dr. Kraven's chair, his thin, delicate limbs convulsing as he cried out in pain, probably calling out for someone. . . anyone. . . .

She winced and shook off the image as quickly as she could.

"D. . . . ," she uttered quietly, almost not wanting to look him in the eye. "Have you had sessions with Dr. Kraven?"

The smile fell off D.'s face. His head dropped down, and he gazed at his hands, clasped in the lap of his green pajamas. "No more," he said. "Nevermore. . ."

Gaia couldn't even be sure what that meant. Had he stopped seeing the doctor, or was he wishing it would stop?

Too painful a thought again. She shook it off and gazed back at the drawings, standing up off the bucket to get a closer look. The more of them she saw, the more she noticed the things they all had common. Of course there were the colors, but that wasn't all.

All the childlike landscapes were obscured somehow. They were like so many children's pictures, with the bright yellow disk for the sun, and a huge blue rectangle for the water, and the swooping double lines for the birds, but still. . . every one of those images of the outdoors was drawn behind the diamond-shaped wires of a fence. Every one of them. Behind a fence or drawn inside a frame. A window frame.

Paris had mentioned all the obnoxious stories they told—the stupid urban myths the patients made up about D.—about how he had spent his entire life in the hospital, "raised in captivity." But could that be true? Could anyone have spent an entire life seeing the world through fences and windows? It made Gaia's chest tight with sadness.

She refocused on the pictures. She'd found another common trait among them. The colors, she realized, weren't just colors. They were, in fact, always emanating from the heads of all the roughly drawn human figures, almost like they were halos—like the circle of light that surrounded all those images of Christ and the saints. Only they were almost all dark halos—dark brown, and dark ugly green, and dark red. Were they even halos? Or spirits? Auras? How would anyone know?

Some of them were done in thick, thick globs of black. One of the black-halo figures was as dark and demonic as any depiction of evil Gaia had ever seen on paper. The black halo dripped over the man's black eyes, with spiked wings unfurled behind his back. The wings were black like a raven's, but his coat was white. A long white coat with a black snake hanging from his neck. *No, not a snake. A stethoscope.*

Dr. Kraven, I presume. . . .

Gaia's hands began to clench in spite of herself, her entire body filling with rage at the thought of him touching D. The thought of him coming near D.'s wide, translucent eyes with that laid-back smile and that sharp green syringe in his hands. . . it was so much worse than any anger she'd felt toward the doctor on her own behalf. She welled up with a shock of protective fury. It took her a little by surprise—just the degree of emotion. The sudden need to protect D. was palpable. It was visceral, running through her veins, pumping through her like blood. It was something more than just the sheer injustice of it—it was something animal.

"Too red," D. said from behind her. He grabbed her wrist and pulled her from the drawing, staring just above her head with a furrowed brow. "Much too red. . ." He shook her shoulders slightly.

"What?" Gaia had no idea what he was talking about.

"No red," he insisted. "Yellow."

"D., I can't understand you."

"*Yellow*," he repeated. He grabbed her hand and turned her to face the back wall, which had been obscured in shadow. He grabbed the metal-encased bulb and shone it on the wall, clasping his long, slim fingers around her head and turning it toward the drawings. "Glorious yellow. . ."

Gaia stared at the drawings on this wall. There were six paintings spread out from left to right. And the figure was the same in every single one. A girl in green pajamas. Every one of them, a girl with long blond hair and a circle of glowing yellow around her head. In half of them she was standing, and in half of them she was sleeping in a hospital bed, but it was still quite obvious: Every drawing on this wall was Gaia.

"D. . . ." His name fell from her lips as she took in this homage. He must have drawn them overnight while she was sleeping—sleeping off that horrible *treatment*, as Dr. K. called it. "You painted these all of me? Just since yesterday?"

"Nuh-uh," he uttered, shaking his head. He stepped over to the wall and pointed out a long piece of tape that ran down its center, splitting the drawings into two groups of three. He pointed to the set of sleeping pictures on the left. "Gaia," he said. Then he pointed to the set of standing pictures on the right. "Ana."

"What?" Gaia didn't understand. How could half of them be paintings of Ana? They were all paintings of the same girl.

"You need to see now," D. said. His expression had suddenly become much more solemn. "You need to see the red."

Gaia searched D.'s eyes again, trying to reach through this unfortunate language barrier. "D., I really wish I could understand you. I really do. But I can't. And I don't understand. I don't understand about the pictures. They're all pictures of me, D. Not Ana. I'm Gaia, not—"

"You need to see the red," he interrupted.

"D.—"

D. turned away from Gaia and knelt down in the corner of the room. He dug his fingertips into a crack in the rotting drywall. At first she couldn't understand, but as she looked closer, she began to make out the length of that crack, running in a full two-foot-square outline. D. tugged out that entire section of cardboard-thin drywall and then reached his hand into the pipe-filled hole.

"D., what are you doing?"

D. pulled his arm back out of the hole with a red spiral binder in his hand. He blew a cloud of dust and filth off the binder and wiped the surface clean. "You need to see," he repeated, looking up at Gaia.

The loud stomps of galloping feet suddenly echoed from the stairwell in the basement. Fear welled up in D.'s eyes as he fell back against the wall, dropping the binder on the floor. Gaia placed her finger to her lips to silence D., and then she stepped to the door and listened for the proximity of the footsteps.

"Do Butch and Vince know about this room?" she whispered.

D. shook his head, darting his eyes toward the door. "Red," he whispered. "You need to—"

"Shhh." Gaia listened through the door again, waiting for the footsteps to head back up the stairs. But that wasn't what was happening. The footsteps were getting closer. "Are you sure?" she whispered. "None of the orderlies knows about this room?"

D. nodded as the excessive terror grew in his eyes. But the steps only came closer.

"Damn it. They're coming. I need to get out of here." But where? Where was she going to go? They were closing in on the room. Now she could hear Vince and Butch's voices just beyond the steam pipes.

No, not just Vince and Butch's. It was practically a crowd of them now. A crowd of gruff voices. Like they'd gathered every damn orderly in the place for their little Gaia hunt. Gaia didn't understand. If the orderlies didn't know about this room, how were they getting so close?

But then there was another voice. A female voice. Rosie? It didn't sound like Rosie.

She had to try to make a run for it. She had no other choice. "Don't worry," she whispered, trying to be as reassuring as possible to calm D. down. "I'll be okay." She didn't know that she believed it herself. But she had to try.

"Nuh-uh," D. uttered, shaking his head. "Nuh-uh." D. shoved the binder back into the hole and slammed the piece of wall back in place. Gaia reached for the knob, but she was too late.

The door slammed open with a horrid metal creak, knocking Gaia flat against the wall. There were suddenly far too many bodies trying to pile into the tiny closet of a room. Gaia couldn't even see past the white shirts and the blur of flesh. She felt what seemed like six different hands grab at her limbs and throw her entire body flat out on the filthy floor.

"Wrists," she heard. "Get the wrists."

"I've got the ankles," another voice shouted. Gaia tried to shove herself up, but two knees had already dug deep into her back, pushing her rib cage flat against the cold concrete. She felt the cold steel of handcuffs dig into her wrists and snap shut. And then her ankles.

"Get off me!" she howled. "Get your goddamn hands off me!"

"It's okay, Gaia," the female voice called from above. "Not so hard, guys! Come on! You're supposed to be *helping* her!"

Gaia strained to force her neck up off the floor. And that was when she saw her.

Tricia. The orderlies hadn't known about the room. . . but Tricia obviously had. Tricia had led them right to her. Gaia's eyes narrowed with rage as she glared at Tricia.

"Oh, Gaia, please don't look at me like that," Tricia pleaded. "Please. They told me you were somewhere in the basement, and I just thought you might be here. Please don't be mad. They're trying to help you. Dr. K. just asked me if I would. . . He's trying to save you, Gaia. He's trying to make you better."

With Gaia successfully cuffed, Butch shoved his arms under her shoulders and Vince grabbed hold of her legs. They began to carry her out of the room as she made pathetic efforts to break free.

"Nuh-uh!" D. hollered, following them, trying to stay close to Gaia.

"D., come here, sweetie," Tricia said, grabbing D. and holding him still in the middle of the basement as they carried Gaia toward the stairs. "You stay with me, honey, okay? Gaia has to get better."

Gaia found D.'s wide blue eyes and focused on

them for as long as she could as they lifted her up the steps. "It's okay," she promised him. She was the one being dragged up to the torture chamber, but all she wanted was to protect D. And she was failing him somehow. She was failing with every step they took up those stairs.

D. tried to drag himself from Tricia's grip, step by determined step, as she pulled him farther and farther back into the shadows of the basement. He stayed with Gaia's eyes for as long as he could.

"I'll be okay," she tried to tell him again. But he'd already disappeared from her line of sight. Besides, it was as big a lie as she'd ever told. She knew where they were taking her. And she was well aware that she was not going to be okay. And there was nothing she could do now to stop it.

that **fantasy**

feeling **persona**

of

perpetual

alienation

"NOW, GAIA, I'M GOING TO SAY

Tough Truths

some things that are going to be pretty hard for you to swallow right now, and I want you to know that's *fine.* You don't have to understand it all now; you don't have to believe it all. You should feel free to voice all your doubts and all your confusion because that's an *essential* part of this therapy."

Gaia tried to follow what Dr. Kraven was saying. Even though her head was still airy and buzzing and Dr. Kraven's face was still out of focus, she forced herself to concentrate.

"I have to tell you a couple of tough truths about your life," Dr. Kraven continued.

"Like what?" She really wanted to understand. Was he talking about the sadness? The loneliness? That feeling of perpetual alienation?

The doctor locked his kind eyes with Gaia's. "Gaia, you're suffering from a kind of mental disorder. It's called DID, or dissociative identity disorder. It actually afflicts a fair number of young females. Now, I'm going to try to explain things in simple terms so that you can easily understand. Basically, what's happened here... You've suffered through some terrible traumas as a child—some very painful events. Events like that night, when you were twelve years old. That night was so traumatic for you, so painful, that it forced you to

189

sort of. . . *step away* from reality. You began to push away your real life, and you took on this. . . well, this 'fantasy persona.' A fantasy persona with a mostly imagined life. Does that make sense to you?"

"No," Gaia replied, shaking her head slowly. Slowly was all she could really manage. "I have no idea what you're talking about."

"Well, like I said, that's okay," he said, reassuring her with an outstretched hand. "A lot of it won't make sense at first. A lot of the truths will upset you at first. They're the truths you ran away from in the first place. The truths you weren't ready to face. But Gaia, once you face them. . . once you come to terms, I think you're going to be so relieved. I think you're going to be happier than you've been in a long, long time. And some of the truths, some of the real truths about your life. . . are going to make you overjoyed. I guarantee it."

"I don't understand," Gaia said. "I don't understand what you're talking about. I was just talking about my dream. I thought we were going to talk about my dream."

"Well, Gaia, that's just it. Your dream was not a dream."

"What. . . ?"

"That was a memory. You're remembering your life, Gaia. You're finally remembering your real life. That's what I'm here for—to help you remember your life before your dissociative split, before this delusional

190

life of yours really set in permanently, when you were still in touch with a modicum of reality. I think this may be the first time you're remembering what truly happened that night—the night your mother was shot."

"What. . . ? I don't—"

"Gaia, you were a very frightened girl in a terribly abusive environment. You'd suffered that abusive home life for years. And when you lost your parents that night, you began to build these. . . 'fictions' in your head, to compensate for all your painful feelings, for your feelings of loss. That's when the primary break from reality took place—at twelve years old. It's completely understandable that you would create this idealized memory of your father and your home life after everything you'd been through. You'd just been separated from your parents—you thought for good. You'd just been put into foster care for years of your life. You'd already invented this 'fearless' persona to cope with your father's abuse. It's completely understandable that you would fully embrace the delusion of fearlessness to protect yourself—to cope with all your fears of loneliness and abandonment living in all those foster homes."

"*Create* this fearless persona?" Gaia was beginning to feel exceptionally dizzy. "What are you talking about? I didn't create anything; I—"

"Gaia, you don't have to listen to all of this now, all

right? Ignore as much of it as you want. I'm not expecting you to understand it all now, but you need to at least hear it. Gaia, your father was abusive. He was a very abusive alcoholic. I think he was an unfulfilled man with some very grandiose dreams, and unfortunately, he took his own self-hatred out on his family. Your story is the story of a lot of children in abusive homes."

"Abusive homes? I don't. . . It was just a dream."

Dr. K. shook his head slowly. "No, Gaia. It's the beginning of your recovery."

Her head was no longer just spinning; it was starting to hurt. She placed her hands over her face and tried to stop it from buzzing like an industrial refrigerator. "My head. . . ," she complained. "It hurts. It's really starting to hurt."

"Well, maybe we should stop for now," he suggested. "I don't want to overwhelm you. Would you like to wait for our next session?"

"No," she muttered from behind her hands. "No, I just want to. . . This is so silly. I know the difference between a memory and a dream. I know. . . . My father was not some kind of. . . Look, my father's not a drunken security guard; he works for the C—"

"Gaia, I know about all about your delusions," Dr. K. interrupted. "Yours is one of the most extreme cases of DID I've ever encountered, but we're going to crack it. Together. Down the line, you're going to understand. Your father was never in the CIA, Gaia; that's just your own way of compensating for his disappearance—that's how you've idealized him in his absence: as the man he always wanted to be, as the man you wished he was. And there's been no conspiracy to capture you or assassinate you. And I *assure* you, you are quite capable of experiencing fear."

Gaia couldn't hear any more of this. Not in this dizzy, half-asleep state. Not with her head burning like this. "I need to sleep," she complained. "Please, just stop this and let me go to sleep. I'm feeling so tired. . . ."

"I understand," Dr. K. said. "Of course I understand. The treatment is very tiring, I know. But Gaia, before you get too upset, at least try and listen to this one last fact."

He grabbed hold of Gaia's hand and squeezed it tightly, looking much deeper into her exhausted eyes. "Try and understand. Your real life, not the delusional existence you've created, but your *real* life. . . it's not all bad, Gaia. It's not all violence and dysfunction and loss. In fact, it's not all about loss at all. You've been suffering for years based on a very essential delusion about that night, and I don't want you to leave this room today without at least hearing about it."

"What?" Gaia choked out weakly.

"Gaia. . . that night. . . the night your father got so upset; the night he accidentally shot your mother—"

"No, that's not what happened. He didn't shoot her. It was my uncle. It—"

"Gaia, please just listen now. You and your father went to the hospital with your mother, and that was the last time you saw your father for years, yes?"

"Yes," she agreed.

"That episode in the house in the mountains; that was the last straw as far as child protective services was concerned. That was the night your father was taken away. He was taken into custody for domestic abuse. That was the night that you were put into the foster care system. But you've blocked something, Gaia. That night at the hospital. . . they told you that the shot to your mother's head wasn't a fatal wound. But you never saw her again. And that was too painful for you. You had to justify her absence in your mind. You convinced yourself that she had died."

The room became dead silent. Even the spinning in Gaia's head seemed to slow to a halt.

"Gaia, after two weeks at that hospital, your mother was released from it. She was sent to live in a halfway house for abused women."

She stared at the doctor without speaking a word. What was she supposed to say to this? How on earth was her half-present mind and her entirely numb body supposed to respond to such a statement?

"Gaia, how do you think I know all these truths about your life? Who do you think has told me all of this?"

"I don't know. I thought—"

"Who do you think brought you here to Rainhill? Who do you think found my name? Who do you think brought you all the way to Florida and asked me to cure you?"

She couldn't answer that, either. Not only couldn't she remember how she'd gotten here, but she was too tired to speak at this point anyway. Too tired to think—there were too many thoughts at once. "I don't. . . know," she uttered.

"Gaia. . . I think maybe you do know. Some part of you knows."

"I. . ."

A smile spread across his face as his brown eyes widened. "Your *mother* brought you here. Your mother brought you to me to try and cure you of these awful delusions. Your delusions of fearlessness, your delusions about your parents and your history—about a huge part of your life. She's alive, Gaia. And I think you know that. Somewhere in the recesses of your mind. . . you know that."

Gaia was frozen in her chair. Everything had stopped. Her exhausted mind and body had been pushed into overdrive, and now they were stalling like a dead car in the middle of the highway.

"It's all right," he said. "We've covered too much today, I know that. Look, Gaia, I'm going to let you go for now, but I want you to take this." He reached over to his metal cabinet and pulled out a small black notebook and a pen, handing them to Gaia. "Like I told you at our first session, it's too early for you to talk to your mother. I don't think you're ready for that yet. But if you want to write her letters, I'd be more than happy to deliver them. I know she'd love to get one. You can write anything else you want in the journal, too. Anything about your thoughts or your confusions. Sometimes the writing helps patients to keep things clear in their heads. And if you and I can do some really great work together. . . Well, let's put it this way: Your mother is pretty damn anxious to come for a visit. And as soon as I'm sure you're ready. . . we'll bring her in. I promise."

She couldn't even listen anymore. She felt thoroughly and completely fried—cooked up until she was burnt. Her head fell back against the chair as she tried to take in the doctor's statements. But she couldn't take them in. She couldn't take anything else in. Not now. No more now.

PARIS NEEDED A GOOD SOLID DOSE

of Gaia. She needed rage bonding. She had just finished session number one hundred million billion with Dr. Pain-in-the-ass

Superstud on the Road

Weissman, and she needed a reality check-in with the girl who had kicked Stephen's butt. She needed to commiserate in true pissed-off fashion.

No, it was more than that. She didn't just want to commiserate. What the hell was the point of commiserating? Commiserating wasn't going to change anything. Commiserating wasn't going to get her Jared's letters or give her any phone privileges. It wasn't going to put an end to these horrific daily sessions with Dr. Pain-in-the-ass or her god-awful evening group sessions. And it sure as hell wasn't going to get her out of this place.

God, that was what she wanted. The real kind of wanting. The kind she'd sworn off for months, ever since she'd lost Ana. She'd forced herself to stop thinking about it for fear of depression. But now. . . now that she'd met Gaia, now that she'd seen her shove their rules right back in their faces and kick their power-trip faces in. . . now it was different. Now Paris's defeatist mentality was really starting to wear on her nerves.

Escape. That was what she needed. Pure and simple. Getting out. Saying good-*bye*. Finding Jared herself. Telling her dad to go screw himself right to his face. Hell, there were a million things she could do out there. She and Gaia and Jared could all do them together. Two escaped mental patient chicks and one superstud on the road. It was an independent film just dying to be made.

Gaia would have some ideas for what they could do. She'd have some great ideas.

Paris bounced up to Gaia and grabbed her shoulders. "We have *got* to talk."

She scanned the hallway for an empty room and then tugged Gaia into Annie Maxwell's. Annie was always sitting out on the deck, looking tragic. Paris slammed the door closed and then turned to Gaia.

"Look," she said. "Forget everything I said before, okay? Forget about all my defeatist crap about not escaping. I had a bad experience, but I'm dealing with two completely different people here. You're not Ana. Ana is in the past. I've got to forget about Ana and focus on the now, you know? *You* are the now, Gaia. And *we* need to get the hell out of here. I am with you on this. I am *so* with you." Paris looked deep into Gaia's eyes and waited for her response.

But that response didn't come for a full three or four seconds.

"What?" Gaia uttered finally. She stared blankly back at Paris, as if she'd hardly even heard a word she'd said.

"Gaia." Paris groaned. "What's your problem?"

"I'm. . . I don't have a problem. I'm. . . What? Wait, what did you ask me?"

"What is the *matter* with you? Did you hear what I said? I'm coming around. I'm *with* you on this whole escape thing. I just gave you my whole 'I'm ready to bust out of here' speech, and you're looking at me like I'm a. . ."

Paris stopped herself midsentence. She had been so excited about her new plan, she hadn't really stopped to take a good look at Gaia—to take a really good look at her eyes. . . those glazed-over eyes.

It was a look she'd seen before. A different face, but the same look.

The Ana look.

Paris hadn't even noticed the little black book in Gaia's hand, either. It was just like the one Ana used to write in.

"Gaia?" Paris placed her hands back on Gaia's shoulders. "Oh, Jesus, they found you, didn't they? You didn't escape that session."

"What?" Gaia looked more lost with each word. "My session with Dr. K.?" she asked, looking unsure as to what Paris was even talking about.

"*Yes*, your session with Dr. K. Did Vince and Butch catch up to you? Did they bring you to Dr. K.?"

"I don't. . ." Gaia's eyes fluttered a hundred times as she blinked. "I mean, I had my session, if that's what you're asking."

God, that look. The ECT look. It was unmistakable. Like a sick puppy that had just woken up from a sound sleep. That was the look in Gaia's eyes. Paris had to wake her back up. Gaia just needed a good, brisk wake-up call, that was all.

"Okay, Gaia, listen to me." Paris pulled Gaia down on the bed and sat close to her, locking onto her glazed-over eyes. "Did you get a shock treatment?"

"What?" Gaia asked.

"A *shock treatment*. ECT. Did that asshole give you the juice?"

Gaia crinkled her eyes in confusion. "I didn't have any shock treatments. . . . I had a treatment with my doctor," she said quietly. "Is that what you're asking?"

"Yes, that's what I'm asking! Can you talk to me, please?"

Gaia only stared with more sleepy-eyed confusion. Paris's frustration was building fast. She grasped Gaia's arms and gave her a firm shake. "*Gaia.*"

"Stop it," Gaia snapped, shaking Paris's arms off her. "God, what is your problem?"

Good. That was better. That was Gaia. That was more like it.

"I was going to ask you the same question," Paris said, breathing out a deep sigh of relief. "Just forget it, all right? Look. . ." Paris checked back through the door and then lowered her voice. "We need a plan. I don't know what; I don't have a clue in the world. Without someone from the outside, it seems impossible. Ana and I thought of everything else, which amounts to nothing. So *you've* got to give me some Gaia-style ass-kicking ideas. You've got to get inspired. Because I am sure as hell inspired. Besides, we've got to get you out of here before they start juicing you every goddamn day. I'm not going to let you go Ana on me, no freakin' way. So hit me with some escape ideas."

Gaia stared at Paris for a few seconds. "I don't know."

"Well, *think*. I don't want to waste time on this."

"Paris, can we talk later? I'm just. . . I'm really tired right now—"

"No, goddamn it, we can't talk later. Just wake up and *think*."

"That's what I'm trying to *do*," Gaia sighed. "I'm. . . I'm trying to think about a lot of things. . . . I'm feeling so. . . I'm confused. . . ."

"It's just the juice," Paris complained. "That's the juice making you feel that way. Just ignore it. It'll pass. We have to stay focused—"

"I need to think," Gaia said, standing up from the bed.

"Good, yes. Think. How the hell are we going to get out of here?"

"Not about *that*. God, there are bigger things than *that*."

Paris went silent. She stared at Gaia incredulously. "What could possibly be bigger than getting out of here? All you wanted to do was get out of here. That's all you've wanted since the moment you woke up in this place."

"I need to be alone," Gaia uttered, her tired eyes roaming down toward the floor. "I just. . . I don't feel like talking right now. I need to think."

"Gaia—"

"*Alone*. I need to be *alone*."

"Fine!"

Gaia turned around and shuffled slowly out the door, leaving Paris alone on the bed in the dark room with very little else to say.

Paris got up off the bed, walked over to the vinyl chair in the corner, picked it up off the floor, and slammed it against the wall. She slammed it against the wall five times.

**Attending
physician:** Dr. Michael Kraven
Patient ID: Gaia Moore 2747
Diagnosis: Acute DID with bipolar II disorder;
recurring paranoia
Treatment: High-impact K-cycle ECT with lysergic
acid diethylamide + phentedrine;
intensive psychotherapy

Notes: Increased lysergic + phentedrine 100 ccs.
Second treatment went extremely well.
Patient was provided with numerous
factual counterpoints to delusional
constructs while in alpha state of
consciousness. All discussion following
the treatment should be retained now as
conscious memory. She put forth mild
resistance to factual information as
expected, but the treatment successfully
kept her nonaggressive throughout the
session.

I know some aspect of her
consciousness has already begun to accept
some of the more challenging
nondissociative truths, but it is one of
the most detailed dissociative constructs
I have ever treated. The idealization of
her absent father and her early family
life are more common. Even compensating

for the absent mother with the delusion
of her death is not uncharacteristic of
DID. But the patient's commitment to her
superheroic fearless identity may require
the most work. This has been her primary
coping mechanism for so many years. That
and the more common delusion of covert
government ties and self-aggrandizing
paranoid assassination conspiracies.

Prognosis: If treatment holds, patient should be able
to gradually integrate new factual
information without excessive resistance.
Confusion and doubt are to be expected,
but aftereffects of second treatment
should continue to expand and accumulate.
Delusions should progressively diminish as
the treatment takes hold.

She should now willingly attend regular
sessions. I think the healing will
progress at an even more rapid rate than I
had hoped. Patient's family should be
pleased. We may even see a full recovery
in as little as a week to ten days, to be
followed by intensive aftercare, of
course.

Future Actions:

1. Possible increase of lysergic and
   phentedrine for next session.

2. Confer w/ Dr. W. regarding group therapy
   participation.

Additional Notes:
1. Reward T. New directives: Increase
   induction efforts/encourage group.
2. R. binder: Inform Y. that process is
   going exceptionally well. Deprog.
   stage 2, complete.

What if it is?

What if it's real? What if that dream is real? What if it really is a memory? That's happened to me before. Did I tell Dr. K. that? Did I tell him it's happened before? With the Soldiers and Sailors monument. I thought it was just a nightmare, but it was really a memory.

What if she's alive?

God, what if she is?

If she's alive, then just let me talk to her now. Don't make me wait. If you want me to get better, then just let me talk to her. Don't make me write her goddamn letters. Let me see her face just once, and I'll believe anything you want to tell me, I swear. I'll believe I'm not fearless, I'll believe my dad was an abusive drunk and he was never in the CIA and whatever else you want—just let me see her. I want to see her now.

What am I talking about? What the hell am

I talking about? This is insane. She's not alive. I know that. I know she's gone. She has to be gone. If she were alive, then why wouldn't she have come to get me? Why wouldn't she have found me and taken me away from any of those god-awful foster homes? Why would she just let me rot out there alone all this time?

Why do I keep talking about it like it's true? I know it's not. Or I don't know—I'm confused. My head is

I feel so fried right now. I just don't feel like me. I don't know.

Maybe I'm not

"GRAY. GRAY-GREEN."

Permanent Happy Face

"What?" Gaia's head popped up off the windowsill. She'd fallen asleep in that black vinyl chair. Her face had been crushed down on her open black notebook, the pen still dangling from her half-asleep hand. She focused her tired eyes out the Plexiglas window of her room and saw that a sliver of gray moonlight was illuminating the dark waves of ocean beyond the fence. The whole day must have passed by. Behind the slightest hint of her reflection in the otherwise dark window she could see someone's silhouette. It was D., hovering over her. There was a heavy sadness in his features as he reached his hand out toward Gaia's aching face and waved it over her head. "Gray," he uttered sadly. "Gray Ana. Gray-green."

Gaia turned away from D. and closed her notebook. Once again the boy was making absolutely no sense, and given the current state of throbbing in Gaia's head, she wasn't sure she had the patience for it right now.

"D., I'm not Ana, I'm Gaia," she explained, rising out of her chair and bringing her notebook over to her bed. She hoped that sleeping on an actual pillow instead of a flat notebook might do something to alleviate her headache. She dragged herself onto the bed and flipped over against the pillow. All she wanted to do was sleep. Maybe then she could clear her head.

Or maybe what she really needed was to talk to Dr. K. some more. Maybe that would help? She wanted to talk about her mother some more. She wanted to know when she'd be visiting.

Wait. No. What am I thinking?

Her mother wasn't going to be visiting. Her mother was dead.

Gaia just needed to sleep. Not talk. Not think. Sleep.

D. followed her over to the bed like a puppy dog and stood right next to her, staring into her eyes.

He was too close again. And his probing eyes were getting on her nerves. How could anyone possibly be expected to deal with this boy just staring and staring like that, like he was some kind of surveillance robot or something?

"So gray. . . ," he uttered, shaking his head. "Gray, gray Ana—"

"D., I'm not Ana, I'm *Gaia*," she snapped.

D. flinched and stepped back from the bed.

Gaia sighed guiltily. "I'm sorry," she said. "I just. . . I can't deal with the staring right now, D., okay? I have a lot on my mind right now." That was a severe understatement.

"Nuh-uh," D. whimpered. "Gray head. You need to see. You need to see the red." He grabbed her hand and tried to pull her off the bed, but Gaia batted his hand away.

"Stop it," she groaned, giving him a harsh glance.

D. backed away again, nearly falling against Paris's empty bed.

"D., can you please just leave me alone? Can you do that for me? I'm *tired*. My head is killing me. I just want my bed right now, all right? I want to lie in my bed, and I want to think, and then I want to sleep. And I can't do that with you hovering over me like this. Do you understand? Can you leave my room, please? I need you to leave my room."

D.'s eyes only grew sadder. He raised his right arm and pointed his finger directly in Gaia's face. "Ana," he said, almost as if he were pointing to a ghost. "Ana gray."

"*Gaia*," she shouted, feeling her head pounding from her own volume. "Not Ana. *Gaia*. What is the matter with you?"

"Jeepers creepers, what is going on in here?"

Gaia turned to the doorway and saw Tricia standing there with her permanent happy face. The moment Gaia saw that freckled nose, a blip of a thought passed through her consciousness. She wanted to be mad at Tricia for something—something she had done. But Gaia couldn't remember what it was. It passed just as quickly, and Gaia let it go. It was probably just Tricia's generally annoying smiley nature.

"Can you take him out of here, please?" Gaia asked. "He's driving me crazy. He keeps calling me Ana."

"Ana?" Tricia walked into the room and patted D.'s shoulder. "You silly-dilly. That's not Ana, it's Gaia, Dee Dee."

"Nuh-uh," D. complained, shaking his head vehemently.

"D., are you bothering Gaia?" Tricia placed her hand on D.'s shoulder, but he shook it off. Tricia shrugged and puffed out a girlish laugh. "Well, that's D.," she said. She lowered her voice to a half whisper. "Sometimes you just need to ignore him." As if D. were a two-year-old child who would somehow not hear this.

"Forget it," Gaia muttered, plastering her hands to her face to rub out the pain.

"Oh, sweetie, are you okay?" Tricia took a step toward Gaia. D. slid down against the other bed and stared at her silently. "You look just awful," Tricia said, oozing with sisterly sympathy. "You had your second session, didn't you?"

Gaia removed her hands from her face. "Yeah," she said. "Yes, and I feel so—"

"Con*fused*," Tricia moaned sympathetically.

"Exactly," Gaia said, actually appreciating a brief moment of identification.

"And your head feels like a big giant bag of microwave popcorn. . . ."

"God, *yes*. Totally."

"Oh, I *know*," Tricia assured her. "*Believe* me, I remember what I felt like after those first few sessions. I mean, they're the most amazing, you know—the first few sessions—they're the real lifesavers, they're the ones that turn it all around, but still. . . they're also the hardest. It's so hard at first, Gaia. When you think you know yourself and then one day you just wake up and you find out that you have it all wrong. Oh God, is it crazy-daisy. And you just want to talk to Dr. K. again. . . but then you don't."

"Exactly," Gaia agreed, actually not hating Tricia's annoying smile for a change. "I mean, I don't know. . . . I feel so. . . *weird*. I have all these ideas running through my head now, and they all seem so insane, but at the same time. . . some of them don't seem so crazy to me. . . . I mean, some of the stuff I think is *real* sounds crazier than the stuff I think *isn't* real. I want talk to Dr. K. again. . . but I also just want to sleep."

"Oh God, I know what you have to do," Tricia said.

"What?"

"You have to come with me to group."

"Group?"

"Yes. Totally. Group therapy with Dr. Weissman. Gaia, when I was so confused and freaked out with my first few sessions, and my head was pounding, and I just wanted to go to sleep, I felt *so* much better when I went to group. I felt calmer, I felt so much less crazy-daisy. . . . It helped me so much. Just hearing everyone else dealing with their own daisies. It really helped. And Dr. Weissman is a real sweetie. You've got to come with me. I'm going right now."

Gaia didn't know what to say. She wanted too many different things at once. She wanted to sleep. She wanted to think. She wanted to talk to Dr. K., but she didn't. Most of all she wanted her mother to visit. Even though it made no sense.

But maybe this group thing wasn't such a terrible idea. If it could really calm her down like Tricia had said. . . if it could really give her a chance to say a few things out loud instead of just letting them incessantly implode inside her own confused head. . . that might be really helpful right now. That might be just what Gaia needed.

"I'll go," Gaia said.

"Oh, *goody*," Tricia squealed, shaking her fists like they were little pom-poms. "We can sit together."

Gaia climbed back out of bed, trying to keep her head balanced to avoid the throbbing. The moment she stepped toward the door, D. bounced right back at her, grabbing her wrist.

"The *red*," he whined. "You have to *see*."

Gaia scrunched up her eyes. She'd heard that before. She'd heard D. say that before. But she couldn't remember when.

"D., let go," Gaia insisted.

"D., honey, be nice," Tricia said. "Gaia's not feeling so good. We're going to group. Why don't you go, D.? You never go to group."

"Too many heads," he said. "Too much black. . . *red*," he pleaded again to Gaia. "You need to see."

"D., let go of my *arm*."

But D. hung on to Gaia all the way to the group therapy room.

THE REPULSIVE POSTDINNER STENCH

was still wafting through the common room. Gaia wished this hospital had just a few more wide-open spaces. She couldn't imagine clearing up her head with the smell of

Drugged-Out Bug Eyes

processed cheese invading her senses. But there wasn't much choice in the matter.

The round wooden tables had all been pushed aside, and a large circle of nine or ten metal chairs now sat in the center of the room, some of them already filled with an assortment of excessively calm or excessively fidgety patients. It was so strange the things Gaia's confused brain could and couldn't remember now. She did seem to remember many of these patients' faces. Soylent James, with his dusty mop of hair and Coke-bottle glasses; Christina Karetsky, the food thrower; Marvin. Even the skinny man with the bright red hair. . . Bible Jerry. She couldn't quite remember how she'd met Bible Jerry.

Why was she forgetting things again?

She really did hope this group thing could help clear the cobwebs out of her head like Tricia had said. Maybe it could bring back some of her damaged memory. Maybe it could stop all those confusing images from bombarding her brain and tugging it in a hundred different directions.

Tricia took Gaia's hand and found three open chairs. D. sat down next to Gaia, holding tight to her arm and scanning the circle of patients nervously. Mostly he looked down at the floor.

"Well, I see some new faces," a voice announced from the doorway. "That's always a good sign."

Gaia looked at the door and saw a young female doctor walking toward the circle of chairs. She had a sort of hipster brunette shag haircut and wore a pair of slim tortoiseshell glasses that were sliding slightly down her nose. She was carrying a styrofoam cup of coffee and smiling at the group. She was obviously Dr. Pain-in-the-ass Weissman, though from the glimpse Gaia had gotten so far, she couldn't see what was so pain-in-the-ass about her.

Dr. Weissman sat down in the empty chair at the head of the circle and set her coffee and a few folders down on the floor. She picked up a clipboard and a pen, crossed her legs, and placed the items in her lap. "Good to see you all," she said.

A chorus of grunts and phrases blended together in

response. Gaia watched Soylent James biting down voraciously on a hangnail, and she quickly turned away. The last thing she needed right now was to throw up.

Dr. Weissman immediately turned in the direction of Gaia and D. "Gaia, are you sitting in with our group tonight?"

Gaia hadn't met Dr. Weissman yet, but she supposed it made sense that all the doctors had some working knowledge of all the patients.

"I. . . I guess," Gaia uttered, shrugging.

"Well, good," the doctor responded. "We're all happy to have you here." The crowd let out another cacophony of grunts and unintelligible phrases. "I'm Dr. Weissman," she added with a bright smile.

"Hi," Gaia muttered.

"And D.'s here, too," Dr. Weissman said. She sounded pleasantly surprised. "Welcome back, D. We haven't seen you in group for a long time."

D. actually looked into Dr. Weissman's eyes and acknowledged her. She was one of the few people Gaia had ever seen him look in the eye besides herself. The doctor nodded to D. with a smile and then turned back to the group.

She did a quick scan of all the patients. "And where's Charlotte Tillson?"

"She's out on a day pass," Tricia said.

"Oh, yes, that's right." The doctor made a small note in her clipboard.

Gaia hadn't even known they gave day passes. Maybe that was what she needed to clear her head. A day pass...

What are you talking about? A day *pass?* She didn't want a day pass, for God's sake. She wanted a *full* pass. She wanted a ticket *out* of this place. . . .

Didn't she? Wasn't that what she wanted? She could have sworn all she'd wanted was. . .

She needed to talk to Dr. K. about it. She'd have to wait and see what he thought about it.

What? What are you talking about? Why do you have to wait and see what he thinks? Why would you possibly care what he thinks?

Gaia dropped her head in her hands. She was so confused, she'd been reduced to having fights with the voices in her own head. Dr. K. had told her she'd be dealing with a lot of confusion at first. Maybe she just needed another treatment? Maybe that would help her straighten things out? Maybe Dr. K. had night hours?

Night hours? Another treatment? What are you talking about, another treatment? Look what the last treatment has done to you. Do you want to feel more confused? More exhausted? You want to have a few more questions about your entire existence?

"Gaia?"

"Huh?" Gaia brought her head up from her hands. Had someone been talking to her? Had Dr. Weissman been saying something she hadn't even heard? Were the voices in her head that loud?

"Gaia, you're looking very upset. Would you like to speak first today?"

"I. . ." Gaia didn't know how to respond. She looked around at all the strange and depressed faces staring at her. Was the look on her face like the look on theirs? Did she look that disturbed? She couldn't help feeling like she fit right in with this group. "I—I don't. . . ," she stammered. "I'm—"

"I'd like to speak first," Bible Jerry announced. "I need to speak first."

Please, Jerry. Be my guest.

"Okay, Jerry," Dr. Weissman said, turning her attention away from Gaia. Gaia felt a wave of tremendous relief pass over her. "We can go back to Gaia."

Please don't. Ever.

Gaia couldn't believe she'd listened to Tricia. (Why *had* she listened to Tricia? Why would she ever have listened to Tricia? That didn't make any sense, either.) This little group wasn't calming her down at all. With all of their drugged-out bug eyes pointed in her direction. All their freakish grimaces and their cold, numb, Thorazine-deadened faces. Was this where she belonged? In a circle with these people, arguing with herself in her own head, playing mental hopscotch between delusions and realities, not even sure which was which?

Jesus, maybe it was. Maybe it was where she belonged. After all, she was sick. She had a mental disorder. DID, it was called. She'd been living some demented lie for years. Thinking she was fearless, thinking her father worked for the CIA, thinking they were all out to get her.

Thinking her mother was dead.

"Yeah," Jerry said. "Well, see, I'm having this problem. Well, not just me, really; it's a problem we're all having. It's a problem we're all *going* to have."

"And what's that, Jerry?" Dr. Weissman asked.

Jerry leaned forward in his chair. He swallowed hard as his eyes glanced to either side of him to make sure no one outside the group was within earshot. "Well. . . I spoke with God and Satan today. . . and they told me to check page one thousand and seven of my *King James* and page three hundred and two of my *Pocket Jesus*. . . . I checked every other word moving backward, and I've gotten the message. Two thousand and six. It's all ending in two-oh-oh-six, people. That is it! That is the end of it! The end of all you sinners and sluts and harlots and psychos—"

"Shut your goddamn mouth, Jerry!" Marvin howled, jumping out of his chair. "You shut your goddamn mouth right now!"

The entire group began to raise their voices in a deafening chaotic mass.

"All right, enough!" Dr. Weissman insisted. "That's enough, Marvin. Sit down, please. Jerry, do you have something constructive to offer the group or not?"

"Constructive?" Jerry squawked. "How is that not

constructive? What's more constructive than warning these dirty sinners about their dying days? Don't they want to know? Don't you all want to know when you're going to *die*?"

"Thank you, Jerry," Dr. Weissman announced. "That's enough."

Gaia's head was throbbing so much harder now. It was aching with every word out of Bible Jerry's mouth. Every word out of all their mouths. Why had she come here? Why would she want to subject herself to this? To any of this madness?

Because she was sick, that was why.

What are you talking about? You're not sick. You're just confused. You need to clear it up. You need to straighten this out in your head.

"All right, does anyone have something constructive they'd like to offer the group?" Dr. Weissman tried to speak over the chaotic hubbub. "Gaia? Didn't you have something you wanted to say? You've been looking very upset over there."

Gaia cringed internally. She didn't want to speak. She didn't want to talk to these people. She didn't even want to look at them. If she talked, then she'd have to tell them. She'd have to tell them about her confusion, about her DID. She'd have to tell them that she wasn't even sure who she was right now. She didn't need to talk to them. She needed to talk to Dr. K.; that was what she needed.

Why? Why do you keep thinking that?

"I'd like to talk," Tricia said, raising her hand.

"Go ahead, Tricia," Dr. Weissman said.

"My treatment's been going really well," Tricia said. "Really well. But I just wanted to say that sometimes. . . I'm still afraid."

"What are you afraid of, Tricia?"

"Well, I've gotten rid of so many of my crazy-daisy delusions. . . but it seems like no matter how hard I work with Dr. K., we still can't figure out what started them all off. We can't figure out what my primary trauma was, and I'm just afraid. . . I'm afraid I'll never know for sure. I'm afraid if I don't know for sure, then maybe my delusions could come back. What if I don't figure it out? What if I never *really* get rid of my DID? I mean, Dr. K. has helped me *so* much. He's made me so happy. But. . . I mean. . . what if I'm never totally cured? If I don't find the primary trauma, will it get worse? I don't want to have to worry about crazy-daisy delusions for the rest of my life."

Gaia's entire body was starting to ache. She didn't want to hear this. "Well, that's a totally understandable fear, Tricia," Dr. Weissman said. "What about you, Gaia?" She turned and looked Gaia in the eye. "I know you're struggling with DID right now. You're looking pretty worried yourself."

Worried? What do you mean, I'm looking worried?

"Are you having some of those fears, too, Gaia? Are

you afraid you won't be able to recover from your DID? Are you afraid you won't be able to find your way back to reality?"

Gaia's entire chest was burning. Her head was throbbing, and her eyes were stinging. . . and they just kept staring. Dr. Weissman, too. Staring at her like she was just as mentally ill as they were. Staring at her like she was one of them. She was *not* one of *them*.

"Gaia. . . ?" Dr. Weissman repeated her name a few times, waiting for Gaia to respond. Waiting for her to say something. But Gaia couldn't say anything. She was too busy clenching her fists and her toes. "Gaia, did you hear me? I asked you if you were—"

"No!" Gaia hollered. "No, I'm not afraid! I'm not afraid of anything!"

The entire group began to murmur again with all their demented, irrational babble. And Gaia couldn't take another minute of it.

"Shut up!" she howled, shooting up out of her chair. "All of you just shut up!" D. curled up into a self-made protective shell behind his arms.

The group became instantly silent.

"Gaia," Dr. Weissman said calmly. "There's no need to—"

"No, there *is* a need!" Gaia hollered. "There *is* a need. Look at you all! Look at you!" She darted her eyes from patient to patient, watching their jaws go slack, from Bible Jerry to Christina Karetsky and all the way back again. "You don't know a *thing* about yourselves, do you? You don't know what's real and what's a bunch of crap in your heads! All you know is your own freakish ideas and the crap these freaking doctors are telling you! What is that? Is that a life? Not knowing who you are, not having a clue? Look at her!" Gaia shoved her finger in Tricia's face. "How long has she been here? And she *still* doesn't know for sure. She's still terrified that she might never know who she is again. Well, that's not me. *I* am not *you*, Tricia. Because I am *not* terrified."

"Gaia," Dr. Weissman began.

"No, that's the point!" Gaia growled. "That's my point! I am *not* afraid. I am in*capable* of being afraid. Since I was born. I know who I am, okay? I know who I am. I have no fear. I'm fearless. And I've never cowered behind any bedroom door and *pretended* to be fearless, and. . . and. . . and. . . my father never screamed at me, and he never drank, and. . . and. . . he *does* have an evil twin brother, and he was one of the sickest sons of bitches any of you have ever seen, and my mother. . . my mother. . . She's *dead*. My mother is dead, dead, dead. And I live with it. I *deal* with it. Because nothing scares me. *Nothing* scares me. Not you, or you, or you, or my life, or my enemies, or being alone. Nothing. I know who I am. I know."

Gaia kicked her chair out of the way and stepped out of the circle. She took two steps toward the common room door, and then the steps turned into strides, and the strides turned into a full-force run.

"Gaia. . . ," Dr. Weissman called.

But she wasn't listening. That was the point. She wasn't listening to them anymore. She was running out. She was going now. Just out. Out, out, and away. Away from this place, away from Dr. K., away from her confusion. Away.

She did hear one last voice shouting after her from way back in the hallway. A raspy young voice fading away under the sounds of her stomping feet.

"Yellow!" he hollered. "Yellow Gaia! Yellow Glorious. . ."

AT NIGHT THE UNPLEASANTNESS OF

Rainhill Hospital was magnified. The day staff had left and the windows were dark, and the fluorescent lights shone harshly. Gaia's footsteps clattered and echoed as she stormed away from the common room toward the veranda doors.

Toward the exit.

I'm leaving, Gaia repeated to herself. *I'm getting out of here right now.*

Good as Gone

Behind her she could still hear the small, sad crowd in the common room. They were already yelling again, about something else. Gaia figured that most of them didn't even remember what had just happened; they had already forgotten that Gaia had just had her tantrum and stormed out.

Because they're crazy.

Gaia came up to the veranda doors. At night, she'd learned, these doors eventually got locked, but not until the patients had all moved into their bedrooms and the night shift began in earnest. Now there was nobody around; just a pair of double doors with hydraulic arms and windows showing black night.

Without slowing down, Gaia pushed open the doors and went out.

The night wind caressed her face, cool and sweet, spiced with the salty aroma of the sea. The sky was black. Gaia's feet slapped the cement as she crossed the veranda, passing the cheap lawn furniture and the rusted-out aluminum folding chairs toward the cement steps to the sand. Now she could hear the distant, hissing roar of the ocean. Ahead of her the hospital's floodlights shone harshly on the chain-link fence—the fence that surrounded the hospital completely.

I'm so out of here. I'm gone—as of right now.

How could she even have *considered* staying? How

could she have lost track of the fundamental difference between herself and everyone else here? Gaia's shoes were filling with sand as she approached the fence. Her ankles hurt from the strain of walking across the thick, soft dunes. Behind her the hospital's lit windows shone weakly, like dismal factory windows. The stars were invisible in the spotlights' glare. Far to the left and right the fence ran up against stone bluffs, a natural barrier that couldn't be climbed. But in front of her, beyond the fence, there was nothing but ocean water. The waves crashed dully against the beach, foam hissing across the flat sand.

Gaia figured she could swim along the shore and find a place to climb back ashore, past the bluffs. Not exactly a walk in the park, but not impossible, either. There were obviously dangers: hypothermia, risk of drowning, even, maybe sharks—Gaia had no idea—but the risks weren't that bad. And she *had* to leave. Now, before she got so confused that she didn't want to anymore.

She stopped, looking up at the fence. Ten feet tall, steel chain link, gleaming support posts every twenty feet. Easy to climb. A diagonal diamond grid of wire, and behind it the endless ocean. Freedom. There was nobody around—and if someone saw her from the hospital windows, it would take them too long to get down here. She was as good as gone. All she had to do was climb the fence.

Go, she told herself. *Now.*

Electrocution

GAIA RAISED HER ARMS AND REACHED for the electrified fence—and stopped.

She had no idea why. It was like some kind of physical force was stopping her. She couldn't make herself grab the fence. *Come on, come on,* she told herself impatiently. *Do it—go.*

But she couldn't. Time was fleeting, she knew—in a few minutes someone was bound to wonder where she was and start looking for her. Lights-out wasn't that long from now—by the time Rosie and Vince and Stephen were hunting around out here with flashlights, Gaia wanted to be miles away. Dripping, cold, wearing a torn hospital outfit, penniless, and alone—but *free*. Every second's delay increased her chances of getting caught.

But she just couldn't do it.

"It's not as easy as it looks," a voice came from behind her. "Is it?"

Gaia turned around.

It was Dr. Kraven. She hadn't heard him come out—the wind had blown the other direction, and the sand masked his footsteps. He was dressed in his usual T-shirt and khakis, like he thought he was posing for a Gap ad. The spotlights backlit his graying hair as he came toward her slowly, his hands thrust casually in his pockets.

"What do you mean, not easy?" Gaia said. She was

thinking of a way to silence Dr. K. A kick in the throat would probably work, but the problem was the sand—it made it impossible to jump correctly. Even Olympic athletes had trouble. "Of course it's easy."

"The climbing's easy." The wind flapped Dr. K.'s clothes as he stepped closer. "But the electrocution part—that can be a bitch."

"Electrocution?"

Gaia had forgotten. Paris had told her, but she'd forgotten. Just like she had forgotten that her mother wasn't fatally shot. Just like she'd forgotten that her father was a drunk. Just like she had forgotten what was real and what was a dream.

Twenty more seconds out on the beach alone and Gaia would have fried. Without Dr. Kraven's intervention, she'd have been dead.

"Oh my God," Gaia whispered. "Oh my God."

Gaia realized that she was sinking down, collapsing onto the beach. She landed on the cold sand, staring out at the waves.

Dr. K. dropped down next to her, sitting in the sand. He put his arm around her shoulders. "Okay," he said. "It's okay."

"But I'm—what am I—I can't—"

"Shhh," Dr. K. said, squeezing her shoulder. "You've got time. You've got plenty of time to think about it. And we're all here for you. All your Rainhill friends."

"Okay," Gaia said. Her voice was quiet and weak.

Suddenly she was tired—so tired, she could barely muster the energy to reach up and brush her hair from her face. "Okay."

"You're taking a big step," Dr. K. said quietly. "Trusting me is a very big step," he added, looking down at her. "A few days ago you might not have believed me. Who knows. . . a few days ago you might have taken your chances, declared you weren't *afraid* of electrocution, and just climbed the fence anyway."

Gaia sniffed, wiping her eyes. She turned her head, looking up at Dr. Kraven. "Thank you," she said. "Thank you for stopping me. Thank you for saving my life."

Dr. K. smiled.

"You don't need to thank me, Gaia," he said, giving her shoulder another quick squeeze. "Just doing my job."

Peaceful, Featureless Blackness

PARIS LEANED HER FOREHEAD ON the glass as she stared out the window. Down on the beach she could see Gaia sitting cross-legged, facing the electrified fence, slumped over and defeated. Gaia's shrink, Dr. Kraven, sat beside her on the sand. That simple tableau said it all—Gaia must have forgotten the fence was electrified and tried to escape, and Dr. Kraven must have caught her in the act.

And Paris knew right then that all the hope she'd been feeling since Gaia came to the hospital was for nothing.

Paris felt the urge to sob but forced back her tears. Which seemed very silly, since nothing had changed. Everything was the same as it had been a week ago. . . a month ago.

But everything was different because she'd been given *hope*. And now that hope had been taken away.

"Stupid," Paris said out loud. "I've been stupid."

And she meant it. Stupid because she'd *told* herself to avoid this. She had seen it coming and had tried to avoid it when Gaia Moore was first admitted to Rainhill. It was the same story as with Ana—it was like a newspaper comic strip. In the first frame you'd see Paris, looking pissed off. In the second frame she'd have a friend, and they'd be doing something, preparing to escape, keeping each other sane. And then in the last frame—punch line!—Paris was alone again. Big laugh—and apparently it just got funnier each time you repeated the joke.

As Paris watched, Gaia stood up, brushing the sand from her green clothes and then crossing her arms against the mild wind. Then Dr. Kraven stood up as well and casually put his arm around Gaia's shoulders. Gaia's blond hair was tossing in the breeze as they walked closer. Paris stared at their footprints in the sand until they were out of view and then turned away from the window.

Damn.

Closing her eyes, taking a breath, Paris went over and got out a sheet of writing paper and a soft pencil. She sat down at the room's small Formica table and turned on the lamp.

Dear Jared, she wrote.

This was the other cartoon strip in her life—and it was even more hilarious than the first one. In this strip the girl just wrote to her boyfriend over and over and over and. . . nothing. No result. She never got to see the replies because they wouldn't let her—but she just kept trying over and over because she couldn't stop. Get it? Hilarious, huh?

Dear Jared,

I guess I'd better tell you about Gaia. She's the new girl here. I didn't want to say anything because we had some secrets, and I know they're reading my mail. But now it doesn't matter.

Gaia showed up a little while ago and they put her in my room. . . .

Paris looked over at the window. She sighed heavily, staring at the peaceful, featureless blackness outside. She kept writing. She did not cry.

Attending
physician: Dr. Michael Kraven
Patient ID: Gaia Moore 2747
Diagnosis: Acute DID with bipolar II disorder;
recurring paranoia

Treatment: High-impact K-cycle ECT with lysergic
acid diethylamide + phentedrine;
intensive psychotherapy

Notes: I think we have a remarkable success story
on our hands.

The last week has been crucial in
knocking down patient's remaining
dissociative walls. Raised lysergic and
phentedrine to 2400 and 450, which have
proven to be the most effective dosage.

Patient is now responding to therapy
with positive and motivated attitude. As
her depressive symptoms have decreased, her
epiphanies and revelations have increased
at an astounding rate. She seems to have
fully accepted the delusional nature of her
dissociative identity. She has come to
terms with the idealized father figure. She
has accepted the delusional nature of this
uncle-/father-as-villain construct
(doppelganger syndrome). And she has
acknowledged in full the existence of her
mother. I'm extremely pleased.

Prognosis: Patient is now focused intensely on making a full recovery. The treatments have gone smoothly without incident, and the sessions have been focused and productive. As the delusions have decreased, patient has now become far more receptive to motivational therapy and a vigilant retraining of the dissociative and depressive mind. I expect to see a marked improvement in her maladjusted habits, antisocial behavior, and leadership skills. She is a remarkably quick learner.

Future Actions:
1. Continue motivational therapy and counterdepressive reconditioning.
2. Provide clothing privileges and other positive reinforcement.
3. Arrange visitation for mother.

Additional Notes:
1. Provide organizational activities. Instruct T. and R.
2. R. binder: Inform Y.: Deprog. stage complete. Beginning reprog. stage 1.

She's coming! My mother is finally coming.

Dr. K. is finally letting her! God, I must have written her about five letters a day, but now. . . Now he says I've made such brilliant progress over the last few days that he can finally arrange a visit.

Ten days. My mother is coming to see me in *ten days.*

It's pretty much all I've been able to think about. It is certainly all I've been able to talk about in my treatments. This miracle. This absolute miracle.

I'm on a massive upswing. It's kind of like I've just put all my old delusions into a big hot air balloon and watched them float into the sky, never to be seen again. It's like I've been reborn. It's like finding Jesus, or Buddha, or the perfect sunrise. But in my case, it's just. . . finding me. The real me. Not that depressive, violent ball of dysfunction I used to be, but the real girl. The real girl with a shot at a real life. It's just like Dr. K. and I always joke:

Gaia's life: take two.

And this time I'm not going to mess it up. My real life has been such a sad one. All that domestic violence and loss—all those lousy foster homes, inventing all this impending doom that never even existed. But now it's going to be different. This time I'm going to make healthy choices.

The first step, Dr. K. says, is acceptance. Acceptance leads to letting go. So I've learned to accept. They were some tough sessions, but they were such life-savers. I've finally managed to come to terms with my past. My real past. My abusive dad and his alcoholic suicidal tendencies— I've even found it in my heart to forgive him now. I have to. It's part of letting go.

It is all just such a glorious, glorious relief. I'm free. Free and clear of all those demons in my head. Free of all those dreams of

the CIA and all those evil freaks
who were out to get me. I understand. I don't have an evil "Uncle
Oliver." There's no "Loki." I was
just splitting my father into two
different people. Dr. K. helped me
understand the entire thing.

My father had finally made it
through years of alcohol and abuse
counseling. But when he came back
last year and asked me to let him
back into my life, I just couldn't
accept him. I couldn't face that
abusive man again. So I created
another delusion. I split my father
up into these two different people
in my head: the imaginary secret
agent I loved and the cruel, abusive jerk I despised. I *turned* my
dad into this Loki character—this
evil mirror image of him, this
"evil father" who was always trying
to "capture" me, always trying to
destroy my life. But really, it was
just my father. My abusive father,
asking for another chance.

I was so insane. I've wasted so
many years already, running from
all these delusions. I don't even

want to think about them anymore. Dr. K. says that's all right. He says that now that I've accepted the truths of my life and let them go, I don't even need to talk about them anymore.

Now it's all about the future. The very near future. I have to make improvements. I have to be my best. I have to get organized. That's what Dr. K. and I have been talking about. Organization and improvement, that's the name of the game.

The main thing is, I need to be more receptive to people. I need to be more social, more involved. I have to be more willing to take on a leadership role. People expect more from me, and I've let them down by being such a loner. I need to "get in the mix." I need to establish goals and then take the reins and develop my leadership skills. Dr. K. and I have been talking a lot about my goals. And we've decided that one day, I'd really like to work for some huge conglomerate company or organization. And once I've had all the

right training, and I'm sure I'm
ready. . . well, then of course I'd
like to run that organization, as
I'm sure anyone would.

That's really my main life
goal: to be the kind of person
who can run an organization.

empty

and

deluded **normal—**

and

angry

and

and **girl**

lonely **attitude**

THIS IS CRAZY.

Surreal Journey

Jake had been telling himself that over and over since he'd left New York. He'd said it as he drained his bank account at the cash machine near Union Square. He'd said it as he got his dad's permission to borrow the car for a weeklong "nature society" trip (lucky for Jake, his father had no sense of high school norms, having apparently blocked out entirely his secondary schooling experience)—fully prepared to swipe the keys and the garage pass if Dad said no—and as he cleared his throat before calling the Village School and, adopting a fake voice, managing to convince the headmaster's secretary that a family emergency was forcing him to miss a week of school.

I-95 south, a green road sign told him. Brunswick 25, St. Simon's Island 62. He was still in Georgia. It were much bigger than he'd imagined, but then, so was Virginia and North Carolina and every state he'd driven through. From New Jersey through Delaware the landscape had changed; the countryside had widened out, the horizon getting farther away as the hours went past and the surreal journey continued.

Gas Food Lodging, another green sign said. Jake squinted at the sign, reading the logos as it flew past: Wendy's, Starbucks, Baskin-Robbins, Lums.

Lums? he thought. He had seen this before; it must be a southern thing. There had been a Lums right across the road from the roadside motel he'd stayed in the first night, near Chesapeake City. He'd lain in the dark, the neon cable TV sign shining through the cheap curtain like a bloodred spotlight, trying to sleep, trying not to think about what a thoroughly crazy thing he was doing, driving south.

Of *course* it was crazy—that had been clear from the beginning. The entire time he'd studied Gaia's answering machine message, with the volume on his father's answering machine turned to maximum, he knew—he could tell that he was on the edge of a fool's errand, that he was putting all his chips on one crazy idea.

This is Gaia Moore calling for Jake, the message started. The connection was bad, and there was a squeaking noise like a badly oiled door that obscured the first two words. Jake had the whole thing memorized—he had listened to it over and over, checking his logic as he came up with this patently crazy plan.

Gaia Moore, Jake's friend from school. Jake, I'm in trouble.

Her voice, Jake remembered, had sounded strange. Not just distorted and muffled by the bad long-distance connection, but different. She sounded confused, tired, disoriented. . . and strange, different in some other way he couldn't put his finger on.

You stay right there, young lady!

A female, adult voice, loud, but distant. Like a

voice from another room, heard through a window or a door. Jake had tried as hard as he could to recognize it, but he couldn't. There was more noise then—clattering footsteps and more clicking and static in the foreground.

I don't remember what happened. I'm sure you're not exactly thrilled to hear from me.

Gaia's voice again. Loud and rushed. Like she didn't have that much time to say what she needed to say. Jake stared ahead through the I-95 traffic, running through it in his head. This was the important part.

But listen, Jake, I'm at a place called Rainhill. Fort Myers B—

The end. That was it. Dad's goddamn answering machine had cut Gaia off. Jake remembered standing in the foyer in their apartment, squinting as he played the message back, playing it a third and fourth time. And feeling the bruises on his arms and legs from the attack. Why hadn't she said anything about the attack? He'd been nearly knocked over with relief once he knew she was at least alive and safe, but couldn't she have said something? Something about that nightmare in the park? Something about how she'd ended up. . . wherever she was?

Rainhill.

The turnoff for the rest area was coming up—Jake signaled and got ready to get off the highway. His stomach was rumbling; it was ridiculous how much bad roadside food he'd eaten since leaving Manhattan.

After an hour at an Internet café on Twelfth Street, doing Google search after Google search on one of the café's web browsers, Jake had found three places called Rainhill. One was a theological seminary in Kentucky; he had called and spent five minutes with the nice lady who answered the phone, finally concluding that there was no "Fort Myers" of any kind anywhere near the seminary. The second Rainhill was a record label in Los Angeles. Jake had no idea how he could possibly get to Los Angeles, but he'd called just the same. There had been a moment when he'd had the sinking feeling that he'd have to find a way when the man who answered the phone had remembered a Fort Myers Boulevard nearby. But the man had checked, and he had gotten it wrong: it was actually Fort Michaels Boulevard.

And finally there was Rainhill Hospital in Florida, and that couldn't be it since it was an institution for the emotionally troubled—a mental hospital. And there was no way that Gaia would be in a mental hospital in Florida, right? It didn't make sense.

"No sense at all," Jake muttered to himself as he nosed the Accord into a parking space near the roadside rest area building. The car seat beside him was littered with road maps and old Dunkin' Donuts coffee cups and McDonald's wrappers. He would get a sandwich and some coffee, splash some cold water on his face, and keep going. And maybe call his dad to tell him he was all right.

Rainhill Hospital was in a place called Fort Myers Beach. Jake had checked three different web sites, and he was sure the information was accurate. It was, in fact, a mental hospital.

I'm at a place called Rainhill.

Why? What would Gaia Moore be doing in a mental hospital in Florida? Did it have anything to do with those men or that car? Were they the ones who had taken her to this place? Even his craziest stories and explanations made no sense.

Walking into the air-conditioned rest area building, past the guess-your-weight scales and vending machines, Jake nearly bumped into a family coming from the other direction, since he was so preoccupied. And ten minutes later, back on the road, with a full tank of gas and a greasy Wendy's burger in his stomach, Jake was thinking it through again. He couldn't stop—Gaia's message was like a tune he couldn't get out of his head.

Jake, I'm in trouble.

And that was it, in a nutshell. He had no idea what kind of trouble she was in or what conceivable connection there could be between that battle in Central Park and a hospital in Florida. . . but there was simply no other choice than to do exactly what he was doing—as crazy as it was. Play hooky for five days and get Dad's car and just start driving toward Florida.

Jake, I'm in trouble.

Jake gripped the Accord's steering wheel, scanning

traffic, looking for the fastest lane. He was nearly there. He would be there soon. And then he'd find out how crazy he was.

Soon.

TIPS. BEAUTY TIPS. HAIR TIPS.

Better with Boys

Clothing tips. Gaia needed them all. Her mother would be coming soon, and Gaia needed to be bright, and shiny and happy and beautiful for the occasion. And that was what led her to Tricia's room.

Tricia knew all about that stuff. She knew how to be a girl—how to look like a girl, and that was what Gaia needed. She and Dr. K. had talked about it. It was one of Gaia's goals. To let herself be vulnerable now that she'd shaken off her delusions of fearlessness. To let herself be a normal, well-adjusted girl. And what could possibly be more normal and well-adjusted than sitting with Tricia and trying out shades of lipstick?

"Hmmm. . . too dark," Tricia said. They sat together on her bed as Tricia sifted through her large metal makeup case to try another shade. Gaia hadn't even known they could possibly manufacture this many different shades of lip gloss. She'd missed out on all of that. She'd missed out on the simple pleasure of trying to decide between Burnt Raisin and Sierra Leone. She'd missed out on *Vogue* and *Cosmo* and all-girl slumber parties. She'd missed out on s'mores and funnel-cake binge fests. In her delusional life, she had always thought of those things as idiotic and shallow, but that was back then—back when she thought things like that sounded ridiculously stupid and immature and stereotypical and arcane. She knew much better now. She knew they were the fun kinds of things that girls were supposed to do. Things like shopping for fabulous designer clothes, and getting your legs waxed, and having six-hour late night phone conversations about liking boys.

Boys. She had to do better with boys. She and Dr. K. had talked about that, too. It was all part of her self-improvement plan. If she wanted to have a well-adjusted and healthy relationship with a boy, then she had to learn how to act like a girl. Boys didn't like sarcastic girls with attitudes like Gaia. They didn't like girls who wore big sweatshirts and old jeans and no makeup. They certainly didn't like girls who could potentially beat them up. But that was old Gaia. Delusional Gaia. New Gaia was going to be a normal girl. With normal-girl clothes and a normal-girl attitude. That was what would lead her down the road to a happy and healthy five-star relationship.

"Ooh," Tricia cooed as she wiped Gaia's mouth clean

and applied a coat of Passion Parfait. She pulled back to get a better look at Gaia's face. "Oh my *God*. . . ," Tricia squealed. "*Gaia*. . .You are *such* a cutie-patooty!"

"*Really?*" Gaia grinned.

"Oh my God, *totally*." Tricia picked up her hand mirror and handed it to Gaia to take a look. "God, when you first got here, you were such a mess. But look at you now. You are so clean and pretty."

Gaia held the mirror up to her face and took a good long look.

It was *true*. She'd spent her whole delusional life thinking she looked like some kind of big-hipped, overly muscular space alien, but Dr. K. had helped her to change her mind. And now Tricia was helping, too. Now Gaia could see it. She looked like the most normal girl in the world—a real girlie-girl, like Megan Stein and Tammie Deegan back at school. Like all the Friends of Heather.

That was kind of mean. Calling those perfectly nice girls the "Friends of Heather." The FOHs. Like they weren't people or something. Gaia would have to watch out for that kind of unnecessary rudeness in the future.

Tricia had straightened out Gaia's tangled hair with a blow dryer and parted it down the middle. Then she'd given her some eye shadow and mascara, and some moisturizing base, and just the right amount of blush, and finally the lip gloss. Bright pink lip gloss.

Gaia liked what she saw. This was what a girl was

supposed to look like. Not that no-makeup, hair-all-over-the-place look Gaia had cultivated back in her other life. It was *supposed* to take an hour for a girl to look like a girl, wasn't it? Of course it was.

"This is *so* your look now." Tricia grinned. "You could be on TV. You could be on a commercial or something. You could be on *Star Search*. You're a brand-new you!"

"Yeah." Gaia smiled. "I feel like a new me. You'll have to do my makeup every day, though. Promise?"

"Totally," Tricia squealed. "Every day."

"You think my mom will like it when she comes?"

"Of *course* she'll like it," Tricia assured her. "Gaia, she'll be so proud of you for getting better."

"I hope so."

"I *told* you, didn't I?" Tricia primped the back of Gaia's hair. "Didn't I tell you Dr. K. was a genius? Didn't I tell you he'd cure your crazy daisies?"

"You did." Gaia smiled. "You were right, Tricia. You were so right."

Tricia checked Gaia's face again and reached back into her bag for a little more blush. She brushed it back and forth on both of Gaia's cheeks. "God," she said, "when I think back to all the crazy stuff I used to think. . ."

"*You?*" Gaia laughed. "Oh, Tricia, you're nothing compared to me. I used to spend all my time looking for people to beat up. I thought my dad had trained me to be some kind of karate master or something."

"Gaia, I thought I was a *farmer*. Farmer Daisy."

"I thought my father worked for the CIA. What's more classic DID than that?"

"That is a pretty good one," Tricia admitted. "Ooh, Gaia, what about clothes?" Tricia was brimming with enthusiasm as she scanned Gaia's green hospital scrubs. "Shouldn't we try some clothes, too?"

"Well. . ."

Tricia stared at Gaia and crossed her arms dramatically. "What? What's wrong?"

Gaia checked outside the door to make sure no one was listening. She didn't want to rub her big news in the other patients' faces. "Dr. K. *did* just give me clothing privileges."

"Yaaay!" Tricia squealed, flapping her hands like wings. "That's great. That's a big step. I didn't get those for a while. I don't really like to wear mine in the hospital, though. I feel more comfortable in my hospital stuff. But Gaia, I'm so proud of you. You have come so far so fast. I have the perfect dress for you," Tricia said as she shuffled through the closet and pulled out a lavender floral summer dress. "What do you think?"

"I love it," Gaia said.

"Well, let's see how it fits. And then we'll go show you off in the common room."

Gaia got up off the bed and walked up to Tricia. She stared at her cute freckled face and smiled. "Tricia. . . you're the best. I don't know how I got so lucky. You know. . . I was just out there floating in my depressing little dream world. My life was just empty. Empty and deluded and angry and *lonely*. It was so lonely out there, Tricia. But now I've got my mom coming, and I've got Dr. K. and Rainhill, and I've got *you*. I just. . . I don't know. . . I feel so blessed."

"You *sweetie*." Tricia smiled. "We are, Gaia. We really are blessed." Tricia reached over and gave Gaia a firm hug.

Gaia rested her head on Tricia's shoulder, and then she caught a glimpse of someone out of the corner of her eye. She craned her neck forward to get a better look out the door, and finally she could see D. He was standing just outside the doorway, looking in.

"D.?" Gaia called. "D., come on in."

D. wouldn't budge. He would only stand there at a distance and stare at Gaia.

"Dee Dee?" Tricia called. "Do you want to come in, honey? Come on in here with us."

"Nuh-uh," D. uttered, taking a cautious step back. He was staring at Gaia like she was some kind of monster.

"What's the matter?" Tricia asked Gaia.

"I don't know," Gaia said. "He won't talk to me lately. He won't even come near me. Every time I try to touch him, he just bats my hands away."

"Oh, that's nothing," Tricia said. "He does that to me all the time. It doesn't mean anything."

"D., come on." Gaia sighed. "Come on in here."

"Black," D. muttered, stepping farther and farther back from the room. "Dark, dark black."

Gone.

Gone black. Just like Ana.
Yellow to black. One, two,
three. . . Kraven says nevermore.

No more yellow. No Yellow
Glorious. No more eyes. She has
black eyes. Black and muddy in the
ugly cloud. Like the monsters.
Like all the monsters.

Just D. again. Only D.

She will go. She will go where
Ana went. She'll be the new Ana.

She is AnaGaia.

Good-bye, Yellow Glorious.

Good-bye.

THE COMMON ROOM WAS EMPTY.

Paris was sitting on one of the tables, her back against the wall, her long legs folded up against her chest. She was gazing out the window down at the beach.

Some Kind of Sick Joke

Surrounded by the rows of empty chairs and tables, Paris tried not to think about what was going on in the other room—how Tricia was turning Gaia into a Barbie doll. Paris had stood outside Tricia's closed door just for a moment, listening. She hated that she was eavesdropping, but she had to know—she had to confirm that Gaia really was inside Tricia's room, laughing and talking and trying on makeup and clothes.

It was like some kind of sick joke. Right after Gaia had arrived, Paris had watched in amazement as she'd leapt in the air and knocked out a full-grown, athletic man by kicking him in the side of the head. It was still the most amazing, the most beautiful, the most impressive thing she'd ever seen in her life. A girl who could do *that*, Paris had thought at the time, could do anything. Not the least of which was escape from Rainhill.

But instead Gaia had turned into a little drone, a zombie, just like Tricia. It was the effect of this place. The corridors and fluorescent lights and doctors and all their privileges and "group" discussions and hypodermics and cheap green clothes and bad food. After enough time, anyone could succumb.

It was like that story about "for want of a nail." For want of a nail, the kingdom fell—that was how it went. If Dr. Weissman had let her communicate with Jared, she and Ana could have put their plan in motion long ago. . . and now she'd be free. Paris had even written out the instructions for Jared, for the part he had to play. But the letters hadn't gotten through, so Jared had never gotten here, and Ana had been taken away. . . and now the same thing was happening with Gaia. No letters, no boyfriend, no escape, no partner. For want of a nail.

"Hello?"

The voice had come from the common-room door. Paris looked over and her heart nearly stopped.

There, right there in the common room doorway, after all this time, just when she was thinking of him—

It was Jared.

But it wasn't Jared. It was a different boy—an unfamiliar high-school-age boy in street clothes. Cute, she supposed, but not Jared. It had been a momentary illusion, Paris realized. She had been thinking about Jared, so when she saw an unfamiliar face, she had naturally thought it was him.

"Is this the common room?" the boy asked, looking around cautiously. He wore jeans and a dark T-shirt. Paris saw the fading traces of a bruise on his forehead.

"The lady at patient information told me to find the common room."

"Yeah," Paris said, sitting up straight. The boy did look a bit like Jared, she realized, but only superficially. Something about his cheekbones or his close-cropped hair. He looked healthy, athletic. . . an all-American boy with an honest face. "Yeah, it's the common room. Can I help you?"

"Maybe." The boy took a step into the room. "I'm Jake."

"Paris."

"Nice to meet you. Listen, this is crazy, but—I'm looking for a girl named Gaia Moore. Is there, like, the slightest chance that she's here?"

Paris nodded coolly. "She's here. I don't understand—are you visiting her? Is she expecting you?"

"Well—" Jake smiled awkwardly, looking at the floor, as if embarrassed by what he was saying. "That's the thing. I'm not really sure. But wait—she's *here*? I'm in the right place?"

"She's here." Paris slid off the table, walking toward Jake. It was so strange to see someone in normal street clothes. It had been a very, very long time. "She's, like, three rooms away."

"Wow." Jake looked amazed. "Is she okay? Is she— is she all right?"

Paris wasn't sure how to answer that. "Are you a friend of hers?"

"Sure. I go to school with her. I'm—I'm here because I got this crazy phone message."

Paris understood. She remembered the day Gaia had made the call.

"Yeah, I was there. I had to scrub some urinals to pay for that message," Paris told Jake. "I guess it was worth it."

"Scrub—what?"

"Never mind."

Paris was looking at Jake again. This boy had driven all the way from New York just because of a ten-second phone message. It was implausible—a crazy thing to do. She believed it, though. Counting back, she realized it was just about the right time for him to show up, if he'd left the day Gaia had made that phone call.

The question was, would Gaia even remember? Or care?

"Listen, Paris," Jake went on, "would you mind taking me to see her? I'm actually pretty worried about her."

"Join the club." Paris could hear voices coming toward the common room—girls' voices. "Maybe you can talk some sense into—"

"*Jake?*"

Paris and Jake turned. Paris saw Jake's eyes widen in surprise.

Gaia and Tricia stood there. Gaia was transformed. She wore a lavender summer dress with spaghetti straps.

Her hair was glossy and smooth, not the tangled mess Paris was used to. Her face was made up, and she looked like a young woman—a beautiful young woman.

"Jake, is that you?" Gaia was gazing at Jake, her eyes wide. She took a step closer to him, reaching to touch him on the arm.

"Gaia?"

Paris could see from Jake's expression how shocked he was. *He doesn't know the half of it*, she thought bitterly.

"Gaia," Tricia said furtively. She was staring avidly at Jake. "*Introduce* us."

Gaia hadn't heard. She stood there in Tricia's summer dress, looking like she'd come from some kind of country club lawn party, staring into Jake's eyes. Jake was floored—he stood and stared back at her.

"Gaia, are you—is everything all right?"

Gaia smiled, a wide, dazzling smile. Paris was amazed at how pretty she looked. The effect of the clothes and makeup was overwhelming. "Everything's fine," Gaia said. "Everything's just fine. It's so good to see you. Are you here to visit?"

Paris could tell that Gaia's behavior was confusing Jake. She couldn't blame him. The boy had driven a thousand miles to answer his friend's call for help, and when he got there, she was acting like it was a cocktail party.

Driven a thousand miles.

Paris looked at Jake again, coolly assessing him. An idea had occurred to her out of the blue.

"Listen, Gaia, what's—what's going on? What the hell are you *doing* here?"

"I'm just learning a few things about myself," Gaia said quietly. She'd moved closer to Jake in a shy, flirtatious way—Paris could barely believe that it was the same person. "Come with me, Jake—let's talk. In private."

"But—" Jake looked at Paris, confused, and then over at Tricia, who was looking at him like he was Brad Pitt or one of the other movie stars she was obsessed with. "Gaia, this is weird. What's going on?"

"Come with me," Gaia told Jake, bringing her face playfully closer to his, "and we can talk about it."

"Well—all right."

Jake gave Paris another glance and then let Gaia tug on his sleeve, pulling him away out of the common room toward the corridor.

"I'll be right back," Gaia said over her shoulder to Tricia. Then they rounded a corner and were gone.

"He's *cute*," Tricia said to Paris. Paris noticed that she was blushing. "Who *is* he? Where'd he *come* from?"

"Get out of my way," Paris said. She pushed past Tricia without even looking. Paris was headed the opposite direction, away from where Gaia and Jake had gone—back toward her bedroom.

There was something she had to do—quickly.

WAS THERE ANYTHING ABOUT THIS

Standing and Staring

girl that ever made any sense? Ever? Jake was beginning to think not. It was like this girl had been invented to confound and confuse him. And Jake fancied himself a pretty unconfoundable, unconfusable person. But when it came to Gaia Moore. . . he was just lost.

First he'd thought she might be dead, or kidnapped, or God knew what. Then there was that message—some kind of cry for help, he thought. Some kind of cry for help from a *mental hospital,* no less. He'd driven a thousand miles just to be sure she was okay. But now. . .

Now she was standing on this sun-soaked veranda like. . . like she was on *vacation* or something. What the hell was the deal here?

Gaia walked out to the edge of the veranda, past the rusted white patio tables and the strewn-out lawn chairs, all the way to the railing at the edge of the sand. She stood there, bathed in a shaft of warm yellow sunlight, looking out at the crystal blue ocean as the strong wind whipped her hair and her dress behind her. Jake followed her up to the edge and leaned next to her against the railing, trying to understand—trying to get any clue as to what was going on here. The white sand was just below their feet, spreading out into a wide expanse of beach, and then the ocean was on all sides, obscured by a tall metal fence.

Jake stared back at her sunlit profile and tried to figure out where the hell to begin here.

"Gaia. . . Gaia, I'm really confused. Maybe you can help me—"

"Shhh." Gaia placed her fingers over her bright red lips and closed her eyes gently. "Listen," she said at a near whisper. "Listen to the wind. Isn't that an amazing sound? The wind and the waves together? I love that sound."

Jake could only stand there slack-jawed. He had no idea how to respond to that statement. It was the most *un*-Gaia thing he had ever heard. Everything about her seemed so. . . *un*-Gaia. The peaceful expression on her face, the purple dress clinging to the contours of her body from the strong ocean wind. . . Had he ever even seen her in a dress? He hadn't even thought she owned a dress. And since when did she wear makeup? And what had happened to her hair? It was always falling over her face in tangled-up tendrils, but now it was so straight. The straightness of her hair mixed with the yellow-gold sun, making it seem even longer and blonder and more. . . well. . . supernatural. It was kind of hard not to just stand there and stare at her.

But all angelic and goddesslike images aside, Jake could still certainly stand to get a little *information* here. And he didn't mean information about the weather or the sound of the wind. He was thinking more in terms of impending death, full-scale attacks in Central Park, and psychiatric hospitals in Florida.

"Gaia, what is going on? I thought. . . the way your voice was on that message, I thought I'd find you here strapped to some—"

"What message?" Gaia asked, turning to face him. Her blue eyes seemed twice their usual size in the sunlight. They were bluer than the entire expanse of ocean that was framing her face. Jake took an imperceptible moment to regain his mental footing. This new appearance of hers was distracting him from the far more important, far more confusing matters at hand.

"What do you mean, 'what message'?" Jake squawked. "*Your* message. You called me sounding, I don't know, desperate. I thought. . ." Gaia's blue eyes showed nothing but calm puzzlement. "I thought something horrible had happened to you. I mean, Jesus, you just disappeared after that night. I didn't know what was going on. You weren't at school, I didn't hear a thing from you, I had no idea if you were alive or what. Gaia, what was that in the park? Who were those men? What the hell was that all about?"

Gaia gazed deeper into Jake's eyes. A slightly bemused smile spread across her face. "Jake, what are you talking about? You're not making any sense."

"*I'm* not making any sense? *Me*? Gaia. . ." He wasn't even sure what to say. Was she screwing with him? Had she called him all the way out to sunny Florida just to screw with him? Was she playing some kind of weird Gaia game that he knew nothing about? That wasn't what this seemed like. This seemed like something else. Something much. . . weirder. "Gaia, I don't. . . I'm not. . ."

Gaia's smile grew even wider. "I can't believe you came all this way just to visit me. I really can't. That's just. . . It's so *sweet*, Jake. I don't think I knew how sweet you were. Did I? Did I know that before?"

Before? Before what? What the hell was she talking about?

Jake had no idea how to answer her. He searched much deeper into her sunlit eyes. A gust of wind blew her hair over her face, dancing in straight little golden strands over the tops of her cheekbones. It was yet another rather dazzling distraction, but still. . . "Gaia," Jake uttered quietly. "Gaia, what's. . . what's going on with you? Are you okay?"

"Oh God, Jake, you have no *idea*." She nearly swooned with joy and relief at the question. "Have you ever just felt like suddenly you were alive? Like someone had just told you a secret and you realized that you'd just had it all wrong your whole life? I mean *all* wrong?"

Jake stared at the bizarre wonderment in Gaia's eyes. "Um. . . no," he replied. "But have *you* ever driven a thousand miles just to talk to a complete lunatic?"

"What?" she asked, looking happily puzzled again.

"Gaia. . ." Jake leaned closer to her face. "*You*," he explained, trying to be as obnoxious as he could. "You are acting like a complete lunatic."

"Oh." She giggled. "Well, that's not very nice."

Jake only grew more puzzled. Frustrated, even. "'That's not very nice?' That's *all* you have to say? Gaia, I just insulted you. I just insulted you to your face."

"Well, I'm sure you didn't mean it."

"No, I meant it," he pressed, getting up farther in her face. "I meant it. You're acting bonkers. Bananas."

"Oh, I don't know." Gaia smiled. "Maybe I am."

"No, Gaia, goddammit, it's *me*, Jake. Jake, the cocky asshole. Jake, the guy you love to hate. I just called you crazy; now you're supposed to call me something worse, something really freakin' scathing. You're supposed to try to kick me in the head or something."

"Why?" Gaia asked.

"*Why?*"

"Yes, *why*, Jake, why would I want to do that? Why do we have to do that?"

"I don't. . . I don't understand. Something's wrong with you, Gaia. Something's different. It's not just the makeup and the dress and the hair; you're. . ."

Gaia took a step closer to Jake and placed her finger to her bright pink lips to silence him. And he went instantly silent.

"Jake. . ."

"*What?*"

She lowered her head for a moment and brushed her straight mane of hair behind each of her ears. Then she clasped her hands behind her back like a schoolgirl and raised her translucent sunlit eyes coyly up toward his. "Jake, do you think I'm pretty?"

Jake nearly fell over the railing into the white sand. He had never been quite so. . . He had no idea how to. . . Speechless. His mouth could not. . . form words.

"Jake?"

"I don't. . . I'm not. . ."

"Oh, no, am I being too forward?" A hint of worry fell over her eyes. "Was that too forward?"

"F-Forward. . . ?" Jake stammered. "Too. . . Gaia, when have *you* ever worried about being too *forward*?"

"I don't *know*." She smiled shyly and looked back down at the sand. "I mean, you still haven't answered the question."

"Well, I. . ." Why couldn't he just answer her? It wasn't like he didn't know the ludicrously obvious answer to the question. But something about this sudden freakish moment, something about her eyes just left him. . . tied up. And Jake was sure as hell not known for getting tongue-tied around women. But this was something else. It was some. . . other Gaia. But still. . . there wasn't exactly any denying. . .

"Well. . . I mean, of course you're. . . you. . . yes, I—"

"Yes?" She looked back up at him with a kind of girlish glee that he didn't even know her face was capable of creating. "Really?"

"Look, Gaia, something is—"

"Because the thing is," she interrupted, "when I saw

you walking into the common room today. . ." She turned her face back down toward the sand. "I thought you looked kind of cute. No." She chuckled. "Okay, I thought you looked *really* cute." She brought her eyes back up to his. "You are, you know? Cute, I mean. You probably know that."

Jake was beginning to feel dizzy and more than a little disoriented. He didn't know if it was his confusion or his heart rate or just this little visit he'd paid to the twilight zone. He didn't know what to say or do. He didn't know what he *wanted* to say or do. He didn't know much of anything right now. "Gaia, maybe we should—"

"Have you ever wanted to kiss me, Jake?" She took another step closer to him. Much closer. Close enough that he could smell the sea air and shampoo from her hair. Close enough that he could see the specks of indigo in her eyes. "Have you?"

Another easily answered question that he couldn't possibly bring himself to answer right now. Right now. There was something about right now. . . something wrong. . . But Christ, was his heart pounding. And he could feel himself leaning. In spite of himself. In spite of all the weirdness and all the wrongness of this moment. Leaning his head toward hers. And her face was rising, her warm breath floating under his chin. . .

"Okay, *stop*," Jake uttered. He stumbled backward two full steps, nearly falling back into the sand.

"What? What's wrong?"

"What's wrong?" Jake squawked, trying to straighten his posture back up. "What's *wrong*? *You*," he announced. "*You* are wrong."

"What? What is that supposed to mean?"

"I don't *know*. I don't know what it means. It's not that I don't. . . I mean. . . I really. . . of course, I— *Obviously* if you were. . . Why are you not doing, you know. . . what you do? Why aren't you shoving attitude in my face, and challenging me on everything I say, and hacking away at my overinflated ego, and *all the things you do*? Why aren't you *you*, Gaia? You're not *you*."

A plump woman suddenly stuck her head out through the glass doors of the hospital. "Gaia. You've got a session with Dr. K. Don't be late."

"Okay, thanks, Rosie." She turned back to Jake. "Look, Jake, I don't know what you're talking about. If you don't want to kiss me, that's—"

"No, that's not the point," Jake insisted. "That's not what I'm saying. Of course I want. . . You're just not yourself, Gaia. You're—"

"Of course I'm me." Gaia groaned. "Who else would I be? Stop being so silly."

"*Silly? Silly?* Gaia, you don't say *silly*."

"Well, obviously I say it, Jake. I just said it. Look, I have to go. I don't want to miss my session."

"Gaia, wait a minute." Jake grabbed Gaia's arm. "I came all the way out here to see if you were okay. I got this message from you. You sounded awful. You sounded like something was really wrong, and now I don't know. I don't understand—"

"Jake, I don't know what you're talking about. I didn't leave you any message. I *thought* you had come out here to visit me, to be *sweet*. But I guess I was wrong. Have a nice stay in Florida, okay? I mean it."

Gaia turned around and floated back toward the door.

"Gaia, wait! Wait a minute. Can't your session wait just one minute?"

She stopped at the doorway with one foot already inside the hospital. "No, it can't, Jake. It really can't. I don't like to keep my doctor waiting."

With that, she turned back around and disappeared, leaving Jake in almost the exact same position as when this inexplicable encounter had started.

Standing and staring.

RUNNING THROUGH THE HOSPITAL corridors, holding her sheet of notebook paper, Paris hoped she could still catch Gaia and Jake out on the veranda.

But when Paris crossed one of the hallway intersections, she caught a flash of

Darkness and Broken Glass

lavender down another corridor. It was Gaia, hurrying in the other direction—she was on her way toward the doctors' offices, probably for another of the sessions she'd become so addicted to.

But if Gaia was gone, did that mean that Jake had left, too? And if he had left Rainhill, would he ever come back?

Paris was out of breath as she got to the glass doors leading to the veranda. It was deserted; Jake was gone.

Where did he go? Was she too late? Paris was about to retrace her steps and head back to the visitors' entrance—the high-security gate with the metal detectors and guards, the place where visitors came and left—when she saw him. Jake was standing to one side, near the stained cement face of the hospital, looking out at the ocean.

"Jake!" Paris called out. "Jake!"

Jake turned around. He had his hands in his jean pockets and a strange look on his face, like he was profoundly confused.

"Paris, right?" He pointed at her as she walked up. "I'm sorry, I don't remem—"

"Listen to me," Paris said urgently. She was still clutching her crumpled sheet of notebook paper—the page that she'd desperately hunted through the hidden belongings under her mattress to find. "Jake, you've got to listen."

"Okay," Jake said dubiously.

They were standing near the veranda's edge, where

there was a wooden railing. Below, down a couple of tiled steps, was a sand-covered path that led to the beach and the chain-link fence that ran along the edge of the water. A couple of Rainhill patients were down there relaxing on the sand. There was more than one way down there—but the fence ran all the way around, cordoning off the hospital completely.

"We both know something's wrong with Gaia," Paris said to Jake. "She's not—"

"*Yes.*" Jake grabbed Paris's arm. "Yes. Exactly. What happened to her? Has she gone nuts? Is that why she's been put in this—"

"You don't understand," Paris said urgently. She was shaking Jake's arm for emphasis. "She wasn't like this when she got here. She's *changed.*"

"What do you—"

"It's this place—it's Rainhill. They're doing something to her. We've got to get her out of here."

"You mean break her out."

"*Yes,*" Paris said insistently. "Yes. Thank God you understand. That's why you're here, right? To help her. That's why you've come."

Jake turned his head, squinting as he looked out at the sea. The wind was gusting, making Jake's T-shirt flap against his skin like a sail.

"Yeah," he said. "That's why I'm here. All right—how?"

Paris closed her eyes in pure relief. The sensation was incredible. *Sanity. I'm talking to someone who understands what I'm saying—who isn't trying to turn this into a Freudian question-and-answer session.*

"Take this," Paris said, handing over the sheet of notebook paper. It was covered in Paris's penciled handwriting. The page flapped in the wind as Jake took it. There was another noise, too—somebody was moving around down on the sand, directly below them. "I wrote this out a long time ago for. . . for someone else. It's the instructions for your part of the plan."

"I don't underst—"

"Just read it," Paris insisted, leaning even closer to Jake so that his smooth, chiseled face was right in front of hers. "It's all there. I can't explain right now; it's not a good idea for us to be talking like this. But it's all there. It'll *work*."

"Okay," Jake said, folding the piece of notebook paper. "But what do I—"

"Leave," Paris said. "Come back tomorrow. Read the instructions; it'll tell you what to do. Do everything I wrote down. Tomorrow at ten you'll be coming back, and we're going to get Gaia and get out of here."

Am I dreaming? Paris thought deliriously. *Is this really happening?* Life could be so surreal—her moment of greatest despair and then, out of the blue, a new hope.

"Ten tomorrow," Jake repeated. "Are you sure this is going to work?"

"I've never been as sure of anything in my life,"

Paris avowed. "I've been waiting for this moment for. . . you wouldn't believe how long."

"Okay," Jake said.

"Thank you," Paris said. She could hear the catch in her voice; she was amazed at the emotions that were flooding through her. *Escape. I'm going to escape.* She realized she wasn't going to get a moment's sleep that night. Before she realized what she was doing, she leaned up and kissed Jake on the cheek.

"What was—what was that for?"

"Nothing." Paris felt her face heating up; she reached to squeeze Jake's arm again. He was in very good shape, Paris realized as her fingers closed on his bicep. "I'm just so glad you finally came."

The clattering noise from the sandy area below the veranda repeated again. Paris leaned over and looked down.

Nothing.

No, that wasn't true. There was a small figure in green just darting away as she looked. Jake leaned over the railing, too; they both looked down, side by side, as the small figure hurried away. "What the hell?" Jake said. "Someone you know?"

"Yeah," Paris said, staring after the retreating figure. "Damn. I should have been more careful. I hope I didn't just make a big mistake."

"That person was listening to us," Jake said with certainty. "Who *was* that?"

"His name's D.," Paris told him. "He's a patient here."

"Is he dangerous? Is it bad that he was listening?"

Paris looked at Jake—and realized that she didn't know the answer to that question.

"You'd better go," she told him. "And I'll see you tomorrow."

"Okay," Jake said. He smiled a lopsided smile, and something about the smile got to her. It reminded her of something—darkness and broken glass. Jake saw something in Paris's eyes and frowned. "Everything all right?"

"Yeah," Paris said. "Everything's fine."

Dear Mom,

I hope Dr. K. has been sending you all of my letters. I don't want to bombard with you with too much stuff. I guess I'm just trying to make up for all the time we've missed.

But you want to know the truth? I'm glad you missed that part of my life. I'm glad you didn't have to see me moping around like a depressed teenage ghost. I can't even imagine what it must have looked like when you found me in the park that night. I can't even remember it. Isn't that sad? I've already seen you, and I can't even remember it.

But that doesn't matter now, because I'm getting better. I really am. And we're going to see each other really soon. I can't wait. I can't. Do I even need to say it? Like I've said it in all the other letters? Oh, what the hell, I'll say it again. I'll say it again and again until I don't need to say it anymore, until it really sinks in that we're finally back together.

I'll say it a hundred million times: I've

missed you. I've missed you so much. It was like a hole in the middle of my chest. A gaping hole in the middle of my head.

And now that's over. That's all over. Because you found me. Because you're coming back.

And I can't wait. I can't wait to see you.

I love you, Mom. I love you.

Love,
Gaia

It was
all
just so
implausible.

show
time

THE BIG WESTINGHOUSE CLOCK ON

A Girl's Prerogative

the wall said it was nine forty-six in the morning. The common room was filled with the usual loud breakfast commotion and the smell of bad food— the runny eggs and greasy sausage that Paris had eaten so many times.

Paris wasn't hungry, though. She had barely slept. She was in the common room for one reason only: to make sure that she knew exactly where Tricia was. If anyone could ruin her plans, it was Tricia.

She saw Tricia: over against the wall, with Christina Karetsky. Tricia was talking animatedly, and it was actually funny to watch Tricia simultaneously hold up her end of the conversation and get ready to duck in case Christina decided to have one of her episodes.

On her way back to the bedroom Paris realized she was trembling. She was breathing quickly, too.

Because today was the day. The day Paris would escape from Rainhill.

If everything went right—which wasn't even close to a sure thing—then she was less than two hours away from seeing Jared.

Paris hurried to Tricia's room, pushing open the door and flicking on the light. She moved past Tricia's neat-as-a-pin, spick-and-span bed and chair and desk and got to the closet.

After all her snide complaints about Tricia—how she dressed and acted—here she was, picking through her closet, trying to figure out which of her clothes to steal. She found a pair of white pants and a yellow shirt that weren't too nauseating and took them. The pants would be too small, but it didn't matter.

Hurry up, Paris told herself, yanking off her canvas shoes and beginning to pull off her clothes. It was hard to keep moving fast—the only way to do it was not to think about what was happening. If she thought about it, she'd get nervous—and if she were nervous, Gaia would be suspicious.

Paris got herself into Tricia's white pants—they were way too short, coming down only to her midcalf—and the yellow shirt. Paris was the last person in the world to wear a yellow shirt, but again, it just didn't matter. She got her shoes back on and gathered up her clothes, making sure that the closet was closed and everything looked normal. Then she flicked off the light and left the room.

Turning the corner, approaching her own bedroom, Paris checked the time again. Nine-fifty. The door was open, and light was shining out onto the corridor floor. Paris stood there, listening—and made sure that Gaia was inside the room. She could hear her moving around in there—and as Paris watched, a shadow moved on the wall, confirming it.

Show time, Paris said to herself. Closing her eyes and rehearsing her lines in her head one final time, Paris took a deep breath, let it out, and then quickly, before she could lose her nerve, launched forward and pushed open the door, striding into the bedroom.

Gaia was on the edge of her bed, writing a letter. She looked up as Paris came in—and then her eyes widened.

"That's a *great* look for you," Gaia said, beaming.

"Thanks," Paris said casually, flopping onto her bed. She was trying to act innocent and excited. The "excited" part was no problem; it was the "innocence" she was worried about. "You look nice, too."

"What happened, Paris?" Gaia was frowning at her. Gaia's hair was still side parted and smoothed out. "Why are you dressed like that?"

"Guess what I've got?" Paris said in what she hoped was an impish voice. This was difficult—she had to make it believable, and Gaia was no dummy. Her heart was beating so fast that Paris was sure that Gaia could hear it from across the room.

"What's that?"

"I've got a *day pass*," Paris said, smiling in a way that she hoped looked genuine. "Dr. Weissman gave me a day pass."

"Oh—" Gaia was beaming at her. "Paris, that's *wonderful*." Gaia frowned. "But I thought you didn't get along with your doctor."

Good point, Paris thought. It was a question she'd

anticipated, though. She had an answer ready. "Watching you yesterday, I changed my mind about a few things. I saw how happy you'd become, and I decided that I was being stupid. So when I had my session, I told Dr. Weissman that I was sorry and that I wanted to try things her way for a while."

The lie was so completely false, Paris could barely get through it with a straight face. Gaia's eyes focused on her as she said it. Paris had no idea whether Gaia was buying any of it.

"Paris," Gaia said, shaking her head in amazement, "I'm *so* glad to hear that. I can't tell you how happy that makes me."

Gaia got up to give Paris a hug. "I'm *proud* of you," Gaia whispered in Paris's ear. "Really."

"Thanks," Paris said, squeezing Gaia's hand. All very beautifully done, Paris told herself, except that they didn't have *time* for this. They had to get moving.

"There's more good news," Paris said, smiling. "I asked Dr. Kraven if you could come with me. And he said yes."

Gaia stared at Paris, and Paris concentrated as hard as she could on staring right back. This was the part she figured she'd have the hardest time selling. It was just all so implausible—the idea that Paris would approach Gaia's doctor, that she wouldn't tell Gaia, that anyone would give Gaia a day pass right after her tantrum in group—none of it made much sense.

But Gaia was ready to buy it, Paris realized, watching her face light up. Something had happened that night that Gaia had sat on the beach by the fence with Dr. Kraven. Her thinking had changed.

"A day pass? You're *kidding*. Paris, that's *really* so nice of you." Gaia smiled. "I knew we could be friends again."

Paris smiled back. "Me too," she said. "So, are you ready to go? I've got my boyfriend picking me up at ten—we've got to hurry."

Outside in the corridor footsteps were approaching. *Don't be Tricia,* Paris thought furiously. *Don't be Tricia— don't come in here, don't notice the missing clothes.*

"I've got Tricia's purple dress here," Gaia said shyly. "Do you think she'd let me wear it again? Those are her clothes, right?"

"Yeah. Go ahead—it looks great on you."
Just hurry up.

Outside the bedroom the footsteps went right past and kept going. Gaia had stripped down to her underwear and was headed to the closet for the purple dress. While facing the other direction, Paris closed her eyes and tried to stay calm. The next five minutes were going to be the hardest part.

I'm coming, Jared, Paris thought. She could picture the beach house so clearly in her mind—the broken shingles, the screens on the windows, the brightly polished doorbell. *I'm almost there.*

"How do I look?" Gaia asked brightly. She was

pivoting in place, showing off the dress. Paris forced herself to answer slowly and calmly, as if it made any difference at all what Gaia looked like.

"You look great," Paris said, smiling at her roommate. "Just great."

"Thanks." Gaia was admiring herself in the mirror. "I just love this dress. I never wore dresses before—I don't understand why."

Who cares?! We have to get to the beach house.

"That's interesting," Paris said, moving toward the door. "Are you ready to go?"

"Just give me one more second." Gaia smiled. "Isn't that a girl's prerogative, to make everyone wait?"

IT WAS A WINDY, CLOUDY, BEAUTIFUL

day. The breeze blew the reeds that lined the causeway leading from the highway toward the Florida shore. Once again, looking around as he drove, Jake was amazed at the landscape. He'd never been this far south before, despite endless boyhood pleas for trips to Disney World. The orange groves, the swampland—it was like a different country.

Jake was running out of cash. After checking out of the motel, paying the bill, and filling the Accord's gas tank, he only had twenty-three dollars left. Not nearly enough to make it back home.

Following the road signs, the same as the previous afternoon, Jake decided that it didn't matter. It was the least of his problems. After spending an hour in the motel room going over Paris's letter—making sure that he understood her plan—he decided that he didn't need money. If this worked or if it didn't, he'd find his way back home somehow. Paris's letter was detailed and precise, but there were parts of it he didn't understand. It kept referring to somebody named "Ana," for one thing—and there were references to a "beach house" that made no sense to him.

Rainhill Center for the Emotionally Troubled, the big sign read. Beneath it said, Established 1975. Jake could see the hospital's concrete roof poking up over the reeds. Another sign said, DANGER: ELECTRIFIED FENCE!

The Accord's dashboard clock read nine fifty-five. Just about right on time.

Jake drove into the Rainhill parking lot. There were several dedicated parking spots with signs that spelled out doctors' names. He saw Westergaard and Kraven and Debakey. All the cars parked in that row were expensive luxury sedans. Jake drove past them and over to the north end of the parking lot. As he pulled into a spot and killed the engine, the dashboard clock said nine fifty-six. Paris's letter stressed that the hospital's shift changes always happened right on time.

Jake locked the car and walked toward the hospital. Nobody was around. The parking lot asphalt was so hot from the sun that he could feel it through his sneakers. And once again, just like yesterday, he could smell the sea.

The main visitors' entrance was a big glass door with a sand-filled chrome ashtray to one side. A woman in blue overalls was just coming out. Jake had gone in that way yesterday. Now he skirted the edge of the building and headed around to the north flank.

Nine fifty-seven.

Jake looked around, wondering if he should try to find a hiding place. There was nowhere he could conceal himself. Besides, the move he had to make was tricky enough. It was probably best if he just stood right there, out in the open. As he looked around at the dirty, grass-punctured asphalt, a rusted metal pipe caught his eye. He darted over and picked it up.

Click. The door was moving. He was surprised; it had happened more quickly than he'd expected. Jake flexed his muscles, raising the rusted pipe, getting ready.

The steel door swung open and a young man in his twenties came out, squinting in the sun. The man was wearing a completely white outfit. Even his shoes were white, Jake saw. He had pale skin and a buzz cut and a nightstick hanging from his belt.

As fast as he could, Jake dove forward and did his move.

With his left hand he threw the pipe over the man's head. It missed him entirely, banging against the door's steel edge with a loud clang and dropping toward the ground.

The white-clothed man flinched at the sound. He was fairly well trained, Jake realized—he was crouching and reaching for his nightstick before he'd even seen Jake or figured out what was making all that noise.

Jake's left arm was still raised from throwing the pipe. Using it for balance, he swung around and gave the man a sharp karate chop on the back of his neck—just below the shaved edge of his crew cut.

The young man's eyes rolled back and he fell to the ground. Jake didn't wait—he darted forward, lunging to catch the door before it swung shut.

He missed. A hand grabbed his ankle, toppling him to the ground. The orderly was better than Jake had expected. He was still conscious. Jake crashed to the ground, flipped over, and kicked the man in the solar plexus. The orderly said, "Ufff," and fell back down. Jake rose to his feet, dust billowing as he karate chopped the fallen man again. The orderly collapsed onto the asphalt, unconscious.

It took a couple of minutes to drag the unconscious orderly to one side and leave him there in the tall weeds. It wasn't a very good idea—Jake had no way of knowing how long the man would stay unconscious—but he couldn't think of anything better.

The door had swung shut, but it didn't matter. The pipe had dropped onto the doorsill, just like he'd planned. The door was propped open.

Jake got his fingers behind the door's metal edge and pried it open. He retrieved the pipe, tossing it far into the weeds, and then went inside and pulled the door shut behind him. Paris had been right, although God knew how she'd figured this out. The door could be pushed open from inside, but a key was needed to get through it in the other direction.

Jake stood in the darkness and waited for his eyes to adjust. He could smell cleanser and laundry and floor polish. Finally he could see.

He was at the bottom of a short flight of linoleum-covered steps. Climbing the steps, he came to a small locker room. There were no windows. The room was empty. The lockers were painted industrial green—they were the same as the ones at the Village School, more than a thousand miles away. A cast-iron sink and a mirror were mounted on the one wall; another displayed a faded poster of Pamela Anderson in a bikini.

Jake's eyes had fully adjusted to the darkness.

Now he could see the room's other door.

This was a nicer door, made of blond wood. Light shone through the crack at its base. Walking closer, he could hear the sound of air-conditioning on the other side of the door.

I did it, Jake told himself. He was mildly proud—but he quickly reminded himself this whole thing was far from over. He had no way of knowing whether the guard he'd knocked out would remain unconscious—and, he realized suddenly, he'd forgotten to take the man's keys. One more thing to worry about. Maybe he could go back out there—

No. There wasn't enough time. It was already ten—it had to be. He had to stay right where he was, just inside the blond wood door.

Jake stood there, waiting. All kinds of dangers were coming into his head that he hadn't predicted or prepared for. What if another orderly came in? What if his car was spotted for some reason and someone started to look for him?

What if the orderly regained consciousness? He just couldn't let that one drop. And just for a second Jake thought he heard a clattering noise from the door behind him. A sound like a key in a lock. He froze, waiting for the lock to turn, but nothing happened. Maybe it was his imagination.

Be cool, he told himself. *Stop thinking so much. Just be ready.*

GAIA FELT PRETTY. THERE WAS NO
other way to put it. It was a good feeling,
too—one she could definitely get used to.
It was part of a whole new life, one she had
been discussing excitedly with Dr. K. She
couldn't wait to thank him for the day pass.
It was a nice surprise, just the sort of ges-
ture she was coming to expect from him.

"This way," Paris said, smiling. Paris seemed especially excited this morning. She looked good, too—the
cropped pants and the bright yellow shirt flattered her
dark hair and green eyes. As they walked together past
the daytime nurses' station, Lawrence actually whistled at them.

Is this so bad? What's wrong with this, exactly?

Gaia had no idea. She'd been resisting this her
whole life for reasons that seemed trivial and selfish in
retrospect. Why had she spent so many years pitying
herself—pushing people away, making everything so
difficult?

Gaia was planning on talking to her mother about
that. She felt a little thrill of excitement every time she
thought about the conversations she was going to have
with her mother. They had to make up for lots of lost
time.

"Aren't we going the wrong direction?" Gaia
asked.

It was true—they weren't headed toward the

reception area. They were going north, toward the utility areas: the kitchen and the laundry rooms and the orderlies' locker room.

"It's easier to go this way," Paris said casually. "Shortcut to the parking lot."

"Okay." That didn't really make sense to Gaia, but after all, she hadn't been here as long as Paris. "Where are we going today, anyway?"

"Somewhere nice," Paris said. She seemed a bit distracted—Gaia noticed that she kept checking the caged wall clocks as they passed. "It's a surprise."

"Cool." Gaia smiled at Paris. "Thanks again for inviting me along—and thanks for talking to Dr. Kraven about it."

"You're welcome."

They turned another corner, and Gaia realized that they were heading straight for the orderlies' locker room. "We can't get through there," Gaia said. "It's a restricted area."

"It's just a locker room," Paris said. She was walking more quickly, pulling ahead toward the blond wood door. Gaia noticed that she seemed even more keyed up and excited than she'd been even moments before. "What's the difference?"

"It's not allowed," Gaia told her. It was irritating: Paris still had these bad habits. She wanted to cut corners, to break rules. "And anyway, it's locked."

Paris wasn't listening. She had bolted ahead and

was knocking loudly with her fist three times on the blond wood door.

Nothing happened.

"Come on," Paris whispered. "Come on, come on—"

What was happening, anyway? Gaia stopped thinking about how pretty she looked in the purple dress and began thinking about what Paris was doing.

"Shouldn't we just go out the front door?" Gaia asked. "I mean, isn't that where we show our day passes? I thought—"

Suddenly the door swung open. It nearly bashed into Paris's face—she pulled aside just in the nick of time. Behind the door stood Jake.

Now Gaia was really confused. And beyond that, she was worried. Because this was getting stranger and stranger.

"Thank God, you made it," Paris said breathlessly.

"Hey." Jake smiled at her. "Good job. Hi, Gaia."

Gaia didn't answer because something had just occurred to her.

She realized that everything that had happened in the last ten minutes was based on things Paris had told her.

A day pass? From Dr. Weissman? For a girl who couldn't even get clothing privileges?

Paris talked to Dr. K.? *Paris?*

They were taking a "shortcut"?

Wait a minute. . . wait a minute. . . .

"Are you sure this is okay?" Gaia asked. She was

pretending to be curious, but she'd already decided something was wrong.

"Someone's coming," Paris said quietly.

Gaia immediately realized she was right—she could hear the clattering footsteps approaching.

"Come on, Gaia," Jake said. "We're going."

And that was another thing—what was Jake Montone doing in the locker room, anyway? Gaia had started to get used to the weird sluggishness of her thoughts these days—Dr. Kraven had told her that it was entirely natural. Normally she would have realized sooner that this all wrong.

The footsteps got louder. Gaia stepped away from the door, looking behind them. Paris's eyes were wide—it was clear that she was frightened. Jake looked nervous, too.

D. came around the corner. He was carrying a small canvas bag. He was running frantically toward them.

"*Ten tomorrow! Ten tomorrow!*" D. yelled.

"Oh, *no*—" Paris was frantic. "D., Jesus Christ, don't—"

"D.? What are you—" This was getting stranger by the minute. And suddenly Gaia had had enough.

"*Help!*" she yelled out. "*Help! Something's wrong!*"

Unfortunately, nobody seemed to hear her. She was getting ready to yell again when somebody's hands grabbed her arm, and before she had time to react, D. and Paris and Jake were pulling her through the wooden door and yanking it shut.

They were in a small, badly lit room. Gaia had a strange moment when she realized she'd been here before, many times. Then she realized that it was just the lockers—they were familiar somehow, but she wasn't sure from where.

"Come on," Jake yelled. He was ahead of them, galloping down a flight of steps. He bashed into a metal door and it swung open. Brilliant sunlight shone through.

"*Help!*" Gaia yelled again. "*Help!*"

Paris was behind her, pushing her forward. Gaia lost her balance and toppled down the steps, and Jake caught her. D. was right there, carrying his canvas bag. . . and smiling.

What were they *doing?* Gaia cursed herself for being so stupid.

Before she could react, they pulled her out into the bright sun, and the heavy metal door swung shut and latched behind them. Gaia immediately turned and tried to get it open—but there was no way. There was no knob or handle.

And then Gaia saw something even more frightening.

Vince was lying in the weeds, unconscious.

Oh, no.

Gaia realized she was going to have to scream as loud as she could. If she screamed and her voice carried across the parking lot, maybe somebody could get here in time and stop these deceitful "friends" from abducting her. She opened her mouth—

—and a hand clamped over it. Jake was behind her, holding her. "Green Accord! Green Honda Accord!" he was yelling at Paris. Gaia couldn't see him, but a set of car keys suddenly whipped through the air past her head. Paris reached for the keys and missed. They chimed against the asphalt, tumbling to a stop. For one hopeful moment Gaia thought the car keys were going to drop off the edge of the parking lot into the tall weeds, but no such luck—Paris snapped them up and sprinted toward the green car that was parked right there.

Gaia struggled, trying to get free of Jake's grip.

If there were ever a moment that Gaia wished her "fantasy persona" were real, this was it. Because "fearless" Gaia could fight. Really well. "Fearless" Gaia could get free of Jake, knock him out, knock Paris out, and be on her way toward the hospital's entrance in less than a minute.

But that wasn't real. In real life she was just a blond high school girl in a purple dress, recovering from mental problems. She bucked and struggled, but Jake held her tight, his hand clamped over her mouth. Their shoes smacked the asphalt, kicking up dust.

Gaia felt like she was hallucinating—the bright, cloudy sky above, the dazzling reflections from the mica in the asphalt, the wind in the reeds, the car exhaust that blew over her legs as a green car backed close to them. Then D. was pulling open the back door and Jake was shoving forward, pushing them to topple into the car's backseat. Gaia was still trying to scream. She *needed* to scream; she needed to be saved.

"*Drive!*" Jake screamed.

Jake was on top of her in the car's backseat. The back door was still open—D. was climbing into the shotgun seat as Paris gunned the engine. The car lurched and then sped forward with Jake's legs sticking out the open passenger door. Paris swung the car sideways—from her position, pinned down against the hot vinyl car seat, Gaia could only see the sky pivoting around out the window as the car turned.

"Get that door closed!" Paris yelled. Gaia was in a total panic. Jake had his hand on her neck, holding her down as he twisted over to pull the door shut.

"*Glorious!*" D. yelled. "*Glorious!*"

The car shook violently as Paris skirted a curb and then screeched around a corner and sped forward. Gaia couldn't see a thing. Jake was still holding her down.

"Drive as fast as you can," Jake yelled.

"*Duh,*" Paris yelled back angrily.

He didn't

look because

he **abducted**

knew what he

was going to

see.

GAIA HAD A PLAN.

She had decided that the best thing was to play along. Paris and Jake were taking her into this beach house. They seemed to have figured out some kind of plan on their own. Gaia was confused; it

What She Wanted

didn't seem to make sense at all. What was Jake doing here, anyway? She couldn't remember.

Something else was bothering her: She felt strangely calm. Not frightened. Of course, she was scared; she had to be. But the fear was abstract. She was aware of it, but it didn't seem to be affecting her. Almost as if her fantasy—her "fearless" fantasy—were real. Jake was moving her out of the car. His hands were on her waist, holding her, his fingers pressing into the lavender cotton. It didn't feel bad at all. His touch was gentle, but she knew what he was thinking—if she started to run, he'd tighten his grip in a hurry.

"Come on," Paris said, slamming the Accord's driver-side door. Paris was making her sad because this was all so unnecessary. If she wanted to wear pretty clothes (and she did look very attractive in those cropped white pants, even though they were too tight for her) and travel outside Rainhill, it was no big deal. All she had to do was cooperate with the doctors. But Paris was a troublemaker and couldn't play by the rules, and in the end, like all troublemakers, she got what she wanted by taking it, not by earning it.

"Gaia, we're going into the house," Jake told her. "We're going to wait for Jared Tyler, Paris's boyfriend. He lives here."

"Okay," Gaia told him. She smiled. "You can let go of me, Jake."

"You're not going to run away?"

"If I ran away, you'd catch me." Gaia swiveled in his grasp so she was facing him. His face was close to hers, just like it had been on the hospital veranda the day before. She could see his eyes looking at her from close up. It made her feel dizzy—the bright, cloudy sky and the sweet Florida air and the sensation of his hands on her. "Anyway, where would I go?"

She kept smiling at him. Jake paused for a second and then took his hands away.

"All right," Jake said. "You're coming inside with us, right? You're going to trust me for five minutes?"

"Yes, Jake." They were still standing close to each other, and Gaia kept smiling. It was essential to her plan that he believed her.

And he did. "Let's go inside, then," Jake said, turning away and heading toward the house. Gaia followed, looking at the house. D. had gotten out of the car, lugging the bag he'd brought. Of the four of them, he was the only one still wearing green hospital clothes. The breeze tossed his brownish hair over his eyes. Gaia couldn't understand what had happened to her friends, why they would endanger a child.

Paris was ahead of them, walking up the porch steps. She seemed very excited. Jake gestured for Gaia to go ahead of him and then followed. Gaia looked up at the house, seeing the windows and the red terracotta tiles and the wires coming from the house's roof, like all the houses in this grove of trees near the beach. Cable television lines and power cables.

And telephone lines.

Gaia quickly lowered her head so that Jake wouldn't notice what she was looking at. She didn't want to give her plan away.

"So this is your boyfriend's house?" she asked Paris, joining her on the porch. "It's very nice."

"I love it here," Paris said absently. She was distracted, looking around at the dusty porch floor—Gaia realized she was looking for something. "That's funny. . . ."

"What?" Jake had joined them. Behind him D. was standing next to the gleaming green car, gazing around in wonderment. "Something wrong?"

"The welcome mat's been moved," Paris said. "The Tylers used to hide a key under the mat. Listen, stay here a second. I've got to find—"

"The door's open," Jake said.

He was right. Gaia followed the others to the door. It stood just slightly ajar.

"That's weird," Gaia said.

"Well, you're from New York." Paris went over and pulled back the screen door, pushing into the house. Inside, Gaia could see floorboards stretching off. "You're not used to neighborly places like this. They probably just went shopping or something."

Gaia tried to appear calm and collected as the four of them entered the house. The foyer was fairly bright, catching the morning sunlight that came in through the porch windows. There was almost no furniture—just a pair of wooden chairs that stood on the bare floor at odd angles and a battered couch. Beside her Jake was looking around. D. was still outside.

Here goes, Gaia told herself. It struck her again—she wasn't remotely nervous. Strange. "Paris?" she said. "Where's the bathroom?"

"What? Oh—go up those stairs," Paris said vaguely. She was pointing to one side—Gaia could see the staircase. The house was pleasant and bright but sparsely furnished. Paris was looking around avidly, like she was in one of her favorite places in the world.

"I'll be right back," Gaia said casually. Trying not to move too quickly, she headed up the stairs. Nobody stopped her.

They're trusting me, she thought. It felt bad to lie to her friends—Dr. K. had talked repeatedly about the importance of telling the truth all the time—but there was no way around it. The situation called for extreme measures.

Once she was out of view Gaia darted sideways into the closest bedroom. Again she was struck by how calm she was—her pulse was slow and steady. The bedroom was carpeted, with heavy brown draperies and an old chiffonier. Gaia saw discolored squares on the walls where pictures had hung and been taken down. The bed was stripped, its mattress bare—and next to the bed Gaia saw what she'd been looking for.

A telephone.

As quietly as she could, Gaia closed the bedroom door and locked it. Walking softly so that her footsteps didn't creak on the floor, she got over to the phone and dialed directory assistance.

Something about that seemed familiar. . . something about phones and calling information. . . a memory of kicking someone or something. . . . Shaking her head, Gaia let it drop. She was getting used to all the strange "memories" that flashed through her head, the symptoms of her DID.

"To report a police, fire, or medical emergency, dial nine-one-one," was all she heard on the other end. "All other calls from this line are restricted."

Gaia frowned. She took the phone away from her ear, trying to figure out what that meant. "Restricted"? Why?

Out the bedroom window Gaia could see Jake's car and D. walking around. She could hear the muffled sounds of Paris and Jake moving around downstairs. She had to hurry—they would get suspicious if she took too long.

She dialed 911.

"Nine-one-one, what's the emergency?" a man's voice said immediately.

"I'm calling from 19 Lapida Road, off State Highway 41, exit 26," Gaia murmured. She was trying to be as quiet as she could. "I'm being held here against my will. I'm a patient at Rainhill Hospital in Fort Myers Beach. I've been abducted."

"I'm sorry; please repeat, ma'am. You say you've been taken prisoner?" the operator asked. He didn't sound remotely skeptical; 911 operators, she assumed, had heard it all. "Where are your captors? Are they there with you now?"

"I've gotten away from them for a moment, but they're nearby," Gaia whispered. "The phone here doesn't work. Listen, this is very important. Can you please patch me through to Rainhill? I need to talk to Dr. Michael Kraven."

"WE SHOULD GET MOVING," JAKE

Golden Pixie Dust

told Paris.

She was looking around at the walls, clearly transported. He could tell from her face how happy she was.

It was almost weird—she seemed to have trouble con-centrating on what he was saying to her. "Paris? We're not exactly safe and sound here."

Jake was very much aware of the situation they were in—that *he* was in. He had skipped a week of school and driven to Florida, and now he was in an unfamiliar beach house with three escaped mental patients. He had pretty much accepted that something strange was going on at Rainhill Hospital, whether on purpose or not. And he was also quite sure that Paris, like Gaia, had been put there by accident or under some kind of false pretenses.

His car was parked outside in plain view. It had been ten minutes or so since they'd arrived here, forty minutes since their escape from Rainhill. His car had New York plates. His name was on record at the hospi-tal from the previous day, when they'd given him his day pass. He was beginning to realize that no matter what happened, he was potentially in very serious legal trouble. And that was just the beginning of their problems. Paris and the kid outside—the strange boy with the letter for a name—might be overjoyed at their newfound freedom, but if they didn't get back on the road and get as far away from here as they could, that freedom wasn't going to last. For them or for him.

"Paris? I said we should get moving," he said again. "They've got to know what happened at Rainhill. I know you want to see your boyfriend, but don't you think we should get out of here as quickly as we can?"

"We can wait just a little longer," Paris said, turning toward him. "You understand; it's been so long since I was here."

"Okay," Jake said reluctantly. "But the longer we wait, the more we're risking getting caught."

"I know." Paris nodded, stepping closer to him. She seemed very preoccupied. "I'm sorry, Jake—you're being great about this whole thing."

"I just don't want to end up in jail," Jake told her. He realized how agitated he sounded; he couldn't help it. "Look, I'm here for Gaia. I'm here because she called me. I still don't get this whole thing. I don't understand it at all. She's acting like a total freak."

"I know. It's weird and scary," Paris said. She was stroking his shoulder, consoling him. "Whatever they've done to her, there's got to be some way to help her."

"Not if we don't get her out of here," Jake said. He could hear a toilet flushing upstairs and footsteps on the staircase. "Something's wrong with her mind, Paris. What if it's permanent? What if she's been brain damaged or something?"

"You're so concerned," Paris said admiringly. Now she was reaching up and touching Jake's cheek tenderly. He was too surprised to react. "You have a good heart. But you need to have more faith in people. Gaia may not understand what you've done for her, but I'm sure she will. I'm sure she'll be very grateful."

Jake took a deep breath and let it out. Paris was caressing his cheek; there was a strange look in her eyes. "Thanks," he said.

"You're welcome, Jared."

"Hi," Gaia said loudly from the staircase behind him. Jake stepped away from Paris quickly. He felt his face heat up. He had no idea how long Gaia had been standing there.

"Am I interrupting something?" Gaia said.

"No," Jake said quickly. He didn't look at Paris—he moved away from her, farther back into the house, toward the living-room area. "Just waiting for Paris's boyfriend to get here. Paris, are you sure they're coming? They could be on a trip or something." Jake reached to turn on a lamp.

The lamp didn't go on.

Jake frowned, clicking the switch back and forth. Nothing happened. *Probably a dead bulb,* he thought. Moving across the living room, he tried another lamp.

Nothing.

"The power's out," he told them.

"It must be the breakers. That happens some-times," Paris said. She headed toward a small doorway set into the knotty-pine paneling. She pulled open the door, and Jake saw a staircase that led down to the basement. "I'll go and turn them on."

Paris went down the basement steps into the darkness, disappearing from view. Jake was standing in the middle of the living room, next to the lamps that didn't work. He was becoming more agitated by the minute. He wanted to get *out* of here—he didn't particularly like this empty house with its sparse furniture and open front door and dead electrical lines.

"You look so worried," Gaia said. She was standing on the bottom step, poised there like a debutante arriving at a ball. The bright late morning sunlight shone through the windows behind her, silhouetting the curves of her body. "And you *should* be worried, after what you've done. You're probably going to get in a lot of trouble for this."

"You read my mind," Jake said weakly. He collapsed onto the couch, avoiding looking at her. The last thing he needed right now was another distracting eyeful of Gaia in her purple dress and straight blond hair. It was definitely not going to help him concentrate. A cloud of dust puffed up from the couch, making him cough. Obviously whoever this famous "Jared" person was, his family didn't dust the house very often.

Jake was picturing what was happening at that hospital, where he'd left an unconscious orderly in the weeds just before leaving with three patients. Probably police were all over that place by now. And they'd been gone awhile—state troopers would be showing up here any minute if they had the slightest idea where they'd gone.

The sunlight danced in the dust motes as Gaia walked through them, coming closer—it was like she was surrounded by golden pixie dust, like a princess in a Disney cartoon. Jake absolutely refused to look. But his plan to avoid looking at her was running into some trouble, because she came right over to him—and sat down on the couch next to him.

IT WAS LIKE LIVING INSIDE THE

pictures. D. couldn't believe it, but it really was. That was all he had ever wanted. The whole time on the rainy hill, it was all he had ever wanted. To live inside his pictures. To walk inside them and touch them and feel them and roll in them. Without the metal wires everywhere. The metal wires in all the pictures. The wall of wires that was always in front of everything. So he couldn't touch it. So he could only see it in pieces.

Hideous Clouds

Now he could touch it and smell it and feel it, too. Now it wasn't paint; it was real. Now he was inside the picture.

D. crouched down in the bed of bright green. He brushed his palms across the tall green blades, and then he fell into them, rolling onto his back and looking up at the sea of blue with the balls of white cotton floating in the sky. No wires or windows. No ugly white lights and hard steel beds. Just blue. Blue and green. That was all he wanted from now on. To live in the green. To smell its sweet and glorious smell, and touch it, and sleep in it all day and all night.

They had all gone into that box. Another big ugly box like the rainy hill. A box with more ugly fake lights and ugly white walls. But D. wasn't going in there. The whole place smelled of black. Black clouds were swirling around the whole place like smoke. That place was nevermore. The only reason he would have gone inside it was for AnaGaia. She was still so gray-black. She still had black eyes.

But he couldn't go in there. Nuh-uh. He never wanted to go inside again.

He had decided. He would never live in a box again. Never evermore. He could never live anyplace with walls for the rest of his life. He would only live in green. Somewhere with even bigger, gianter beds of green. Where there were no more monsters and no more vicious black heads.

He couldn't ever be anyplace with too many heads again. All of those heads with the hideous clouds floating over them. Why were so many heads black and gray and vomit brown and bloodred? Why couldn't there be more yellows and purples? So D. could stand next to them. So he could live with them and see their eyes and not be afraid. He would never understand.

D. got up and roamed around the air, keeping his distance from the black box. He found a patch of green with all sorts of new colors. Colors growing out of the big bushes. Yellow and pink petals. They felt softer than the softest white sheets. They smelled sweeter than anything. Sweeter than sugar. He could have smelled them for days. He would have, too.

But something had changed.

It had changed on the ground. A new rumble. A new sound. It was getting louder and louder, coming from around the other side of the box.

D. ran around to the front of the box, and that was when he saw it. He saw it far in the distance, down the long road, coming toward him, moving slowly, as in a dream.

A car. A big white car with mean glass eyes.

A white car that was black. Vicious, vicious black.

Far away. Moving closer.

Distracting Thoughts

"I DON'T UNDERSTAND YOU," GAIA said to Jake. "How could you be such a nice boy, such a cute boy. . . so earnest and kind. . . and then do something like this? What were you thinking?"

"I wanted to help you," Jake said doggedly. He was staring at the floor. "You called and asked for help and I came to help you. Paris and I put this plan together so—"

"*Paris?*" Gaia was very close to him; their legs were touching. He was forcing himself not to look at her. "When did you suddenly become president of the Paris fan club?"

"What?"

"Well, the two of you have obviously gotten very friendly," Gaia went on. Just like the day before, on the veranda, she was confusing him completely. And filling his head with all kinds of distracting thoughts, just when he most needed to concentrate. She was close enough that he could smell her clean hair. "I mean, I'm not blind. But she's bad news, Jake. She's a troublemaker."

"'Troublemaker'?" Another distinctly non-Gaia word. Next she would tell him he was being "silly" again. "She seems fine to me. Listen, Gaia, I think we should go. I think we should get on the road and—"

"Not yet," Gaia said quickly. "Not just yet, Jake. As long as we're here, let's relax. Let's stay awhile. It's a nice house, don't you think?"

"I guess."

"Jake, look at me."

There wasn't the slightest chance he was going to obey this request. He didn't look because he knew what he was going to see. He remembered from the veranda, at the hospital, the day before. He was not going to walk down that road.

He jumped as he felt her fingers on his chin, gently turning his face toward hers.

He really, really wished she hadn't done that. Because it ruined his whole state of mind. He had been furiously thinking about how to get this whole crazy caravan of people back into his car and onto I-95. He wanted to be in Georgia by noon at the latest. But now, suddenly, it was like all those ideas were on the other side of the planet somewhere.

Because who was he kidding? She was absolutely beautiful. She was the most beautiful girl he'd ever seen. All the messy, tangled haircuts and baggy sweatshirts and worn-out jeans were like a life preserver he'd been clinging to without even realizing it, hopelessly trying to convince himself that she wasn't interesting, wasn't fascinating, wasn't capable of running through his thoughts nearly nonstop.

"Jake?"

Hadn't he driven a thousand miles for this girl? Hadn't he risked getting expelled from school and broken what must have been ten separate state and federal laws for this girl? Who was he kidding?

Gaia's wide blue eyes were inches from his. Her hand was still on his chin, now moving down to caress his neck. Her eyes were narrowed, her lips parted as she moved her face close to his, slowly, haltingly. The room was quiet; the only sound was the distant moan of the ocean's waves, breaking against the shoreline just outside.

And in the end he wasn't even sure which of them moved, closing the tiny gap between them. Their lips touched, and Jake closed his eyes and kissed Gaia, and nothing in that moment could stop either of them; their lips pressed together and her arms moved to his wide shoulders, pulling him closer. He could feel her slim, smooth hands trembling as he reached up to her face, caressing her smooth cheek, feeling her face press forward into his as the kiss went on, and again he thought, who was he kidding? Hadn't he wanted this since the moment they'd met?

With some reserve of willpower that he'd never known he had, Jake did the most difficult thing he'd ever done in his life. He reached up, took Gaia's shoulders, and pushed her away.

Gaia's eyes were closed, her lips parted; she was so stunning that he nearly lost his resolve and leaned forward to kiss her again. But he didn't. He held her away from him, and after a moment Gaia opened her eyes.

"Jake?"

"No." Jake let go of her, edging away from her on the couch. "No. Stop."

"What? Jake, don't you want to—"

"No!" Jake stood up, his head reeling. This was all wrong. Wrong in every way. It was like stealing something—like taking advantage of something you hadn't earned, didn't deserve. "No. Damn it, Gaia, it's not fair. This isn't you. You're—there's something wrong with you."

"Oh." Gaia looked hurt. "Oh."

"That's not what I meant," Jake said quickly. "There's actually nothing wrong with you. You're. . . you're perfect, Gaia. But something's different. I wish there was some way I could get you to wake up from whatever this is."

Gaia looked unhappy—he'd hurt her feelings. She was looking away from his face down at the bare, dust-covered floorboards.

"You're really annoying me," Gaia said quietly.

"*Yes!*" Jake pointed at her urgently. "Yes. I annoy you. I always annoy you—that's why we argue. Come on, Gaia, don't you remember? Don't you understand?"

"No."

"You don't like me, Gaia," he insisted. Behind him he could hear Paris coming up the basement stairs. "In real life, when you're not being crazy, you don't like me at all. You would *never* kiss me."

"That's what *you* think."

"The power won't come on," Paris said loudly.

"Really?" Jake gratefully turned away from Gaia. "Listen, I don't think we should wait any—"

And he stopped. Because there was no mistaking the sound outside the house.

The hum of an approaching car.

The front door burst open, and D. stumbled in. He

was clutching his canvas bag, looking positively shaken. The screen door slammed behind him.

"*Vicious Black! Vicious Black!*" he shouted. Everyone could hear the car now. It was pulling up into the driveway in front of the house. The unmistakable sound of slamming car doors echoed through the open door.

"*Jared!*" Paris squealed, running toward the door. She was wide-eyed, nearly hysterical. Someone was coming—there was no question about it. Jake could see a shadow on the screen door. "*Jared! Jared!*"

Paris got to the door, her arms out—and stopped. Jake watched her freeze in place and then take two steps back.

The screen door opened, and Jake saw a tall, dark-haired man in a white lab coat enter the room.

"Thank God!" Gaia shouted, leaping to her feet. She looked overjoyed. "Thank God you got my message. Thank God—"

And that nearly made Jake collapse to the floor in shock. *Stupid, stupid,* he told himself. Gaia had gone upstairs by herself. . . and called the hospital. Neither he nor Paris had caught it, and Gaia had done an amazing, incredible job of delaying everything, of keeping them there for the crucial few minutes it took for these people to arrive. He couldn't believe it. He couldn't believe he'd let it happen.

Behind the man in the lab coat was the plump woman Jake had seen at the hospital the day before.

She was holding a strange device that he suddenly realized was a stun gun. The orderly Jake had knocked out was there, too—and another orderly who looked much stronger. And behind all of them was the auburn-haired patient—Jake remembered that her name was Tricia.

"No," Paris uttered, backing away. She looked pissed beyond belief. Pissed and a little scared. "No way," she hissed, backing farther and farther from the door.

"You must be Jake," the tall man said. "We haven't met—I'm Michael Kraven. I'm here to bring my patients back home."

In this
bizarre
frantically
unraveling
state **holding**
she was
on
in. . . . she
remembered.

"DR. K.," GAIA CELEBRATED, RUSH-
ing toward him. She had never
been so happy to see someone
in her life. He had come when
she called, just like he'd always
said he would if anything went
wrong. He was right here to
save her. Her plan had worked.

This Nonsense

"You called him. . . ?" Paris asked incredulously.
She looked more than a little angry. And disappointed
and frightened and hurt. More than anything she
looked hurt. But it served her right, Gaia thought. "I
can't believe it. . . . You actually called Rainhill. . . ."

"Hey, those are my clothes!" Tricia yelled at Paris.
"How dare you take my stuff?"

"I'm so glad you're here," Gaia said, reaching to
hug Dr. K. Soon she'd be back at Rainhill, and this
nonsense would finally be over. Dr. K. squeezed her
shoulder absently, looking around at the others. "You
have no idea."

"Oh, I have some idea," Dr. K. said calmly. "Okay,
Vince, Butch—we need to take them all home."

"You stand right there, young lady," Rosie snapped.
She had her stun gun pointed right at Paris. Gaia
wasn't sure that was necessary.

"Come on, kid," Vince said. "Back to Rainhill—here
we go."

Vince was reaching for D., trying to pull him

toward the door, but D. kept trying to back away in terror.

"D., it's *okay*," Gaia assured him. "There's nothing to be afraid of. We're just going home."

"Well, Jake," Dr. K. said. "I certainly have no authority over you, but I will say this. I think you should be ashamed of yourself."

"Why?" Jake asked. "What do I have to be ashamed of? Gaia shouldn't be—"

"I don't want to argue with you, Jake," Dr. K. interrupted. "But I have a responsibility here. And whether you realize it or not, so do you."

"Come on, kid. Let's go," Vince was saying. D. was frantically holding on to the staircase banister as Vince and Butch tried to pry him away. Butch's hands were tangled in the straps of D.'s canvas bag.

"D., don't be scared," Gaia implored him again.

But D. wouldn't listen. He tried to wrap his hands tightly around the banister, as if he might drown from letting go. Vince and Butch had been reduced to yanking at his canvas bag just to shake him loose.

"Nevermore," D. shouted desperately. "Kraven says nevermore!"

"D., *please*. They just want to help—"

"Ana nevermore! Gaia nevermore!"

"D.—"

A sudden ripping noise filled the air. Butch pulled so hard on D.'s bag that it finally just split open. Its contents burst out all over the dusty floor: D.'s paint set, a roll of drawings and clothes, and then a red binder.

Gaia's eyes were drawn to that red binder as it tumbled across the floor and landed on its side. The cover fell open as the loose front page skidded across the floor and fell within inches of Gaia's feet. She stared down and saw that the page from the binder was nearly filled by a large color photograph that was pasted in. The picture was a close-up of a young blond woman staring straight at the camera.

And as Gaia leaned down even closer, she began to realize. . .

She knew this girl. She knew the girl in the picture well, she thought. If she could just get her stalling, scatter-brained memory to work. She knew her name. . . .

"Ana," D. called, grasping desperately for the pieces of the binder. "The red. No. . . Ana's red. . ."

Ana? Was that the girl in the picture's name? This girl was Ana? *No,* Gaia told herself. It *sounded* like Ana, but it was longer. Her name was more like. . .

Tatiana. That was the girl's name. *Tatiana.* Not *Ana.*

There was no question about it. Gaia was sure—that girl's name was Tatiana. Her mother was named. . . Natasha. The names popped into her head immediately, as though they'd never been gone. Gaia knew them both in New York. She just had to remember. . . .

"Give that to me," Dr. K. shouted. His usual composure seemed to have suddenly disappeared. He stretched his arms out furiously, trying to retrieve the book. "Where did you get that, D.?" he snapped, whipping his head back to Gaia as he approached her at near full speed. "Gaia, leave that alone," he ordered.

But Gaia was struck with a sudden overwhelming need to see that binder.

Moving at a speed that surprised her completely, Gaia lunged down and snapped the book off the floor just as Dr. Kraven tried to nab it—and missed.

"Gaia!" Dr. K. shouted. Why was he suddenly so furious? It was so unlike him. "Give that to me! Give me the book now!"

Vince and Rosie were closing in on Gaia now. Rosie had even begun to wield her stun gun. But Gaia *needed* to see this binder—she had to understand why everyone was calling Tatiana *Ana*. Gaia darted right past Rosie before she could react. She bolted up the stairs, and before anyone could follow her, she swung around into the bedroom she'd been in earlier—the room with the phone. And the lockable door.

"Gaia!" Rosie yelled from behind her. "Get up there!" she ordered Vince and Butch.

The orderlies were barreling up the stairs. Gaia pushed the heavy bedroom door around and slammed it shut. She locked the door, leaving Vince and Butch pounding away, but Gaia didn't care. She stood there in her borrowed lavender dress, opened the red binder, and began to read.

TRICIA HAD WATCHED GAIA ROCKET

up the stairs with the red binder. She didn't understand. What was the big deal? What had happened to Gaia? Why had that picture of Ana made Gaia react like she'd just seen a ghost, or worse?

Unusual Genetic History

"Dr. K.?" Tricia began. "Why did she do that? What's going on?"

Strangely, Dr. K. completely ignored her. Instead of answering, he pulled a black walkie-talkie out of his coat pocket.

"Tac squad move in," Dr. K. yelled into the machine. "Upstairs and downstairs. Secure the house."

Tac squad? Secure the house?

Tricia didn't understand. Rosie had yelled for Vince and Butch to follow Gaia, and they were galloping up the stairs right behind her. Gaia's friend Jake was moving forward, toward Dr. K. Paris and D. were trying to pick up all the remaining stacks of papers.

"Dr. K.?" Tricia said fearfully. "What's going on?"

Again Dr. K. ignored her completely. Around the house wild scuffling noises were getting louder and louder. Shadows moved over the windows. Tricia realized that several men were out there, surrounding the house. In the living room Jake was the only one moving—he was striding toward Dr. K.

But Tricia couldn't believe what she saw next.

"Stop right there," Dr. Kraven told Jake. As he said it, he reached into his jacket, and as Tricia watched incredulously, he pulled out an automatic handgun. A gun. He pointed the gun at Jake's head. "Hands on top of your head. If you even *look* like you're going to try something. . ."

"Dr. K.?" Tricia whispered, looking up at him. She could hear the panic edging into her voice. "Dr. K.? What are you doing?"

"*Shut up*, Tricia," Dr. K. snapped. Tricia recoiled as if a rattlesnake had reared up in front of her. She was stunned.

The front door crashed open and three men in black uniforms with machine guns came into the room. Each had a belt radio that was blasting static. They wore boots and gloves, and their guns were drawn.

The ceiling started to shake as trampling footsteps echoed through the house. More of those armed men were upstairs.

Tricia had to scream. She couldn't help it. Her fists were pressed to her mouth; her eyes were wide. Her entire world had turned upside down in just a few seconds. It was like some kind of nightmare DID episode or something.

"Report," Dr. K. said into his walkie-talkie. He was still pointing the gun at Jake. Jake was staring at him, not moving, his hands on top of his head. His eyes were blazing.

There was another blast of static. "Target in bedroom; she's locked the door," a voice came over Dr. K.'s walkie-talkie. "Window secured; entrances secured."

"Move in. Move in. Break the door," Dr. K. ordered. "Don't harm the girl. Bring her down here."

ADVANCED MEMORY/MOTIVATION REALIGNMENT PROJECT

Dr. Michael Charles Kraven, M.D., Ph.D.,

supervising operative

ABSTRACT

This technique exploits the combined effect of lysergic acid diethylamide + phentedrine treatment, repeated high-impact electroshock treatment (the "K cycle"—see appendix II, pp. 221–26), and conventional psychotherapeutic techniques to in essence remake the personality, motivations, fears, desires, and memories of a test subject.

When perfected, this technique will have many beneficial applications; specifically, the creation or alteration of personnel for high-level espionage and clandestine intelligence-related missions. AM/MR will ultimately allow the Organization to achieve 100 percent control of the motivations, knowledge, and capabilities of each high-level operative, allowing the creation of extremely advanced espionage programs.

TEST SUBJECTS

Four persons have been selected as unknowing test subjects in the initial AM/MR series of experiments; their individual histories are outlined below. All experimentation and research was performed by Dr. Kraven in a controlled environment created for this purpose within a Florida psychiatric hospital; various techniques allowed the experimentation to proceed without the surrounding hospital personnel ever discovering the true nature of the work being done there.

Subject 1. **DAISY KELLER**, female, 18, American born. Ms. Keller represents the initial testing stage of the AM/MR project; she is the experiment's "control." An unremarkable teenage girl selected for the initial "test run" of the K-cycle techniques, Ms. Keller was abducted from her farm home in Oklahoma by Organization operatives. Ms. Keller was then "reprogrammed" with a synthesized identity, "Tricia Keller." Although the experiment was in essence a complete success, Ms. Keller's intrinsic limitations as an "average" test subject severely limit her value to the Organization; she is currently performing a trivial monitoring and surveillance role at the facility and may be terminated at any time.

Subject 2. **D. MOORE**, male, 13, American born. Stage 2 of the AM/MR project represented an ambitious attempt to exploit the intrinsic capabilities of an unusually young man. Moore was taken at birth from his natural parents, who were informed that their child was stillborn; the child therefore had not been named. From birth Moore displayed a remarkable capability to perceive human psychological "auras" and understand their meaning. However, this extraordinary property was severely hampered by Moore's additional psychological idiosyncrasies, including a diagnosed aphasia and an erratic antisocial behavior pattern; these drawbacks render Moore unworkable in any field-operative sense, and the experiment was abandoned. (Some theorize that Moore's interpersonal impediments are simply the result of a lifetime spent within the confines of a mental institution; the prevailing opinions, however, go the other way.) Although he is for these reasons utterly useless to the Organization, Moore's unusual capabilities prompted a keen interest in his immediate family's genetic composition (see below).

Subject 3. **TATIANA (or ANA) PETROVA**, female, 18, Russian born. Stage 3 of the project represented a more ambitious and pragmatic attempt to create an idealized "field agent." Ms. Petrova represents the program's first unqualified success: Upon her completion of the experimental treatments at the same facility, Petrova has been successfully deployed as an Organization operative, accomplishing a series of delicate and subtle missions with generally high degrees of success. The initial success of stage 3 revitalized Organization interest in the project as well as demonstrated the flexibility of the technique.

Subject 4. **GAIA MOORE**, female, 17, American born. The older sister of test subject 2, D. MOORE (see above), Ms. Moore is targeted as the fourth subject in the AM/MR project, following her abduction and assimilation into the facility. If successful, Ms. Moore's assimilation into the project will represent a major triumph. Ms. Moore's manifestation of her family's unusual genetic history is extremely exciting for the Organization. Ms. Moore is potentially the ideal operative in that she is endowed with a complete absence of fear, the hybrid human property that can limit performance and drive. It is hoped that experiments on Ms. Moore will begin as soon as acquisition of the test subject can be arranged.

GAIA'S HEAD WAS SPINNING. IT

was like all her ideas were
unraveling and coming together
a different way. The entire docu-
ment had left her dizzy with
confusion, but one phrase had
damn near knocked her off her
feet.

Fairy-Tale Scenario

The older sister of test subject 2. Gaia was test subject 2. *D. Moore...*

Moore. D. Moore. The older sister...?

*Me. I am D.'s older sister. D. is my brother. How is
that...?*

Taken from birth, it had said. The Organization
had taken him at birth from her parents. Gaia's
mother had never even known about her son. Her living son. Her son named D.

Oh God. Her mother. Gaia's mother...

Her mother was dead. Again, still, always and forever, her mother was dead.

It hit her like a battering ram—but the pain was
blunted by the fact that at heart, she knew already.
She'd known since the real weekend, the weekend Loki
shot her mother. Not that fairy-tale scenario Dr. K.
had concocted.

The Organization. They had tried to convince her
that her mother was alive. They had done all of this.

There was a sudden, tremendous crash. The bedroom

windows smashed open and two men in black clothes with machine guns burst into the room.

Before Gaia could react, they had grabbed her arms, taking the book out of her hands. Roughly, they pushed Gaia toward the bedroom door, one of them reaching to unlock it.

My brother. He's my brother. . . .

Gaia stumbled as they pushed her forward. Her head was spinning. Faces and names and sounds and images were cascading through her mind. Even if she'd been able to fight, she was too confused and dazed to try to get free.

But it's all lies. Everything out of Dr. K.'s mouth. Lies. . . I can fight.

Where had *that* thought come from? Gaia wasn't sure. She was so confused.

The men were pushing her forward, around the corner and down the stairs.

"Target secured," one of them said into his walkie-talkie. Gaia nearly fell, they were shoving her so hard down toward the ground floor. She could see more men in black down there. Rosie was pointing a stun gun at Paris and D. . . . Dr. K. had a *handgun* trained on Jake.

"Gaia!" D. squawked. "Gaia!"

I'm not afraid.

Another thought that had popped into her head out of nowhere. Gaia didn't understand it at all. She was still reeling from what she'd just discovered.

As hard as Gaia was trying to concentrate on that astounding fact, it was very difficult. Her head was spinning, and on top of that she was afraid. Wasn't she afraid? The machine guns were so big, so scary looking. Downstairs she could hear voices yelling and the trampling footsteps of more gunmen arriving. She *was* afraid—she had to be.

Wasn't she?

"Well done, Carter," Dr. K. told the man who was pushing Gaia down the stairs.

Gaia suddenly looked down at her body. *Why am I wearing this stupid dress?*

She didn't pay any attention to that question because something was dawning on her. It was fleeting, infuriating, like trying to remember a name that was on the tip of her tongue. They got to the bottom of the stairs and the men in black pushed Gaia over toward Paris and D.

"What are you doing?" Tricia was yelling. "What's going on?"

"Gaia!" Jake yelled. He was standing in the middle of the room, right next to the couch where she'd kissed him, his hands clasped on top of his head. "Gaia, look at the men! Look at the men!"

What?

Soldiers in black outfits. Ribbed Kevlar vests, military boots, machine guns.

"*Central Park!*" Jake yelled. "I know you remember. *Remember Central Park!*"

He barked it like an order. So loud and harsh. And somehow, suddenly, in this bizarre unraveling state she was in. . . she remembered.

THEY'D APPEARED LIKE GHOSTS. A

Faceless Assailants

black-masked army. Right there in the middle of Central Park. Converging on Gaia and Jake from the surrounding trees. More men than she could even see, moving so quickly through the dark grass, shining their glaring flashlights, blinding Gaia as they aimed the beams directly into her eyes. Some of them had guns; some of them didn't. Their feet moved so fast, they barely touched the ground. They were closing in so fast. . . .

And Jake still wasn't moving.

"*Jake*," Gaia hollered again, staring down at his unmoving body on the grass. She shook his shoulders as hard as she could. She had to get him out of there. She had to get them *both* out of there, and she had about two more seconds to do it before this shadow army ripped them to pieces. Next to his head, on the damp grass, she saw a rubber bullet. It confirmed her

327

suspicion—the Organization men wanted *her*, not him. And they didn't want conscious witnesses. Or live ones.

"Jake, get up!"

Jake's eyes finally fluttered open. "What. . . ? What happened? What hit me?"

"Jake, we've got to move," Gaia ordered. "*Now.*"

She tugged Jake back onto his feet, but by the time they had him upright, it was already too late. They were already surrounded by this SWAT team of gun-toting men in black.

They were Organization thugs. There was no question about that. Gaia knew how they moved; she knew how they planned. They must have been watching her this entire time. Waiting for just the right moment to move in. But why now? Loki was out of commission. What the hell did they want from her now?

There was no way to find out. Organization operatives didn't discuss their plans or orders. Especially with their intended victims. Gaia knew that even when Organization gunmen were captured, they would go to incredible lengths to avoid saying what they had been ordered to do. It was a big part of the Organization's strength: You could capture dozens of them and still not figure out what they were doing.

Jake, of course, didn't know any of this. He was looking around at the ring of faceless, motionless assailants like it was some kind of nightmare come true. It gave her a sinking feeling. Whatever happened,

Jake was going to suffer. He was going to get killed or hurt or maimed, and in the end he'd be added to the long list of people whose lives had taken a turn for the worse just because of bad luck—the bad luck of happening to know Gaia Moore.

Hadn't she entered Central Park to avoid that problem? To get away from her nonlife and find strangers to hurt?

I'm sorry, Jake, she thought sadly. *I'm sorry you decided to follow me into the park. Maybe it'll teach you that I really am hazardous. So you can avoid me in the future.*

If they let him live.

Gaia realized then, glancing over at Jake, that she'd gotten it wrong. He wasn't looking around like he was trapped in a nightmare.

He was getting ready to fight.

It bothered Gaia, for a bad reason. She didn't want him to think he was protecting her. As if the sparring were just a game and real danger demanded old-fashioned chivalry. So she struck first.

The closest gunman had trained his gun on her. She grabbed the barrel and twisted it down as the man fired and then rammed the gun upward, slamming it into the man's face. He was down, and Gaia was already spinning out of the way of the second gunman.

Beside her Jake was in motion. And all her regret about involving him melted away as she watched him.

They weren't going to kill him, she realized. He was too fast.

She'd experienced some of Jake's considerable skills in their little bout at school, but she honestly hadn't understood his level of proficiency until this very moment. Each kick and jab, each swivel of his hips was successfully warding off the attackers or knocking them down. This was no sparring match. This wasn't breaking boards for a crowd of proud parents. This was full-scale combat against full-scale killers. And Jake was holding his own.

The thumps and cracks and grunts of the fight went on, echoing against the park's dark, empty spaces. Nobody was around to hear or see any of it, but nobody ever was. Gaia knew this from experience. Gaia and Jake were fighting well, keeping out of each other's way, picking up each other's rhythms. It didn't matter, though. There were just too many Organization operatives here. It was pure math: Gaia and Jake were outnumbered. Her kicks and jabs got weaker, and her breath got hoarse and ragged. Beside her Jake struggled on, but he'd been knocked out by the rubber bullet—the sniper's version of a knockout punch. It was slowing him down.

They weren't going to win, she realized as blow after blow connected. Jake and Gaia were down now, and the sky was blocked by the thugs' looming shadows as they closed in. Gaia heard a new sound in the distance—an approaching car.

Here we go, she thought dismally. *Now we'll see what this is all about.*

Jake was in bad shape beside her. He wasn't moving quickly anymore. She realized that he was starting to lose consciousness. Finally she couldn't muster the strength for one more punch, and they grabbed her arms and pulled her upright, and headlights shone in her face as a dark luxury sedan cruised up, driving right up onto the pedestrian path and cruising to a stop in front of them. Gaia stumbled groggily as the men ushered her forward.

Jake was on his back in the mud. She couldn't tell how badly injured he was, but he was moaning slightly as his head wove back and forth. The thugs weren't dealing with him at all now. They were concentrating on moving her toward the car. Gaia was suspended by her arms, being dragged forward by at least four Organization men. Even though she was done, with no fight left at all, they were taking no chances. They got her to the car just as the sedan's gleaming back door swung open.

"Hurry up," a female voice snapped from inside the car. "Get her in here."

Gaia was pitched forward. Two men inside caught her by the armpits. Gaia was passing out. Her vision darkened as the door slammed behind her, and she felt a dizzying lurch as they started moving.

Jake, she thought dazedly. *Jake, did they kill you? Did they knock you out?*

"Haldol," the woman's voice said beside her. The car interior was warm and quiet. Gaia could only see dark shapes; she had no idea who she was traveling with. "Knock her out. She's got a long trip ahead of her."

Gaia could have told them that the drugs weren't necessary. She could never stay conscious after fighting. Already she was fading into a dream. The car's motion carried her off into sleep. Just as she was losing consciousness, the dome light clicked on. It was brief, just long enough for a black-gloved operative to load a syringe. But Gaia saw the light flash over the woman's face. She was the only one not wearing a black mask.

"Lights out!" the woman snapped.

The operative complied, and they were back in darkness.

Gaia had only seen the woman's face for a moment as the light flashed. A plump face, with dark hair tied back in a bun.

The car hummed, thumping over curbs, jolting her. They were back on the park's roads, speeding up, racing away from the dark clearing where Jake lay passed out in the dirt, abandoned there like a discarded action figure. Then waves of gray washed over Gaia's mind and she faded into the darkness.

Rosie.

Rosie was the Organization operative who abducted me. Rosie was the one who put me to sleep the night before she woke me up in Florida. At Rainhill.

It's all starting to make sense. Slowly, though. . . so slowly in my head. . .

This was an Organization trap from the moment it started.

I was Dr. Kraven's *fourth* test subject. Another one of the Organization's guinea pigs. After Tricia, after D., after Tatiana. . .

Tatiana. Every time anyone talked about Ana, they were talking about Tatiana. A different version of the same girl—the real Tatiana, before the Organization flushed her identity down the toilet and turned her into this. . . this trained assassin. Was that what they'd been planning for me? Was that what this was all about?

And Tricia—poor Tricia was just a test subject. A discarded plaything in the Organization's arsenal of human espionage tools. Not even worth bothering with once she'd served her essential purpose. Tricia, Ana, D., and now me. . . all these innocent people chewed up and spat out like overcooked meat.

I have to wake up. I have to wake up now and make my head work. I have to remember everything. How to *do* everything. . .

Jake, just give me a chance. Give me a chance to wake up.

JAKE HAD HIS HANDS ON HIS HEAD.

Thoroughly, Completely Magnificent

His heartbeat was thwacking in his ears. He was trying not to think about the black hole at the end of the gun that Dr. Kraven was pointing at his face—the hole that was like a tunnel into darkness.

"Gaia!" Jake yelled again. "The park!"

Gaia was at the foot of the stairs, flanked by the two gunmen. Three other gunmen were behind Dr. K. Jake was doing furious distance calculations in his head. He remembered sparring matches and karate training, when you had to take on several assailants at once. In class if you made a mistake, they tossed you to the mat, and you gave them the point. Here it was different.

"D.? Paris? Tricia?" Gaia said. She sounded weak, confused.

"Gaia, you realize you're not in any trouble with me," Dr. K. said. "Or with anyone, really. You've got this thing all wrong. What's going on here is something I think you'll come to appreciate a great deal once you understand it. I'd love to have a chance to explain it to you."

"Gaia!" D. yelled.

Gaia looked at Jake and then at D. And then a most unexpected word fell from her lips.

"Duck," she uttered, staring into D.'s eyes.

D. immediately tugged on Paris's yellow sleeve, pulling her downward. Rosie turned, her eye obviously catching the sudden movement.

"Now, don't move," Rosie warned. "Do not move."

"Jake," Gaia said quietly, lifting her head straighter and higher than he'd seen it since he'd gotten here.

Jake had his eyes fixed on Dr. K. "Yeah."

"Move," Gaia said, locking her eyes on his with a surprisingly familiar expression.

"What do you m—"

"*Hai!*" The guttural sound came from the deep center of Gaia's chest.

Jake only had a peripheral view of her, but he could see how she'd twisted her arm behind her and grabbed the arm of the gunman to her right, pushing him sideways to stumble against the other gunman to her left. The men behind Dr. K. reacted, raising their machine guns, but they were too slow—by the time they'd trained their guns on Gaia, she wasn't there.

The first gunman was toppling down the stairs—Jake had missed it, but somehow she'd struck him in the solar plexus. The other gunman swung around and Gaia pushed him forward, swinging vertically in a backward somersault over the staircase banister. As he fell, Gaia tore his gun away from him and threw it. The machine gun sailed through the air across the room and banged loudly into Dr. K.'s arm.

Dr. K.'s gun went off, firing a bullet that whistled past Jake's head and exploded into the knotty-pine paneling behind him. Dr. K. yelped as he toppled backward, landing on Tricia, and Jake was moving—he was ducking to one side as the three gunmen at the door sprayed machine gun fire where he'd just been standing. The room was full of the smell of gunpowder and the deafening blasts of the machine guns.

Gaia was still moving—after throwing the gun, she completed the same motion and catapulted into the air, her hands gripping the banister, swinging around upside down like an Olympic gymnast in a lavender summer dress, dodging the bullets that the other gunmen were firing at her. Jake kicked out three swift blows to the gunmen one by one, desperately pushing the machine guns so that the bullets would miss Tricia and Paris, who were cowering on the floor. The deafening spray of machine gun bullets shattered the windows all around the living room, creating a waterfall of broken glass.

Gaia completed her aerial spin and landed in the middle of the living-room floor next to Jake.

Dr. K. was rising to his knees, cradling his injured arm. Jake spun around and kicked at the head of the gunman who was coming up behind him, knocking him out, while Gaia leapt upward and kickboxed the three gunmen near the door, bashing her hands and feet into their heads until they had all fallen to the floor. The machine gun sounds stopped. Jake's ears were ringing painfully.

"Hold it, young lady."

Rosie was training her stun gun on Gaia. Jake didn't even have time to help. He could only watch as Gaia kicked Rosie's arm away, striking Rosie in the throat with a jab and then catching her stun gun as she dropped it to the floor. A quick glance confirmed that Paris and Tricia had crawled together to one side behind the couch—they were unhurt. But what about D.? Where was D.?

"Gaia," Dr. K. said, rising slowly to his feet. He was wincing as he nursed his arm where the gun had hit it. "Gaia, that was extraordinary. That's precisely the kind of skill that the Organization can—"

Gaia fired the stun gun into Dr. Kraven's face.

His entire body convulsed and shook until he fell back against the wall and slid to the floor, unconscious. A sliver of drool ran from his open mouth down the side of his cheek.

"You talk too much," Gaia said firmly.

Now it was quiet. Jake's ears were singing. He and Gaia stood panting in the center of the room. Smoke and plaster dust and broken glass were everywhere. The house was completely trashed.

Jake turned and looked at Gaia. She looked back at him. She had a thin cut across her perfect cheekbone. The lavender dress was torn from her incredible inverted swing around the banister. Her hair was tangled around her face, and she held the stun gun down beside her bare thigh. Jake didn't dare speak. He had never seen anything as thoroughly, completely magnificent in his entire life and figured he never would again.

"I'll find some rope," Jake said quietly. "To tie these guys up. Okay?"

"Good," Gaia said distractedly. She was looking around. "D.?" she called out. "Where are you?"

Jake wasn't sure where D. had gone. He couldn't see him anywhere. Then he noticed another door that he'd missed. The door stood half open; through it he could see a kitchen table and the edge of a stove.

"Gaia," Jake said, pointing. "He must have gone into the kitchen."

Gaia didn't even look at Jake. She brushed right past him, moving toward the half-open door.

"D.!" Gaia called out. "D.! Are you in there?"

Painful and Palpable

"D.?" GAIA SHOUTED, STEPPING INTO the kitchen and darting her eyes in every direction. "D., are you okay?"

She hurled open the pantry door and any other

door she could find. She had to see him intact. She had to see him safe and sound and in one piece, and she had to see it in the next two seconds or her heart was going to fall right out of her chest.

It was the most bizarre sensation. The heart pounding in this particular way, the lungs almost completely unable to contract or expand, her temples pulsing incessantly. If she hadn't known any better, she would have thought this must be what fear felt like, but Gaia's relationship with fear was no longer up for debate. That was no longer in question, and it never would be again. No, this sensation wasn't fear; it was something else. Something painful and palpable, but not fear. Urgent, maybe even bordering on desperate, but not fear.

And when she saw him crawl out from the one closet that she hadn't yet checked, looking positively terrified, she knew suddenly what the sensation had been.

Worry. Not the normal kind of worry. Not the worry about a friend's health or an injured animal on the side of the road, but something else. Something Gaia had never experienced in her life until this day. A kind of worry that she instantly knew was specific to only one situation.

It was a sister's worry for her younger brother.

It was overwhelming. The urge to protect him—to literally shelter him from the remotest possible harm—was coursing through Gaia's veins at an almost unbearable level.

Unbearable and. . . glorious.

D. had barely made it back to his feet when Gaia practically tackled him. She fell toward him and wrapped her arms around him as tightly as she could without actually crushing his skinny thirteen-year-old frame. It seemed that sisterly relief was even more overwhelming than sisterly worry. D.'s arms wrapped around her shoulders, and he squeezed.

She finally released D. from the hug and grabbed his shoulders to get a good look at him. She checked him from head to toe for scrapes or bruises, and then she looked into his eyes. His bright blue translucent eyes.

Now she could see it so clearly, so completely. She could see it in every speck of his being, every single detail of his face. Brownish blond hair just a shade or two darker than hers, bright blue eyes just like her father's, her mother's perfect and elegant nose.

Her brother. Her flesh and blood. Somehow, due to a pack of horrible tragedies and some of the most sadistic people in the world. . . she had found him. They had found each other.

D. still looked shaken by all the violence. His body was still shivering slightly with fear.

"D, it's okay now," she assured him. "We're okay."

His expression began to relax as he stared into her eyes. And finally the smile began to creep back over his face. He reached his hand forward and brushed his fingertips gently over Gaia's forehead. "Bright," he uttered, marveling at her face like he'd just seen his first glimpse of sunlight in days. "*So bright.*" He seemed almost awed by her entire countenance. Almost as if he hadn't ever really seen it before. "White and yellow and gold. . . glorious gold. . ."

Gaia thought back to all of D.'s pictures at the hospital. All her memories seemed to be returning now. She'd seen all the halos he'd painted over their heads in various colors. She knew that the colors he saw told him something about the person and that yellow was clearly a good thing to be. It was good to be glorious yellow or glorious gold. But right now, at this moment, Gaia wished so much that D. could say more. That he could say something more to her. Did he know? Did he somehow know the truth about their relationship?

"D. . . . do you know who I am?" She searched the blue mirror image of her own eyes.

D. nodded. "Glorious," he said.

"No, D., not the color. Me. D. . . . I'm your sister."

D.'s eyes widened. He leaned forward and stared much deeper into Gaia's eyes. And quite suddenly, with his face only an inch from hers, a tear fell from the corner of his eye.

"Did you know that?" Gaia asked. "Did you know I was your sister?"

D. shook his head slowly. And then he nodded.

"I don't understand. You did know, or you didn't?"

"I did," D. uttered. "I didn't."

"No, D., please. I need to know if you understand what I'm telling you. I need you to say something that *I* can understand. Can you do that for me? Can you say something that will let me know whether you understand?"

D. tilted his head slightly. He reached out his hand and brushed his finger over her cheek. "You are me," he said. "And I am you."

He did understand. He understood it perfectly. She leaned forward and wrapped her arms back around him. When his skinny arms wound around her neck, she was quite sure she was going to burst into tears.

But then there was the sound of Jake's voice from the other room. Calling for her urgently. She could hear it instantly in his tone. Something was wrong.

She grabbed D.'s shoulders. "Stay here."

GAIA CAME BACK OUT INTO THE

Massacre

living room. The smoke was still in the air, making her eyes water. She was swaying on her feet as she walked. Gaia knew she wasn't going to be able to stay awake much longer. It was incredible that she was still conscious this long after a fight. Her hearing was returning finally. The ringing in her ears was subsiding.

And she could hear crying.

Paris was curled on the floor, in near fetal position, her face a heartbreaking picture of grief. She was sobbing gently, rocking back and forth. Tricia seemed too stunned to notice—she was leaning against the wall, trembling.

Jake stood over Paris, holding a sheet of paper. A large cabinet to one side had a single drawer pulled open, containing a stack of yellowing newspaper clippings. Gaia realized that Jake had opened that drawer, looking for rope to tie up the gunmen, and had found the clipping instead.

"Paris?" Gaia said. She crouched beside her, reaching to touch her shoulder. "Paris? It's over. It's over—you're safe. We're all safe now."

Paris's eyes were squinted shut, leaking tears. She was sobbing so hard, she couldn't make any sound—her mouth was forming the words *no, no, no* over and over.

"You'd better look at this," Jake said quietly. He handed over the clipping.

It was an article from a Florida paper—Gaia could tell from the Miami Beach restaurant ads across the bottom. She read the first few paragraphs:

CORAL SPRINGS (AP), FEBRUARY 12—
Tragedy struck the Denny's restaurant yesterday evening as a lone gunman opened fire with a concealed automatic weapon, killing five and critically

wounding 11 patrons of the family franchise restaurant before ending his own life.

According to local police and eyewitness reports, unemployed former tool-and-die technician Pierre M. Truitt, 43, entered the Denny's establishment at approximately 7:25 P.M., wearing casual clothes and carrying an M-1 assault rifle concealed beneath a poncho or coat. After making a cursory inspection of the premises, Truitt opened fire without warning, unleashing sustained bursts of gunfire that shattered the establishment's windows completely, showering the terrified patrons with broken glass. Truitt then began walking through the dining area arbitrarily firing into booths while the terrified patrons attempted to flee the scene. After several minutes of continued gunfire, Truitt allegedly shouted an unintelligible epithet and turned the weapon on himself, dying immediately.

Among the dead were Allstate Insurance regional manager Oswald Dolan, 56, and his wife, Sun City bank teller Mary Ann Dolan, 55. Also slain was student Jared Tyler, 19, who had just begun his spring term at the University of Florida. According to police, Tyler was accompanying the Dolan family for dinner because of his romantic involvement with their daughter, survivor Paris Dolan, 18, who was visiting the restaurant's public rest room at the time of the massacre. Ms. Dolan has been hospitalized for psychiatric counseling and treatment.

Also slain were Coral Springs public school teacher Wayne Turnow, 28, and his wife, Lydia Turnow, 26, also a teacher. All the victims died instantly of gunshot wounds to the head. Truitt's rifle had been legally purchased in Tallahassee last March.

"Oh my God," Gaia whispered. She was really starting to faint now. The room was growing dim. With a tremendous effort of will she kept herself awake. But now she was beginning to see. . . .

This was the *real* reason Paris never got letters back from Jared. Gaia was reeling from the scale of the tragedy. Paris's mother and father and boyfriend shot dead, practically right in front of her.

And this house. Nobody lived here. Not now.

"Oh, Paris," Gaia whispered. She could feel her own eyes filling with hot tears. "Paris. . ."

"Mom," Paris whispered. She was shaking her head back and forth over and over. "Mom. . ."

Gaia knelt down and hugged Paris as hard as she could. The borrowed, bright yellow shirt collar poked into Gaia's face. Paris hugged her back—she was shaking like a leaf. Gaia was crying now.

"Mine too," she whispered in Paris's ear. "Mine too. Gone. Dead."

Paris squeezed Gaia so hard, it nearly hurt. They were both rocking back and forth gently, holding each other in the middle of the empty beach house, the deserted living room filled with bullet holes and smoke and broken glass.

"Dad," Paris whispered. "Jared. Jared."

"It's okay—it's okay to let it out," Gaia whispered. She held Paris as tightly as she could. "Let it out, and you can make it through. You can do it."

"I *can't*." Paris sniffed. She was barely audible now.

"Yes, you *can*."

Gaia squeezed Paris a final time and then gently pulled away. She was really starting to faint; she didn't trust herself to try to stand.

"Phone," Gaia whispered to Jake. Tears were running down her face.

"Yeah." Jake looked around quickly and then dashed to one side. It didn't take him long; there was a maroon-colored phone right there on the floor, where a coffee table had probably stood. He brought it over to her. Gaia lifted the receiver—it felt like it weighed twenty pounds—and brought it to her head.

"Nine-one-one," she told Jake. His finger stabbed out quickly and hit the three keys.

"Nine-one-one," the operator said. "What's the emergency?"

"Central Intelligence Agency," Gaia rasped. Her head felt light. "Code Mayberry 12."

"Yes, ma'am," the operator said. There was a quick series of clicks and electronic beeps and then a different, male voice came on.

"Branch office 27," the voice said. "Agent Rennie."

"Six-two-five-eight-one-nine-two-four," Gaia recited

carefully. The room was spinning. "This is a class-five alert."

"Yes, Ms. Moore," Rennie said. "Go ahead."

"Alert Agent Rodriguez in New York," Gaia whispered. She was sliding to the floor—Jake leaned down quickly and caught her. "Then send a team here. Stand by for my friend. . . to tell you the location. Passing out. . ."

Gaia never even knew if Agent Rennie—whoever he was—said anything in response. She felt the phone being gently taken from her fingers, and then she was plunging into the deep, soothing darkness of uncon-sciousness.

Her heart
was truly
breaking
for Paris.

queen
of
sanity

I have a brother.

Not a fake brother. Not a foster brother or a half brother or an adopted brother. A real brother. My own flesh and blood.

The Organization stole him. They stole him from my mother. My parents never even knew. They told my parents that he'd died at birth. And then they threw him into Rainhill just to start experimenting on him. Another one of Dr. K.'s *projects*. Thirteen years ago.

Why? What would they want with D.? Why would they start with him so young? How would they even know what he could see in people? How would they have any clue? It doesn't make any sense.

But I can't figure it all out now. I just need to be with him right now. And he needs to be with me. In the city. He needs to come home with me. So he can draw beautiful pictures of something other than steel beds and white walls and evil-son-of-a-bitch

G A I A

doctors. So he can breathe real
air and walk on real grass and
eat a real Krispy Kreme doughnut.

Home. A real home with a real
family. I know it will come back
to me. Piece by piece, moment by
moment. I'll remember what it
feels like to wake up for breakfast and actually want to leave
my room. I'll remember what it
feels like to actually want to go
home at the end of the day. I'll
remember caring about little
things. Things that aren't about
living or dying. Things like what
teachers he likes, or who the
assholes are in his class, or
what to buy him for Christmas.
Things like what groceries to
buy, and what kind of dog we
should get, and when we should go
the dentist. . .

Home. D. and I are going home.

CIA File # BFO-P922304-L
Rating: Classified
Administrating: Agent Martin Rodriguez
Reporting: Agent Duncan Sanderson
Subject: Rainhill Incident Aftermath

The Central Intelligence Agency has completed its exhaustive investigation into the recent events in and around the Rainhill Hospital in Fort Myers Beach, Florida.

After a thorough examination of the facility and the removal and analysis of the materials found there, it has been determined that **the Center's psychiatric caregiving programs were essentially isolated from, and unaffected by, the illicit activities being performed.**

All hospital personnel have been cleared of charges. The Agency has determined that with the exceptions of Dr. Michael Kraven (see accompanying file #56546FI-MK), Rosalyn (Rosie) O'Rourke, and two other orderlies, **nobody on the staff of the hospital had any knowledge or understanding of the Organization's surreptitious activities there.**

Dr. Kraven has been taken into federal custody (as has Ms. O'Rourke) and will be transferred to the Agency's Guantanamo Bay holding facility, where he will be subject to in extensive fact-finding interviews and experimental psychotropic procedures intended to maximize his usefulness to the Agency as a source of detailed, high-level Organization-related counterintelligence. Dr. Kraven has been charged with 271 separate criminal charges, predominantly involving his egregious misuse of psychiatric facilities and his exploitation of unknowing test subjects. It is speculated that several of Dr. Kraven's crimes represent violations of international human rights laws; in the face of such prosecution, Dr. Kraven has agreed to provide exhaustive details of his inside knowledge of the Organization's newly discovered (and presently terminated) "Advanced Memory/Motivation Realignment Project."

The remaining patients at Rainhill will continue to receive the outstanding treatment for which the facility has become well known throughout the worldwide medical community.

The Central Intelligence Agency is prepared to regard this matter as closed.

AT LEAST A THOUSAND THOUGHTS

were spinning through Gaia's head. Thoughts and feelings and revelations. So many questions answered. So many more questions to ask. But she had put them all on hold right now. Because right now was not for her. Right now was for Paris. Right now was for saying good-bye. And Gaia despised good-byes.

Tragic Loss

They'd spent hours in that house just waiting for agents to arrive and then hours more answering their endless questions. It must have been such torture for Paris. It must have been hell. Sitting in that abandoned house where she and Jared had spent so much time together, understanding for the first time in God knew how long that he wouldn't be coming home. That he would never be coming home. That he was gone. Her boyfriend and her parents gone in a heartbeat. It seemed unthinkable, unimaginable.

But not for Gaia. Gaia knew that feeling. Maybe not exactly, but close enough. Close enough that she didn't even want to think about it right now. Close enough that her heart was truly breaking for Paris. Maybe some part of Gaia had even known that when they'd first met. She'd known that they were connected in some deeper way than just a rebellious attitude or a need to escape. Loss had so much to do with the people they were now. Tragic loss.

They were standing face-to-face just outside the Rainhill parking lot. Jake, D., and Tricia had said their good-byes in the car and waited out by the road. None of them wanted to come within a mile of this place again. Gaia certainly hadn't wanted to, either. But she wanted to stay with Paris for as long as she could now. She wanted to see her through this. And she wanted to postpone the good-bye.

But this was as far as they would walk together. This was where their paths had to diverge. Gaia would be getting back into that car and going home. And Paris would be walking back through the doors of Rainhill. Gaia didn't know what to say about that. She didn't even know what to think about that. And neither, it seemed, did Paris. They had stood there in silence for at least a full minute before Paris finally spoke.

"So, I guess I was wrong," she said, staring down at the gray asphalt of the parking lot.

"About what?" Gaia asked.

"About knowing."

Gaia wasn't sure what she meant.

"You know. . . ," Paris muttered. "Knowing. Knowing I was sane."

"Oh." Gaia searched desperately for the right response. She just had no idea what that might be. "Well. . . but now—"

"No, it's okay," Paris said. "You don't have to say anything." Her eyes were still glazed and bloodshot from so much crying. She crossed her arms tightly over her chest and gazed over at the hospital entrance. Then she looked back at Gaia. "I mean. . . you're not exactly the queen of sanity, either." She lifted a corner of her mouth with the faintest hint of a smile. Gaia puffed out a half laugh of acknowledgment.

"No," she agreed. "Pretty far from the queen."

"Yeah. . . I guess maybe we have a few issues."

"A few, yeah. . ."

"You want come back with me?" Paris joked, her bright green eyes bathed in irony.

Gaia smiled and looked back at the entrance. "Um. . . I think I'll pass on that one."

"Right. Probably a wise choice."

The comic relief seemed to fade away in their silence. And Paris's eyes grew much sadder. The look in her eyes made Gaia's entire body ache. It was much too painful. She wanted to do something to make it go away. Anything she could think of to just fix it right now. "Paris. . ."

"Yeah?"

"You don't have to go back. You can just come home with me. You can get in the car and we'll all head back to New York, and we can find you someone to—"

"No," Paris interrupted. She looked deeper into Gaia's eyes, acknowledging what they both knew. And just in case it wasn't clear, Paris chose this moment to say it. "I need this, Gaia. I need to be here. I think. . . I think I need help. I need to figure some things out."

"Yeah," Gaia said. "I know."

"And I think. . . I can't believe I'm saying this, but. . . Dr. Pain-in-the-ass. . . I think she's been trying to help me. I think maybe she can help me."

"I think so, too," Gaia said.

"Yeah. . ." Paris shook her head to herself. "I just wish the food was a little better."

They stood through another short silence, but there was something else Gaia wanted to say. Something she needed to say, really. She'd been wanting to say it the entire car ride back from the beach house. "Paris. . ."

"Yeah?"

"Thank you."

Paris's eyes widened slightly. "For what?"

"For what?" Gaia looked deeper in her eyes. "Paris, you got me out of there. I was gone. They had me right where they wanted me, and I wasn't going to do a thing about it. But *you* did. You knew what I needed. You knew what had to happen, and you made it happen."

"Hmmm. . ." Paris seemed to consider this for a moment. "Yeah, I guess I did, didn't I?"

"You did. And I don't really know how I'll ever repay you for that."

"I know one way," Paris said.

"How?"

Paris suddenly looked incredibly uncomfortable. She turned her head away and began looking in any direction but Gaia's. "Well. . ." She took a deep breath and squeezed her arms tighter to her chest. "I need. . . someone to write to now. Now that. . . you know. . . . I need someone else." Gaia could see Paris's jaw clenching. "Someone who's going to write me back," she said. In spite of all her efforts, one last tear did fall from her eye. She quickly swiped it from her cheek and looked back at the ground. "So, if I write. . . will you write me back?"

Gaia could feel tears hovering just behind her eyes. It might have sounded like a simple request to someone else, but Gaia knew better. She knew how much this meant. For the first time in her life Paris was trying to accept it. She was trying to accept that the boy she'd been writing to all this time wasn't there.

And in that moment Gaia knew. She knew that Paris was going to find her way back. Back out of denial and back to reality. "I will," Gaia said. "I'll always write you back." Gaia felt compelled to hug Paris, but she held back. Hugging wasn't exactly either one of their styles.

But she hugged her anyway.

And Paris hugged her back, strong and firm. After everything they had been through in the last week. . . perhaps their styles were beginning to change.

Their hug completed, Paris stepped away from Gaia and wiped the tears from her face. "Okay. I'm going in. Wish me luck."

"You'll be okay," Gaia said. "And if not. . . just call

me. I can always come back and bust you out."

"Nah." Paris shrugged. "I think I'm going to try and do this the hard way."

With that, Paris turned around, and step by determined step, she marched herself through the parking lot, straight toward the entrance of Rainhill Hospital.

That girl is brave, Gaia thought as she headed back toward the car to go home. *Not fearless. Brave.*

Fearless was easy. But brave. . .

Brave was hard.

all those
auras, all
those
different
practically
colors,
right **swooning**
there,
around him,
all the time

HOME AGAIN.

Incredible Treasure

Gaia gazed through the car's tinted window at East Seventy-second Street. It was a beautiful Manhattan afternoon. The sky was bright—the sun shone on the buildings' painted brick faces.

D. sat beside her, looking nervous and brave and excited, just as he had on the CIA charter plane they'd taken back to New York. His blue eyes looked very large. He stared past Gaia at the enormous passing buildings, with their hundreds of windows. It was impossible to guess what he was thinking.

Jake was across the car, against the other window. The entire trip he'd been quiet. . . friendly, but quiet. He seemed to be avoiding eye contact with her.

D. was in real clothes for the first time—a blue T-shirt and jeans. Gaia couldn't get used to it. He had picked them out himself at one of the Florida airport's stores. He seemed to really enjoy being able to choose what colors he dressed in.

Gaia reached over and squeezed his shoulder fondly. D. turned his solemn eyes on her and smiled. She smiled back.

The car pulled up to the curb and stopped. The driver had been given the address. He waited, idling, while Gaia opened the door, admitting the traffic noises and the unmistakable New York air.

Jake was climbing out of the car on the other side. He had a small travel bag. The Agency was taking care of shipping his car back—he only had a few things with him on the charter jet they'd taken home.

Gaia took a slow, deep breath, held it, and let it out. She closed her eyes and opened them again. She gazed around at the residential street, at the people who got to live ordinary lives all around her.

"Happy?"

At the sound of Jake's voice Gaia turned and looked at him over the car's roof.

"What?"

Jake shook his head, looking away. "Just the look on your face. You look happy. Or you did for a second there. Never mind; it's a stupid question. I forgot who I was talking to."

Gaia kept looking at Jake. "Very funny."

"What were you really thinking of?"

"The phone booth at Rainhill," Gaia said. The memory was clear. Running down the endless corridors, with Paris following, trying to stop her, and then standing guard. Wedging herself into the tiny, smelly booth and practically swooning at the sound of a New York phone ringing far away. "Realizing how much I missed the city."

"When you left the message," Jake said. "When you called me."

"Well, I didn't exactly *choose* you as the person to

call," Gaia said quickly. "You followed me into the park—you were there when Rosie's team abducted me. It wasn't like I could call anyone else."

"All right." Jake smiled pleasantly enough.

"I just wanted to clear that up."

He came around the car, his bag slung over his shoulder, and stood next to her.

"So you remember calling me now."

"Yeah." Gaia brushed her tangled hair away from her eyes. "Clearly."

"Everything's come back to you?"

Gaia didn't answer that. She looked down at the pavement, enjoying the beautiful New York grime.

"I've got to take off," Jake said.

"Okay. Thank you, Jake," she said. "I mean, really. Thanks for everything."

Jake shrugged. "Don't mention it."

"See you in school," Gaia said.

"Karate class?"

"Not likely."

Jake reached up and ran his hand through her hair. "Next time we meet in the park," he said, "I'll make sure you see me coming."

Then he smiled and walked away.

Gaia looked after him for a moment and then ducked her head and climbed back into the car.

D. was shivering. He trembled violently, pulling his arms over his head. He was in the very center of the car's backseat, cowering like an animal caught in a thunderstorm.

"Bad colors," D. whimpered. "Too many. Dark colors everywhere."

"D.?" Gaia reached out and hugged him. He felt cold, feverish. He trembled uncontrollably. "D., what's wrong? What's the matter?"

"Vicious black."

"D., it's all right. We're away from all that—we're home." She was patting his back, trying to soothe him. D. squeezed against her, shivering. "Everything's fine— what's wrong? What's wrong, D.?"

Gaia wondered what to do—what this meant. There was nobody left to ask. "D., we have each other now. I won't leave you alone. You don't ever have to go back there."

D. seemed to have calmed down—he was still shaking, but less violently. "Bad colors," he murmured.

It's the city.

All the people—all the auras. Gaia thought about it. The city was filled with people. Even the most crowded parts of Rainhill had only a few dozen people. But New York had millions—all those auras, all those different colors, right there, around him, all the time.

And Gaia realized something else.

"You can't live here," she whispered, hugging D.

She realized that he would have to be indoors all the time if he lived here. It would be no better than the hospital. In fact, it would be worse—trapped in a vast, unfamiliar city, surrounded by the colors of New York strangers.

So she would lose him.

That was the truth—that was what it meant. Gaia felt a sinking feeling. To have found this incredible treasure—her own brother—only to lose him again was unbearable.

Except she *wasn't* losing him, Gaia told herself. He just needed time—he needed to be protected, just a while longer, until he could learn to adjust.

"I understand," Gaia told D. She tried to hold back her tears. "We'll find a place for you. We'll find another place."

D. looked her in the eye, as if he might cry himself. "Thank you," he said.

Dear Gaia,

I got your letter today. Actually, like five minutes ago. Lawrence came through as he always does with the mailbag, and when he held up that blue envelope and yelled, "Dolan," I nearly had a heart attack. Actual mail! I had to write back immediately.

I was already thinking about you today. I was in the common room, having breakfast. Vince was there, ready to play gin rummy. He usually wins, but I'm getting better. I'm going to be able to kick his ass by next summer.

Anyway, a new patient arrived, and she's all attitude. She spit on Lawrence and hid under her bed. So I went to talk to Maria. That's the new patient's name—Maria. I got her to come out. She's so angry, but I'm sure that underneath, she's just scared. The first night here can be rough. I still remember it.

Wanda—Rosie's replacement—officially gave me clothing privileges. It's funny, not wearing those pajamas anymore.

So it turns out that getting better's not such a big deal. I mean, it's not so hard. It's just a step at a time, like anything else. Like escaping—you start by making a plan, and then you fill in the details. I'm just as determined as I ever was to get out of here—but I finally know how I'm going do it. One day I'll just open the front door and walk out into the sun.

Things keep reminding me of Mom and Dad. I think they always will. Little things, like getting pancakes with butter and blueberry jam, or seeing a lady the other day with glasses just like Mom's. It hurts, but also it feels good to remember them. I'm glad they're still with me, in my heart.

I miss Jared. That's the hardest part. I've told Dr. Weissman all about him. I've told her so many stories, she must be sick of them. I miss D., too. And of course, I miss Ana. You know what's funny? I even miss Tricia. The place isn't the same without her. There's another ass-wipe goody two-shoes in training here—a girl named

Rita—but she's not in Tricia's league. I hope she's happy on that farm of hers. Maybe she's bossing the animals around.

And I miss you, Gaia. I don't know how long I'll be here, but when I get out, I'd like to see you again. Someday I'll hop a Greyhound bus to New York and come see you and Jake. Someday soon.

Until next time, bye, Gaia. I'm proud that you're my friend.

Paris Dolan

Dear Gaia,

Things are so wonderful here. Dorothy really had it right: There's no place like home. My parents still can't believe that I'm back. My real parents, Merle and Nellie. For so many years they thought that they'd never seen me again. One night I woke up at four in the morning and caught both of them together in my bedroom doorway, just looking at me the way (mom said) they used to do, soon after I was born.

D. is very happy. He loves the clean country here—the flat fields of corn and barley that go on for miles. The doctor from the university drives out once a month and charts his progress—but mostly everyone leaves him alone. Nobody's sure if he'll eventually be able to go to school and learn to communicate with people in a normal way, but it's clear that he's a very gifted boy.

Speak of the devil—D. just came into

the room from finishing his evening chores with Jill and Jack. He's wearing his sheep's-wool sweater mom knitted for him. I can tell from his face he got to spend time with the horses again. The animals make him happy. He draws them all the time. He knows I'm writing to you now. I think he can see it on my face. I'll give him the pencil so he can write his greeting at the bottom of the page.

For so long I thought my real life was a dream. Thanks to you, I know better now. It's funny: Sometimes it's not so easy to see the truth as you think. I guess I didn't really know that before.

My parents want me to invite you to our farm. If you're ever tired of New York and want to take an Oklahoma vacation, we'd love to have you. We've got plenty of room, and you're welcome anytime.

If you talk to Paris, please give her my best.

Thanks for everything as always, Gaia.
I'm thinking of you. D. wants to sign
this, so I'll hand it over to him. I miss
you!

XOXO
Daisy

GAIA GAIA GAIA
BRIGHT GREEN ALL GREEN GLORIOUS
BROTHER FAR AWAY
MISS YOU SISTER LOVE LOVE LOVE

Dear Mom,

   If it's all right with you, I wanted to write you one last letter. Don't worry, I'm well aware that you won't be receiving it. At least not until heaven and earth get back on speaking terms. But I guess it's really more for me.

   Someone tried to take away my memories, Mom. Dr. Kraven tried. The Organization tried. They tried to convince me that the family I remembered was a fake. They tried to convince me that the me I remembered was a fake. But I just wanted to let you know. I just wanted to say it once and for all and for the record:

   I know who I am. And I know what my family was. And what it is. I know how happy we were together. And no one is ever going to be able to touch those memories. No one is ever going to take them away from me. Because in certain unfortunate cases, they're all I have.

   Memories are all I have of you now, Mom. But you want to know the truth? I'm starting to believe that I just might be able to live with that. That the memories might just be enough to get me through.

I hope that doesn't hurt your feelings up there. I don't think it will. In fact, I think maybe you've been waiting for me to discover the power of memories for a long time.

You know what else I discovered, Mom? I discovered that I have a brother. That's the other reason I'm writing you. That's the other thing I wanted you to know. I found my brother. I found your son.

I know you never knew him. They told you he'd died at birth, those sick, twisted Organization sons of bitches. But he's not dead, Mom. He's alive. I lost you again, but I found him.

His name is D., and he has crystal blue eyes like mine, like Dad's. And he's a freak like me. Both of us God's freakish little mistakes. Both of us mutants. Both of us totally alone in the world. Until now.

And now everything seems possible. Everything has a purpose again. I have a purpose. I have a full-fledged, irrefutable, actual reason for living.

D. is the reason I've survived all this time. He's the reason no one has pulled the plug on me yet, no matter how many times they've tried, no matter how many times I've wondered why I didn't just go ahead and let them pull it.

I'm still here so I can take care of him someday. So I can show him the world and teach him all the things that you and Dad have taught me, and tell him all about his beautiful, glorious mother.

And whenever D. is ready, that's just what I'm going to do. Believe me, Mom, I'll do it. I'm going to take down all of this family's enemies, and I am going to find Dad, and I am going to bring us all together. All of us. Call it a mission or a calling or whatever you want.

I still miss you. I miss you every day, and

I'll miss you every other day after that. But I'm going to try now. Just like Paris is going to try. I'm going to try to move on.

But don't worry, Mom. I'm taking all my memories with me.

Love,

Gaia